HOT CHOCOLATE THIS WINTER

BOOK 2 OF SAG HARBOR BLACK ROMANCES

LULA WHITE

CONTENT WARNING, COPYRIGHT & DISCLAIMER

THE SAG HARBOR COMMUNITY

Books In The *Sag Harbor Black Romances*

Brown Sugar This Christmas - Maddy & Jerrell

Hot Chocolate This Winter - Chrissy & Sheldon Part 1

Flinging All Spring - Adella & Desmond

Overheated for Summer - Chrissy & Sheldon Part 2

Rouse Family Christmas - All Couples

Books in the spin-off series *Explore Men of the Hamptons*

Explore You - Kevin & Cher

One Tasty Night - Solomon & Chaitra

Taste You - Solomon & Chaitra

Drink You - Lion & Kamila

See Through You - Keenan & Eugenia

Find You - Roland & Neeraja

Books Related to Sag Harbor

A New Life for Christmas - Odell & Tazima

The Sag Harbor world includes two book series- nine books and three novellas.

The events do not occur based on order of the books. Here's the order in which to get acquainted with this world:

Brown Sugar This Christmas

Hot Chocolate This Winter

Flinging All Spring

Overheated for Summer

One Tasty Night

Explore You

Rouse Family Christmas

Christmas Down Under (Web site only)

Taste You

Drink You

See Through You

Find You

It all started with 3 childhood friends
Books 1-4

Maddy **Chrissy** **Adella**

The Old Hamptons Money

ELLIS/PAGE BLOODLINE

Maddy marries Jerrell
William
Marguerite

MIDDLETON SONS

Lion marries Kamila
Brendan
Kevin marries Cher

TOWNSEND COUSINS

Chrissy marries Sheldon
Cher marries Kevin
Neeraja marries Roland

These Black families have thrived in New York since 1700s & 1800s.

The English family arrived in the 1970s & 80s during the real estate boom.

Explore Adventures is created by Keenan, Solomon, & Kevin

ENGLISH FAMILY

Solomon marries Chaitra
Lonnie
Constance
Rachel
Martin
Adella marries Desmond
Ilyana

New Hamptons Money, Books 5-12

ROUSE FAMILY

Roland marries Neeraja
Sheldon married Chrissy
ex-wife is Eugenia

Etta
Kamila marries Lion
Jerrell marries Maddy

These Black families arrived in New York after 2000.

MCLAIN FAMILY

Chaitra marries Solomon
Desmond married Adella
Keenan loves Eugenia

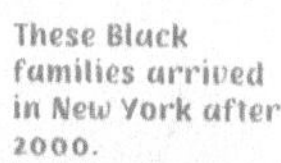

www.lulawhitebooks.com

email: lula@lulawhitebooks.com

CONTENTS

LULA'S HOT CHOCOLATE PLAYLIST

Hey Loves, I have a playlist for all books in the series. These are the songs I listened to while writing this story, and am sharing with you if you're wanting a sexy, grown, mostly 90s vibe. In my Loves Letter and on my web site, I'll share which songs go with which scene.

On Spotify it's free to set up an account. I will also send out the list of songs to my Loves, and will make the list available in the Books section of my web site.

Hot Chocolate This Winter on Spotify

PROLOGUE

GUARDIAN ANGEL

CHRISELLE

"*E*xcuse me?" Chrissy asked the bank officer on the other side of the counter. She suppressed her growing ire.

The officer in heavy makeup spread her strawberry-red lips into a fixed smile. "I said, Mrs. Mason, I regret to inform you that your ability to use the account has been frozen."

She would not give her audience the pleasure of hearing her voice elevate one decibel. Besides, Chrissy could easily convey her point with a raised eyebrow.

"I'm sure that's not what you intended to say," Chrissy replied, letting her thumb glide across her sharp nails in a veiled message. "What you meant to say was, now that you've seen my ID, you will give me access to my account immediately, before I call my close friend, who is the Regional Vice President. In case you're not aware of your bank's structural hierarchy, that would be your boss's boss."

The bank officer appeared as if she had sucked on vinegar. The woman did not back down.

"I'm afraid the only way you can regain this account is with an order from a judge, or with special authorization from our regional office. My boss would tell you the same thing."

Ugh! That damn Blake. He had frozen her out. Chrissy and Blake had agreed they would not touch the children's account, as a condition of keeping their marital differences out of court. How had he done this? Without a judge?

"I never received lawful notice of this freeze on my funds. You all should have informed me. Therefore, statutory notice is lacking. I request you respect my legal rights. And because you have not, I'd like an explanation from your Regional Vice President." Chrissy seethed.

Where did Blake get off? Her estranged husband's domination and control tactics rivaled those of any zookeeper. Of course, Blake was not answering the phone.

Two minutes later, the associate returned with the branch manager, for whom Chrissy had no time.

"Mrs. Mason, we apologize for the inconvenience today," the branch manager with a bad comb-over said. "Unfortunately, we have spent quite some time looking into the situation, and this is a unique hold on the account. We have no say in the matter. I believe you are going to need an attorney. You should have received some papers."

"But I received nothing."

"You are correct. You should call the regional office. Here is the number, as it involves higher authorizations we do not have access to."

She ignored the piece of paper. Enough heat and electricity might have cracked through her eyes that they could bolt out lightning.

When she turned around in her Carolina Herrera burgundy suit and pink pearls, a small waiting area of other high-income account holders sipped their complimentary coffee and offered her fake sympathetic smiles.

Ensuring that she glided and did not stomp, Chrissy began her humiliating exit several long yards to the door. Already, she wondered how the conversation with Blake would play out, and which version of her husband she would get this time —the relentless devil or charming liar. How much longer would she let this go on before she finally took this to court?

"Excuse me," a male voice said behind her. "Hold up. Wait."

Great. The deep baritone indicated an ambitious brother, perhaps overly confident in himself. This was all she needed right now, a dude who thought he would shoot his shot simply because he had a black credit card. She kept strutting.

"Mrs. Mason, is that her name?" the male voice asked in a low tone, as if speaking to someone else, and then to her, "Ma'am, have you changed your mind about your account?"

Chrissy stopped in her tracks. Her Prada shoes pivoted to face a dapper pair of Berluti Scrittos underneath a crisply lined Ermenegildo Zegna wool mohair suit, topped with a silk square tucked in his breast jacket pocket. A set of teeth smiled at her that could light up the Times Square ball on New Year's, not to mention a bald head, shaved clean enough for fingers to skate across. But he must have been some years older than her, with flecks of salt-and-pepper whiskers winking at her from his goatee.

"Um…" she started, taken aback to find this steaming cup of hot chocolate appear from nowhere.

"Your account?" he repeated. "I can probably help you with that. Come on. Let's open it up."

Open it up?

This gentleman's long legs took off, brushing past the astonished branch manager and the branch officer.

The manager objected, "But, sir, no one may gain access to—"

"I'm well aware of the rules, Martin. Thank you very much," Mr. Christmas Dessert declared in an unbothered tone that gently chided them to fuck off.

As they proceeded, her eyes dropped to the sculpted ass strolling toward the largest corner office. Once inside, photos on the desk displayed a smiling, picturesque family belonging to the same Martin who had just shaded her. Mr. Christmas Delight closed the door to Martin's office. "Coffee?"

"No, thank you. I'm trying to quit," she confessed, nearly forgetting why she was there. *Blake who?*

Within moments, this holiday stranger was inside Chrissy's account. "Oh, you share this account with someone. Maybe your parent? But then, you are quite confident, so I'm guessing not a parent. Your spouse."

She linked her hands together, trying not to let his velvet voice wrap around her. Chrissy remembered to focus. "Wow, you have apparently done this a few times before."

"Not really," he replied with an easy smile. "I build the bank's technology. So I'm aware of procedures for freezing an account. I overheard you say that you never received notice. One should have automatically gone out," he noted as he continued to type.

Chrissy watched aghast at the big red letters crossing the screen, with blocked access and blurred lines that prevented her from seeing the status of her and Blake's joint funds.

Christmas Dessert's fingers moved deftly, as if he did this in his sleep.

"I'm sorry, sir, but who are you? And why couldn't the branch manager do all this?" she asked.

"Because the branch manager's job is to run the branch, and my job is to know the bank system's infrastructure," he answered with yet another Times Square-illuminated ball drop of a smile. "My name is Sheldon Rouse."

She breathed a quiet sigh of relief. "I appreciate you coming by when you did, Mr. Rouse. Wherever you came from."

"I see what your problem might be. This is strange. I'll need to investigate it. Seems we sent you a letter to a 43586 Bedford Avenue, Los Angeles. Ah! Ladera Heights. Black Beverly Hills." He laughed. "I've got a few friends in that area."

The heat of potential humiliation rose from Chrissy's chest and crawled up her neck and face. She prayed her expression did not betray her fear of more gossip.

Mr. Rouse stopped laughing when he caught the irritation she didn't meant to serve in her eyes.

Damn. So much for keeping a good poker face.

He cleared his throat. But rather than returning to the screen in an awkward moment, his gaze deepened. "Not to worry. Our clients' circumstances remain confidential. However," he said as he turned his attention back to her account, "there may be an issue of who in our bank approved this. I will dig around some more to see if there's a court order somewhere. If not, this action was unauthorized, and I'll be happy to restore your access to the account."

Chrissy reeled. "Unauthorized freeze? So if there was no court order, how could this have happened?"

"That's what I plan to find out. In the meantime, I am

going to recommend someone back in L.A., whom you might want to contact." With that, his elegant, well-moisturized fingers scribbled out a name and a phone number. "One of my good college classmates out there takes care of bullies with her eyes closed."

The thick, ivory parchment paper had bad handwriting on it, drawing a snort from Chrissy at the man's chicken scratch. "I'm guessing your degree was clearly not in writing."

Laughter flowed easily from deep in his chest, and she imagined what that chest looked like.

His relaxing smile returned. "And now my technology salary makes up for the handwriting fail." He got up to open the door for her. "Either I or someone from our team will be in touch with you. I was just on my way out. Let me get you my card."

They headed back toward the front of the branch. The original bank officer's eyes escaped everywhere they could to avoid Chrissy's glare.

Not that Chrissy was interested to stare any place other than Mr. Rouse's fetching derriere, anyway.

After grabbing his briefcase, he whipped out another fine, parchment business card with beautiful raised lettering.

Sheldon Rouse
Chief Technology Officer
Executive Management

It listed three different phone numbers, including his cell and direct line.

"I will try to contact you in twenty-four hours. But don't hesitate to use it if I don't get back to you before then," he said, waving goodbye to the bank employees and then holding open the exclusive backdoor entrance for her.

Chrissy almost hated to leave. On the way out, she caught a whiff of woodsy, rich cologne that placed her inside a cabin in the mountains.

"Thank you. I appreciate your being there today," she replied, concentrating on her step so she didn't lose it.

"And likewise. Not too often I see our people walking through that door. Glad I happened to be in the building when I was."

When she turned to wish him a Merry Christmas, she noticed his eyes leap up from her hips. A self-conscious grin spread across his lips in a subtle acknowledgment she had caught him. Somewhere inside her heart, and perhaps between her legs, a gush of warmth lightened her mood. She still had it.

Chrissy managed to hold in her appreciative snort this time. "You enjoy a Merry Christmas, Mr. Rouse."

"And you try to also, Mrs. Mason, despite the circumstances."

They went their separate ways as she headed to the guest parking and he toward the employee spots.

She wondered if it was safe to peek at him one more time, but her phone vibrated in her purse.

Her mother. "I know you said you wouldn't go, but come to the debutante ball with me this weekend. I don't want Neddy Watkins yapping all night."

Chrissy winced, irritated at her last shot of Mr. Rouse being interrupted.

"Mom, there's a lot going on right now." She rattled off every excuse, any excuse, so *she* wouldn't suffer three hours of boring upper class diamond-flinging, fur-swinging, and car-parading.

"Chrissy, please. You've been absent from Sag Harbor for years. People want to see you."

"No, Mom, you are showing off your daughter who was recently in the *Wall Street Chronicle*." Her mother would not pull any fast ones on her.

"And? Can you blame me for being proud? You're finally making something of yourself after all these years of letting Blake do the heavy lifting." The old goose clucked from her end.

Ouch. The words stung. But the woman was not wrong. Now, more than ever, though she longed to hide out in remote shopping boutiques and nail bars, Chrissy needed to be front and center. Strong and vibrant, rather than cowering to Blake in fear of the drama he might bring.

"All right. Find me a dress and I'll pick it up?" Chrissy asked.

She drove through the bustling streets of her beloved New York City she missed so much, and her thoughts drifted back to the tall chocolate bar she'd just met. A tiny twinge of disappointment twisted her chest. Like most corporate types at big companies, he'd probably never call her again.

SHELDON

Sheldon let out a tense breath behind the wheel of his Maybach.

Before starting his car, he took a moment to shake off the memory of a womanly waist enclosed in a single-breasted pantsuit that flared out at the hips, teasing a very voluptuous posterior.

Poised, well put together, and calm, Chriselle Mason had almost snuck by him.

But standing in the exclusive section of the branch reserved for high-net-worth clients, her stiff-armed stance showed she was reaching a boiling point. At which damn near every black woman prepared to go off, without the poor person in front of them having a clue. He'd initially jumped in to rescue the branch officers. But once Sheldon had sat down with Mrs. Mason, her tense smile screamed she needed saving herself.

Even the most successful bank clients rarely got his attention, regardless of what country they visited from, what job they did, or which celebrity they hosted at their homes. Sheldon had done and seen it all the last fifteen years, from the White House, to The Met Museum, the Kodak Theatre, Buckingham Palace, and the Taj Mahal.

And yet, here in the plain old bank waiting room, a precious ruby had snagged his eye.

His phone vibrated with a text message from his younger sister. *This Saturday night. We're going to support Jerrell. Oasis Cove, Sag Harbor, @ 7 p.m.*

Irritated, Sheldon texted her back. *Busy. It's the weekend after Xmas. Why? What is that?*

He got a final response. *Cancel. Debutante ball. Family table.*

Sheldon sighed. Same eye-watering social functions, different day. He was happy for his little brother starting his own business, but he wanted to relax after all the Christmas engagements.

While he had the phone in his hand, he called up his ten-year-old son in Chicago. Though Hadar spent most of the year with his mother, they still alternated holidays, and Eugenia got Christmas this year. He should have been at his grandmother's house playing video games. The phone rang continuously. Sheldon tried two more times.

"Hello?" a deep male voice finally answered, stunning Sheldon.

"Um, yeah, I am Hadar Rouse's father. With whom am I speaking?" he asked, suppressing his fury.

"Don't matter who I am, man. Hadar's not here right now. I'll tell Genie you called."

"Where is my s—"

Click.

Sheldon had a mind to get on a plane and go see for himself what that woman was doing in his son's presence. But if he did so, she'd jump at the chance to haul him before the judge and request a modification of visitation. He intended to file for shared custody next year and didn't want to give Genie a confrontation she could use to strengthen her hand. Hadar was getting older, and within a couple of years, Sheldon expected his son to soon tell the court for himself that he wanted to return home to New York.

Steaming, Sheldon drove to the next branch on his list of visits that afternoon. Another surprise check-in. Pressing more flesh. Meeting new starry-eyed tech boys who had taken the bank job with fantasies of Silicon Valley. More bank tellers batting their eyes, "accidentally" showing off their cleavage, and leaving their numbers and social media handles inside their printed reports.

As he wondered which houses he'd hit up for Christmas, the phone rang again. Looking at the name, he hesitated to answer.

"Hey," he said, hoping he sounded as upbeat as he intended.

"Hey yourself," his girlfriend's voice greeted him from the other end. "I don't hear you outside among ocean waves, near seagulls, or in the dead quiet with snow somewhere. So you're still here in town."

He cringed. "Yeah, yeah, but I'm doing a lot with family. On my way to pick up my nieces from school and I'll take them to buy a few things for Christmas. And then I'll kick it with fam for the next few days." So it was partially true. He wasn't due to get the girls until tomorrow. But after hearing another man's voice on his phone, tonight he wanted to stew alone.

"You sure have been busy lately. Anything I should worry about?" Darian asked. "My bath tub has missed you these past few weeks."

"You know how crazy things get during the holidays, with employees leaving town and I have to cover. Then the family gets super needy."

His parents couldn't have cared less where he was. Sheldon was the second eldest of the five Rouse children—not their first son, with all the responsibility and the perfect family setup. And he wasn't the last son who pissed everyone off. Sandwiched in the middle, Sheldon was more the forgettable, call-at-the-last-minute child.

"Well, just don't forget that certain other people need you too. Speaking of family, mine would like to meet you. Annnnd," she paused, and Sheldon braced himself, "I was wondering when you would introduce me to yours."

He sighed, staring out the window at the humming downtown traffic before he squeezed into it. How did he lie his way out of this one?

"Hmph," she scoffed after several painfully long seconds. "That certainly is not a good sign. Sheldon, if there is something you have to say to me, I really wish you would just tell me."

As she said the words, he entered the gridlocked New York City traffic that seemed to represent his life. "I thought I already did, Darian. You know how I feel."

"Actually, I don't. We've been together almost a year. You said at first that you didn't want your ex-wife to find out about significant others. Then, you told me you weren't over the divorce and losing your son, and it's hard for you to trust. Now the job is taking a lot out of you. Let me grab a pen so I can mark on my calendar when you'll be ready to move us to the next level. What day will it be, Sheldon? You tell me."

He pinched the bridge of his nose. "Baby, I won't lie to you." Sheldon considered Darian more of a little sister or a close friend than wife material. Sweet and loyal, she simply didn't hold his attention. What else did she do with herself besides waiting for him to call her?

A small, muffled cry vibrated across his car speakers via the Bluetooth.

"I have to go," she said. "I have a family of my own that needs me for Christmas."

But laced within her words was the wishful tone, hoping he would stop her.

"You have yourself a good Christmas if we don't talk, baby, okay?" Sheldon wouldn't string her along for the convenient sex. She deserved better. Especially at thirty-four. Up to this point, she'd chosen to stay. But over the last couple of months, her demands had grown from a whisper to a roar. If she stayed now, he would be reduced to telling her lies. And he couldn't. Even if her leaving came with a little lonesomeness.

Another shriek, this time not so muffled.

Click.

A tiny pain shot through his heart. But if a woman was with him, he held out no false promises. She would likely text him next week.

That left one final call to make. A conversation he'd longed for all day.

"Mr. Rouse, you're still working two days before Christmas," his secretary greeted him.

"I live on the clock, Lela. You know that. Could you be a dear and patch me through to that one client, Chriselle Mason? That'll be my last business of the day. Standard drill. Answering service is to call me if any issues pop up. Thank you, and your Christmas gift should arrive in the morning."

Lela patched him through. The delay that afternoon hadn't been necessary. Sheldon could have resolved Mrs. Mason's issue easily that morning.

But he'd chosen not to.

"Hello, this is Chrissy," a voice answered that sounded like its owner needed a rubdown.

"Yes, Mrs. Mason. Mr. Rouse here. New York Bank calling you back."

"Oh," came a new energy. She may have been shuffling, and getting up.

"I hope I don't have poor timing."

"Of course not."

"So, I spent more time wrapping my head around your issue. And I've straightened out your account status."

"You did?" Her tone perked up more.

"Yes, although I'm afraid you'll have to watch the account, in case this person you're dealing with asks to change the code on it again. I placed a note in the system that no one should touch this. But your co-holder may try this again later," he posed. Why did he kind of feel heroic at the moment?

"Oh, my goodness. Thank you so much. But do you know why the bank is restricting my access without a judge?"

Sheldon bit his bottom lip. He definitely had a theory but wanted to deal with that part himself. "I'm not sure. There could be a ton of reasons that banks authorize a freeze. It's what I plan to investigate. But for now, I hope getting your access back helps some."

"Absolutely, it will. I really appreciate your assistance." The uptempo in having more to say. "And I'll also connect with this divorce attorney you gave me."

Sheldon hadn't told her it was a divorce attorney, so Mrs. Mason must have already looked her up. "No problem." Intrigue sat on the tip of his brain, fantasizing of those luscious thighs on the other end, what she was wearing over them. Where were they sitting? Or lying. "You have yourself a nice Christmas… Mrs. Mason."

A pause….

Sheldon smiled, recalling her sucking her bottom lip as she had sat on the edge of her chair nervously at the bank.

"You too, Mr. Rouse." Her voice had dropped to a sultry murmur before she disappeared from his screen.

He sat back and imagined her. Or maybe reimagined her. For what must've been the umpteenth time that day.

A text from Darian came through disrupted his daydream. Make that several texts of angry pleading and vitriol, intermittent, one after the other. All for which Sheldon had gotten too old.

Stopping himself from redialing Chriselle Mason,

ignoring Darian's incoming calls, Sheldon headed to his next destination—an empty mansion.

To his surprise, at the end of the litany of texts from Darian, was a lone text.

From Mrs. Mason.

Chriselle Mason: *Can't tell you how helpful that was. You didn't have to. Don't know where you came from, but you're the guardian angel before Christmas. Thanks again.*

Christmas sweetness seeped through Sheldon's chest.

She was thinking of him too.

SWAN LAKE

SHELDON

That Saturday night, Sheldon's fingers hovered over his phone.

He sat a few minutes longer before exiting his car. Inside the *Oasis Cove Hotel*, his family awaited, the people he loved most on the planet. But for the past several days, and at this moment, his mind had lingered on one person.

He rarely researched most bank clients, and preferred to keep them all at arm's length.

But this individual had lived in his head all week, stoking intrigue he couldn't shake. He pressed the "Search" icon.

Chriselle Mason's social media accounts popped up. A married mother of two children. Skiing in Wyoming. Yachting in Florida. A home in South Hampton. A budding talent agent career in Los Angeles. The wife of Blake Mason, a rising talent agent in Hollywood. Sheldon knew a few Hollywood folks, and he'd never heard of this cat.

But his wife, on the other hand, Mrs. Mason, stood out prominently in the *Wall Street Chronicle*. *"One-hit wonder, or Hollywood's newest star-whisperer?"*

Sheldon grinned. She was ambitious. A budding talent agent in her own right, she'd recently signed on six new actresses and a singer in L.A.

Now the picture was filling out, and things made sense. Jealous husband was salty that Wifey was giving him a little competition, so he punishes her with the bank account. *What a damn chump.*

Shel recalled how her burgundy suit had flowed over her thick, buttermilk-biscuit thighs like brown gravy. The way she'd strutted with her back straight, chest out and commanded the bank's attention. She moved with cool reserve. Graceful, elegant, she'd been trained, *raised* even, in an aristocratic environment. But behind her eyes, past those soft eyelashes batting through one bank officer after another, Sheldon sensed she wasn't so soft. He detected burning embers, maybe a lake of fire inside her. And she was firing up the wood on Shel.

Bam!

His bones practically left his skin when an object smacked against his car. He peered down at a small body glued to his door, a cute face gazing up at him.

"Little girl," he said, staring down at his four-year-old niece, Halle, "you'd better be glad I love you. Because anyone else who slams into my paint like that is going to miss those hands come next Christmas. I'll eat 'em right up."

She threw her head back and laughed while he scooped her under his arm, pretending to bite at her. They entered the *Oasis Cove Hotel* in South Hampton, where his younger brother's new hustle sprawled across tables along the breezeway.

Sheldon hadn't wanted to come tonight, but he knew his younger brother, Jerrell, needed him. Since Sheldon was the middle brother, he often mediated between headstrong

Jerrell and their overly cocky eldest brother, Roland. Though he would rather have been nestled on his couch doing tech work and watching a game, Sheldon begrudgingly entered the little girls' ball to offer Jerrell an assist. Their dad and brother were giving Jerrell shit for starting his own business.

Roland Rouse, the eldest of the five Rouse siblings, chortled. "Damn. So this is how dude rolls these days? From an office in Manhattan with an expense account to selling pies at prom dances?"

"Roland, shut it. We're here to be supportive, okay?" their younger sister, Kamilah, chastised, turning to Sheldon for help. "Shel, will you please tell him not to start any mess tonight?"

Shel returned his niece, Halle, to her father, Roland. Then, Shel ignored his brother and addressed his sister-in-law, Princess. "P, tell your man to keep a lid on it."

Princess smoothed over Halle's hair and cut a side-eye at Roland. "Baby, be nice to your brother. Don't get popped."

"Thank you, P," Sheldon said. "Ro, give J his props for having the balls to do something we never did."

Roland kissed his teeth. "That Negro should write Dad a check for wasting good money on Brown, just so he could be a damn beggar. Makes zero sense."

Jerrell had broken out of their father's chokehold on all their life paths and forged ahead on his own. Shel had even loaned J a few racks of cash, and now, he was interested to see how the youngest Rouse fared.

His mother kissed his cheek and warned all of them, "We will all be on best behavior. No arguing. Let your brother know you're proud of him. Tonight is not about who is right and who is wrong. It is about all of us being together."

Before entering the main ballroom, Sheldon headed to the bar for a drink.

A few familiar faces mingled in the lobby, and he waved. Colleagues from other ends of the tech world he'd met at conferences and had joined on speaking panels. A smattering of fellow Brown University alumni. A former parent, who shared carpool duties for his son, Hadar, asked about him just then, cutting Sheldon's heart two days after Christmas. Sheldon had barely spoken with Hadar for five minutes before he was off to the movies with his cousins.

To salve the sting still in his chest, he downed a whiskey shot.

"Sheldon!" a voice bellowed. A real estate investor who dealt in commercial properties.

"Brent!" he called, happy to see his energetic college classmate with whom he'd rowed in school.

"What are you doing way out here in this bitter-ass cold ocean air when you could be in a warm cabin or at the beach in Malibu?" Brent asked, a wide smile on his face as he turned to the bartender. "Eh, sir, whatever he just had, get him two more of those!"

Sheldon threw his head back with laughter. "No, no, man, can't do it tonight. I'm with the fam. My young nieces and everything. What are you doing here weekend after Christmas? How did you escape Emily and the kids?"

"Sweet business deal. A restaurant space in a hot area just opened up, and I've got eyes on it."

"Really? What restaurant?"

"A soul food place called *The Ivory.* Ever eaten there?"

This was news to Sheldon. *The Ivory* was historic, a part of New York history.

"Whoa. *The Ivory.* I've gone a few times. It's going up for sale?" He was sad to learn it. Black-owned, it was one of only three spots in the Hamptons that could serve up good creole-flavored seafood dishes with a spicy kick. "What happened?"

"The owners are retiring or something like that. Kids don't want it. My crew and I plan to snag it, tear it up, and turn it into a nightclub. There's an open house Monday. Come with me! Get in on the action."

"I'm not too sure I've got energy for that." Sheldon had made some sweet money on Brent's investment deals, but he was growing bored with random investments that did nothing for his true love of technology.

"Oh, energy, my ass," Brent challenged, nudging him. "Come on. Make some money. What else do you have going on besides chasing tail, you single bastard. Must be nice not to answer to anybody."

Shel turned up another whiskey shot. And choked.

A vision in navy blue floated on the other side of his shot glass, stunning him.

Her head held high, curls pushed up with tendrils cascading down her neck, full breasts busting out of a tuxedo bodice, diamond and sapphire choker tight around her neck, she swept across the lobby floor like a swan over a lake.

He couldn't believe his eyes. She was here. Chriselle Mason.

Sheldon's drink trickled down the wrong pipe. Coughing, he pumped his chest as fumes of the burning liquid traveled up to his eyeballs and ejected fiery tears. He unsuccessfully tried to stifle the burn, and Brent slapped his back. Sheldon raised his hand to stop him. How embarrassing.

But while he nearly died, Sheldon's neck craned for him to glance around the lobby area again, checking for her.

She was gone. Had he really seen what he thought he had? Was it somebody else?

"My bad, man. I thought I saw a chick I know," Shel said.

"Yeah, bruh. You good?" Brent asked.

No, Sheldon was not good. He needed to find the lake of fire he could have sworn he'd just seen flaming by him. Sheldon scanned the room desperately for a curvy set of hips, fulsome backside, and a strut like she was marching straight into Heaven with her crown atop her head.

But near the door, the ballroom entrance, around the lobby area, nothing.

"Um, y-yes, I'm okay," he stammered, lying. "It was good seeing you again, Brent. We should do lunch soon after the new year," he replied, as deflated as a balloon with its air released.

"Uncle Shel, come on! I want you to sit with me." Halle ran to him, pulling him off the barstool.

He kept scouring, and finally, he gave up.

"The Ivory," Brent offered. "Monday at five. Call me if you change your mind."

The best part of the next three hours was the finale. Sheldon honestly did not understand the point of debutante balls, not even when his sisters had done it back in Louisiana.

After showing Jerrell some love and seeing that he and Roland and their father hadn't gone to war, Shel was ready to cut out.

He started toward the sliding doors.

There she was again. No mistaking now. Shel's heart rate hammered across his veins and up to his head.

A clutch purse tucked under her arm, swaying as if strutting on a catwalk, she flaunted her floor-length navy-blue gown like a royal robe. His eyes did not fail him. It was Chriselle Mason.

Shoulders straight, she glided through the double doors of the ballroom. But the strain on her face was even greater than when they'd first met. Before Shel went to speak, she rounded up two small children, and steered them forward. One of them scowled and jerked away from her.

Shel hung back. Those were obviously her kids. She didn't seem to be having an easy night.

Another young woman joined them, someone Sheldon had just met moments earlier. *Oh.* Jerrell's girlfriend—or whatever he called her—was friends with Mrs. Mason.

Shel slowed up and assessed how to approach her. A busy mother with two irritable children, and a man jumping on her nerves, didn't have the time or headspace for a come-on right now.

"Say, bartender, that lady over there, in the blue. Can we have a server take her a cocktail?" he asked.

He would not distract her from her current situation. But definitely a small gift to help her through the night. From parent to parent.

"And what kind of cocktail shall it be, sir?" the bartender inquired.

Sheldon's eyes drank her up, while he bit his bottom lip, wishing he could bite something else.

"Mm, send her a Painkiller."

He wouldn't be so quick to leave. Maybe if he was patient and bided his time, he might steal a couple minutes of hers.

THE PAINKILLER

CHRISSY

Chriselle rushed her son out of the ballroom so she didn't snatch him up in front of the ball guests.

Her husband had done this on purpose. With no warning or prior discussion, he'd simply dumped them on her. Eight days early. This should have been her free week, and she desperately needed to catch up on work.

Blake answered his phone when she called. "What's up?"

"I thought you said you wanted the kids through New Year's," she huffed, trying and failing to keep her cool.

"I did, but you were the one who complained they needed to be ready for school, and you didn't want them around my female friend. So there you go. You've got them now."

The nerve over Chrissy's eye twitched. "Don't play, Blake. We agreed to next Sunday afternoon, after I return to L.A. from New Year's. You knew when you showed up in New York unannounced and took the kids last week, that you weren't keeping them. Do you ever think of how your games affect your son's mental health? He wants to be with you and have your attention, and you only use him as a yo-yo to screw with me."

"I don't know what you're talking about. My children had a stable home and father, and you took that away from them. Now who's fault is that?" Blake challenged on the other end of the line.

"You said you wanted to keep this out of court, but you are working on it. Do this one more time—touch the account, stop paying into it, switch their schools, go outside the agreed visits, anything else, Blake, and..." Chrissy pressed her eyes shut. Fury shook in her voice.

"And what?" he asked. "You're going to do what, Chriselle?"

She bit her tongue. Ten long years, since she was at Spelman and he at Morehouse, pregnancy in her junior year, marriage in their senior year, uprooting all she knew on the East Coast and relocating her whole life to Los Angeles, a decade of sacrifice to build his Hollywood dreams, never having given herself to another, Blake had eaten her entire existence. He was still eating away at her.

"I didn't think so," Blake concluded.

"Daddy!" Little Blake screamed, his small feet taking off through the lobby, and exiting the door.

All while Chrissy still held the phone.

What? She whipped around, confused. "Blake!" Chrissy called after her son. But she and their daughter rushed after him, into the bone-chilling cold. "You're not wearing your coat."

Outside, in the parking lot, there stood her husband. Dropping to one knee, he opened his arms wide. Little Blake went running right into them.

An infuriated Chrissy fumed at big Blake playing more

custody games. He'd dropped off the kids earlier than agreed and hijacked her free time, and then come back to get them with no warning. And he was doing it all just to get in Chrissy's head, as punishment for leaving him.

"Did you say goodbye to your mom, before we leave for skiing?" Blake asked, shooting her a mischievous stare over their son's shoulder.

"Daddy," Little Blake cried, wiping his eyes, "I thought you were leaving us here."

"Of course not, little man, I just brought you to hug Mom before we go have some fun. You'll see her next weekend."

Their daughter, Kara, turned to an infuriated Chrissy. "Mommy, why don't you come?"

Enraged, Chrissy held in angry tears that she refused to let him see, her arms frozen at her sides. She wouldn't go off in front of the children. "This was so unnecessary. Wasted time. And why?"

Blake walked to meet her. Taller, beefy, and far less mesmerizing than he had been in college, he leaned toward her. "These are *my* kids. You're kidding yourself if you think they'll be happy with you. Come home with me. It's not too late. And I'll forgive you for thinking you could make a decent life without me."

"And your side piece? Where will she stay?" Chrissy asked.

"Don't worry about that. She'll never be in your way. I told you. You'll have everything you could ever want or need. Come to your senses, baby. And stop this independent woman bullshit you're running. It won't work."

Chrissy was the one to hug the children this time. "Babies, you have fun skiing. Send me lots of pictures, okay?" Tears fell that she could no longer control. Sending them away with a maniac rocked her body at its core. She trembled from more than the cold drifting in off the ocean.

Blake's side piece got out of his truck and opened the door, smiling at Chrissy's children and promising them hot chocolate and hamburgers.

"I'd better talk to them every single day, Blake," she called after her husband. "Do you hear me?"

He walked away and his truck door slammed.

"You good, girl? Want to get in the car and hunt him down? Take the kids and then run him off one of these cliffs?" a voice asked behind her. A hand touched her back. Her childhood friend, Maddy, offered support.

"Somehow, his evil ass would still manage to survive. Pieces of shit like him always make out just fine. And live another day to torture the rest of us." Chrissy turned to go back indoors.

The icy cold of Sag Harbor floated through the doors, freezing her stiff veins into numb icicles.

"You're shaking," Maddy said. "Let's get some drinks and you take a moment before you go back in the ballroom."

"Thanks, love," Chrissy said. Just as Maddy started to get up from a cushioned bench, a server approached them.

"Mademoiselles, I have two Painkillers for you."

"We didn't order drinks," Maddy replied.

"They would be courtesy of the gentleman at the bar," the server replied, and gestured to a handsome man wrapped in a crimson velvet jacket and skinny black slacks.

Every one of Chrissy's blood cells must have jumped to attention.

Oxygen emptied from her chest, vaporizing into white puffs. *No.* She wasn't seeing what she thought she was seeing. How had a dream boat sailed right into her harbor?

Chrissy barely heard whatever Maddy said. How could this be happening? Speechless, she stared. "What?"

"You know Jerrell's brother?" Maddy asked.

"Huh?" Chrissy absently replied.

The man raised his glass. Same gorgeous clean head, salt-and-pepper goatee, shining and disarming eyes. It was him. He got up and began walking toward them.

"Oh, my God." The words tumbling from her head were her body's reflexive response to… something. "He's coming."

"Mrs. Mason." Same sexy voice.

"Mr. Rouse," Chrissy said in a breath, as much as her hyperventilating lungs allowed. "Why are you here? I-I mean 'hello' and Merry Christmas." She shook her head. *Ugh. You are a grown ass woman.*

His lips spread into a stunning, one-thousand-wattage grin that reminded her it was indeed the holidays. He motioned toward the breezeway. "That guy over there is my brother, and the young lady with him is my grandmother."

"Get out." Chrissy laughed. "Poppin' Pauletta's Desserts? Jerrell Rouse is your brother?"

He chuckled too, and she could have sworn fireworks burst in the sky behind him. "Yes, he is. Our family is here tonight to show him and Gram some love. I hope he hasn't been around here embarrassing our name too much."

Chrissy fished for her big girl words. "Oh, no, to the contrary, Poppin' Pauletta's is all we've been talking about these last couple of weeks. Those are your folks. What a coincidence."

Maddy's eyebrow raised. "You two are familiar?"

Sheldon smiled. "We met at the bank a few days ago. Things still okay with your, uh, affairs?"

Chrissy's insides melted when he cast her an intimate

look, as if promising he would not betray her. "Yes, they are. Thank you. And thanks for this drink. It came right on time."

With a knowing grin, Maddy got up. "I'm going to find my family. It was good meeting you tonight, Sheldon." She turned to Chrissy and winked. "Later on, let's you and I talk?"

"Maddy, don't go away," Shel said. "I was only saying hi. I didn't mean to break up the girls' meeting here."

"You weren't breaking up anything." Maddy's gaze skipped back and forth between the two of them. Chrissy's old friend wore an amused grin as she sipped her drink. "She's all yours."

Sheldon's attention returned to Chrissy.

Why did the weight of his eyes feel as if he saw underneath her dress? Did she want him to… see underneath her? See inside her… repeatedly.

His eyes roamed over her. "You wear that royal blue well. Is that your favorite color?" he asked. His thumb strummed his glass. And her imagination.

"Yes," she answered. A natural smile rising from a deep spot inside her, far beyond her lips. Which set of lips… she still wasn't sure. "And you are rocking that Christmas crimson. Definitely a distinct look from the bank, although both looks are very… complimentary." She hoped all thirty-two of her teeth weren't flashing.

He laughed. "Thank you. Crimson is my favorite color. So what are *you* doing here?"

"I have a goddaughter who's a debutante, and a cousin. Plus, my good friend, Maddy, is one of the judges, and I wanted to grab a little more time with her before she heads back to D.C. tomorrow. If I didn't have people here to support, I would have been perfectly happy not wearing these heels and relaxing with a movie."

The banker's eyes crinkled at the edges, and he nodded as

if he understood. "Same. Same. But my little brother needed me here. So, lucky me, here I am."

Damn, he was even more fine when he laughed.

"I always wished for a little brother."

"Don't," Mr. Rouse replied and glanced back at his brother, Jerrell. "Not worth the trouble." They both burst into more chuckles. "If you ever want to borrow one of mine, I have plenty. Never a dull moment, I guarantee it." Again, his amusement was easy and unnerving. "What kind of movies would you be watching if you were home? And please don't say chick flicks."

Chrissy wrinkled her nose and faked like she was hurt. "What's wrong with chick flicks? I like the Hallmark channel," she lied.

He rolled his eyes, sipping his drink, picking up on her playful vibe. "Nah. I don't buy that. You don't cross me as the type."

"Oh, really?" she asked. A mesmerized Chrissy observed his tongue hit his glass, and then his lips before he sipped. In an effort to keep her head straight, she averted her eyes. "What type do I cross you as?"

In his eyes, tiny lights reflected off the ceiling mounts and shined on her. "Maybe one day, I'll get a chance to tell you."

Her throat beat with all the energy her heart was pumping, and it spilled in her bottom lip. She tried to control it with her teeth, but Chrissy's little-girl reactions to him had a mind all their own. "Wow, sounds mysterious."

"I like mysteries." Once again, his stare dropped and took a tour down her bodice, over her rack, past her waist, and parked at her hips. Before they returned to home base, her eyes.

His lips then started moving, and Chrissy imagined what them moving on her...

Stop acting like you've never seen a man.

"I must be honest, Mrs. Mason. I'm aware you have children. And also, that you have a man who wishes he knew how to be your husband, but... I'd like to take you to dinner."

She gasped.

He strummed.

You mean you want to eat me for dinner? Or you want to eat food with me?

Chrissy hadn't been on a date in... almost twelve years.

She'd never slept with anyone besides Blake. And had kissed no one other than him since age twenty.

"I..." What did she say? She swallowed, eyes fluttering, the earth shaking under her feet. If she did this, what would it mean? Would Blake hire a private investigator to watch her, the way he had two times before when she'd tried to leave? If people found out, what would they whisper and repeat? Sororities and clubs, and memberships she held in L.A., how would they treat her?

Her reputation, her children's lives, her new career, depended mostly on her marriage to Blake, her status as Mrs. Mason. She would risk an entire life they had built together over ten years, inseparable, as a single entity in Southern California.

"My bad," Mr. Rouse said, his face scrunching up. "I'm probably being too forward. Totally unprofessional on my part. If I crossed the line, then—"

"No," Chrissy replied, and rushed to correct him. She didn't want him to feel bad for shooting his shot. Not when she had simply fallen dumb and was still so astonished that she simply didn't have words. While men hit on her all the time, Mr. Rouse's heat was hitting different. "You didn't. I'm glad you asked. Really. I just… my work schedule."

Who the hell are you fooling, heffa? You're scared AF. All the fantasies in her head for over ten years, Sheldon Rouse was serving up energy that he could satisfy every single one.

"You mean as a new talent agent making headlines in the *Wall Street Chronicle?*" he asked. The way his eyes shined at Chrissy, she could have been the only person in the room.

That might have been her heart slinking down her thighs. He'd looked her up.

"Yes. You know?"

"Of course, I do. A baddie like you shows up while I'm in the building, hell yes, I'm checking for her," he replied. More fireworks erupted in his smile. "So am I still being forward if I ask when you're returning to California?"

"Next weekend." Which meant she had plenty of time for dinner.

Her thoughts spiraled out of control as liquid entered those gorgeous lips sipped on the glass. She couldn't help feeling like she was falling into the ocean of his curiosity.

"But you're originally from around here? Sag Harbor? Visiting just for the holiday?"

Maybe not just for the holiday. Not if Chrissy had her way.

"Yes. My ancestors helped build Sag Harbor. So a lot of people who vacationed here for years, we all know each other… our parents, grandparents, great-grandparents, going way back to the early and mid-1900s. The history is important to us."

"Now that's what's up. I visit here on occasion, and have heard stories about Black Sag Harbor, even met a few folks here and there." He studied Chrissy once more. "My family comes from Louisiana, and we've been in New York a long time. But it's rare that I hear about the upper-class blacks, the lineage, straight from the people themselves. I'd love to see more. And maybe I can find out what movies you do like."

From her knees, Chrissy's heart screamed, *Yes*.

"I really wish I could but I'm afraid I can't right now."

Blake would go nuts if he found out.

What was she doing? She was crazy. Insane. *Stop thinking of yourself as Blake Mason's wife.*

A shadow of disappointment crossed Mr. Rouse's face, and he served up a gracious grin. "I understand," he replied, staring out the exit door where Chrissy had confronted Blake minutes before. "I hope at least the drink helped ease your stress a bit."

He knew? Her face grew hot with increasing self-consciousness. Had he seen that awful display with Little Blake and his father?

"Don't worry," Mr. Rouse continued, his easy mocha eyes deepening to comfort her. "I'm a divorced dad myself. It happens to the best of us. As time goes on, and you're better off, it gets easier."

Chrissy wanted to swim in those eyes. She'd never swam in anybody's eyes. Not even Blake's. Yet, here, this stranger could easily suck her into his.

"I certainly hope it gets easier sooner than later, before one of us winds up in jail," she joked with a snicker and a laugh.

He joined her laughter. "Please, don't hurt him, sweetheart. Just move on with the life you deserve." Mr. Rouse's tongue slid over his lips in an epic lip-lick for the history books. "With someone who deserves you. *All* of you." His eyes flashed. "Every stunning inch."

No, you will not change your mind. But her nipples had

something to say about this decision. "Th-thanks for the drink. It helped."

She had to be a responsible mother. With a new career, working again for the first time in years, she needed to focus on a stable life for her children. There was no time or space for romance right now. Not until Blake was out of the picture and she had figured out her life.

"I'm glad. I won't hold you. Since this is your stomping ground, I know you have social calls to make. Thanks for chatting."

Mr. Rouse stared at her again, as if he could read Chrissy's internal conflict. As if he had x-ray vision and could *see* the wet spot in her panties.

Stay strong, Chris.

His gaze drifted from her eyes, and over her nose, her mouth, her hair.

"I hope you have a happy New Year's, Mr. Rouse." She averted her eyes, hoping to avoid his x-ray vision, praying he would turn and walk away.

But suddenly, Chrissy found her face buried in the warm citrus and cedars emanating from his jacket. Crushed crimson velvet brushed her cheek. He had closed the space between them, and his six feet and three inches now towered over her.

"Just so you know, Mrs. Mason," he murmured, his mouth swiping her ear, "this won't be the only time I ask." He didn't pull away. They stood so close he only needed to lift her face so their lips could meet. But he spared her. "And I won't stop asking until you say yes."

The intensity in his eyes signed off on his promise like it was one he intended to keep.

When he finally released Chrissy, and she tried to escape,

so stunned was she that she tripped. She had to grab a lounge chair to keep from falling on her ass.

"SO, DID HE ASK YOU OUT?" Maddy asked, clutching Chrissy's arm as they exited the ball with their families at the end of the night.

"Yes," Chrissy answered. Her fingers shook from more than the cold. She squeezed her nervous disbelief into Maddy's arm. "Chile, oh, my goodness. I couldn't even get my words out straight. That damn man is so…"

Her childhood friend laughed. "Oh, most definitely. Every single one of those Rouse boys. Even their father is fine. It's like he was Geppetto who sat and carved them up himself. So, what happened?" Maddy asked, her neck craned, her eyes dancing and waiting for the exciting story.

Mrs. Mason breathed in a dream-crushing blast of cold air. "I turned him down."

Maddy's cheer fell, and she offered Chrissy's shoulder a supportive squeeze. "I understand. You have a lot on your plate as it is."

Chrissy batted back unexpected tears that started rushing in. Sheldon Rouse's invitation had completely caught her off guard. Even the way he'd looked at her. Behind her eyelids, in the corners of her mind, he still gazed at Chrissy. For five precious minutes, *she* existed. More than a wife and mother. More than a servant to everyone else's needs. He had stared at her like *she* had needs.

Foreign territory to her. But she shook the expanse of his gaze from her head.

"You don't have to make me feel better. Yes, I'm crazy for

saying no, but with Blake giving me hell every time I turn around…"

"No, I get it. Ultimately, you're doing the right thing for you and the kids. What's for you will be waiting when you're ready."

"Thanks, boo," Chrissy said. But her lead chest dragged the ground behind her. "How crazy is that? The same guy you're talking to has a brother who asked me out."

A mushroom cloud could have risen over Maddy's face.

"Uh-oh. How are things going with you and Jerrell?"

"Things are not going with Jerrell," Maddy answered. "He won't talk to me. The whole Kevin Middleton thing."

"Oh, damn, Maddy." Chrissy winced. "Sooo… which one of them did you choose?"

"Not Kevin. I told him a few minutes ago. That ship has long sailed. If it was ever there at all," Maddy said with a sigh.

"Good for you, sis. There's nothing to like about that fool. So glad you ditched him."

The two turned to hug before saying goodbye.

"Chrissy, we don't need to wait so long to talk to each other. I really enjoyed hanging out with you and Del this week. We shouldn't have let so many years go by." Maddy held Chrissy's hands.

Chrissy agreed. Over the last ten years, she had gotten lost in Blake and his Los Angeles life. Chrissy missed her home of New York, and the quaintness of her beloved Sag Harbor. Though she'd made friends and connections in L.A., the vibe from West Coast to East was definitely not the same. She had not attended high school with the Angelenos, or college at UCLA or USC, nor grown up among those families. She still longed for her old Spelman classmates and friends on the Eastern seaboard.

"For sure, lady," Chrissy said, her arms around her child-hood playmate.

"I'm serious." Maddy squeezed and held on while saying so much more in the embrace. "No matter what it is. I'm here for whatever."

"I'll call you," Chrissy whispered.

"Especially if you and Sheldon hook up." Maddy laughed. "I want to hear everything."

A juvenile warmth rolled through Chrissy as the possibility crossed her mind. Chrissy's smile was weak while she tried to stay strong. "No, ma'am. There will be no anything with Mr. Rouse. But *you* call *me* if Jerrell comes to his right mind."

The two clung to each other a final time in front of the *Oasis Cove*, where hers and Maddy's own debutante ball happened thirteen years before. It almost seemed they were clinging to a girlhood long gone. Chrissy would have given anything to feel that giddy excitement and hope for the future just one more time.

Once she left with her mother, she couldn't help wondering if she should race back to Sheldon Rouse and accept his invitation. Bask under the brilliance of his eyes again. And feel like she was in Heaven.

How would she say goodbye to New York next Sunday? And return to the other side of the country, to a husband and a life that gave her hell?

HER BACKBONE

SHELDON

So this Ivory spot is in a decent location?" Sheldon asked, dribbling the basketball against Jerrell that Monday afternoon.

"Yep. Prime real estate, near the water. Close to other restaurants and shops. We all had dinner there a couple times. Roland and Princess's engagement party, remember? Owners are nice. Good people, getting up in age. Probably tired of keeping it up," Jerrell replied, panting as he tried to block Sheldon's shot. "If your guys are offering you a piece of the action, you need to take it. I can see that place striking gold with a solid concept."

Sheldon faked until he shook Jerrell off, and then pulled up. "Boy, get out of here with that." One-handed throw, and the basketball hit the rim before tumbling in. "I'm thinking about it. I'll go look."

For the last forty-eight hours, Sheldon's head flooded with thoughts of Chriselle Mason. He'd gone to bed and awakened reminiscing of her bottom lip disappearing under her teeth, the intent way her eyes scrutinized his when she wanted him to answer her question, how her eyelashes swept around, and her chest shook when she laughed. Her bronze irises danced with his, and they told him so much more than her mouth was willing to reveal.

"Ayo, Shel? Negro, you there?" Jerrell asked, and snapped is fingers. "You taking the ball out, or will I have to go on a treasure hunt for it or some shit?"

Sheldon grinned and tossed his little brother the ball. He'd remained in the Hamptons since the gala, sleeping at Jerrell's crib, hoping he'd run into her again. Now that he knew this was her neck of the woods.

"What's to think about?" Jerrell challenged. "It's the same as every other investment you've made."

"Yes, but I'm bored, though," Sheldon answered. "Tired of funding everybody else's dreams without starting my own thing."

"Ha!" Jerrell scoffed. "Really? You mean you don't love riding around town fixing people's computers all day, thinking of a million ways to screw bank customers out of their money?"

"Dude, come on, you know I've got more weight than that. Just because your rinky-dink ass was stuck in a job with training wheels, it's not everybody else's situation. The rest of us are doing fine," Sheldon clapped back.

He leaped in the air to block Jerrell's shot. The unhappy heaviness in his chest brought him back down.

"I just figured at this point in life, I'd be settled with my kids and wife, and we'd be traveling the world when we're not at little league games and ballet recitals. I expected my evenings to be homework and school projects. I never imagined, for a minute, calling my son's phone and some other dude picking up." Sheldon slammed the ball on the floor so hard, it ricocheted into the air, soaring toard the ceiling lights.

"Aw, you're bullshitting! No, she did not." Jerrell huffed.

"Damn straight, Genie did. And what can I do? If I go get him and bring him here, he might hate me, and I don't want that. Dad always forced us to do things his way. I won't force Hadar."

"I know that shit burns, bruh,, but good on you for waiting it out. It's rough if Hadar has to figure out a new city," Jerrell added.

Jerrell's pain was evident in his voice. When their family had moved from Louisiana to New York sixteen years earlier, Jerrell was still a kid. Sheldon and Roland had already entered college, so the change was easier for them. But not for Jerrell, who struggled to fit in among New York's elite. As the youngest Rouse children, Jerrell and their sister, Kami, had to endure much of the transition on their own.

"So what's up with you and this new chick? Maddy?" Sheldon tried to redirect his brother's mind from the memories. He also wanted to feel out a path to Chriselle—since Jerrell was now seeing her friend.

At the mention of Maddy's name, Jerrell's expression plummeted from the basketball goal with the ball.

"I don't want to discuss her."

Sheldon released a low whistle. "Oh, damn. Somebody got hit this Christmas. Mom and Dad like her."

"Dude, you know the last thing I care about is what Dad thinks," Jerrell said. He fired the ball at the basketball goal, and it ricocheted off the rim.

"Yeah, I see it's pretty clear you're not into her." Sheldon grabbed the ball. "I'm feeling her friend, Chrissy."

Flashbacks danced through Sheldon's head of her soft

skin, so supple he could bite it... in front of his fireplace, while tender moans escaped her smooth lips and made love to his ears. How long had it been since he'd made sweet, slow love? The past year, his rounds with Darian had been good enough to get him by, but not satiating.

Jerrell snatched the ball and threw it at Sheldon, snapping his elder brother back to attention. "She's married. With kids. Please tell me you're not that desperate."

"Her man is crap. She's making moves. She has drive and is demanding. I'm feeling it. Invite Maddy to dinner, so we can all go out." Sheldon suggested.

Jerrell chuckled and stole the ball. "Dude, don't lie. The only reason you like that woman is somebody's already got her. If she was free and hot for you, you wouldn't give her the time of day."

"I won't know unless I find out. So call up Maddy. Apologize for being a dick, because I'm one hundred percent sure you were. And let's all hit a cool spot this week."

"Man, that's a nope. Maddy should've gone back to D.C. already. I sent her ass packing." Jerrell took his final shot.

"What for?"

"She was trying to play me and some other guy, from their childhood. Some buppy dude who wears his slacks up his crotch and makes computer chips in Silicon Valley. I wasn't having it. That's what for," Jerrell answered, clearly seething as he wiped off sweat.

"Oh, wow, she got you good too. So you're telling me you hit that?" Sheldon cracked.

Jerrell's smile reappeared instantly, spreading so hard in his cheeks it almost broke his face. "None of your damn business, Negro."

Shel burst into laughter, rubbing his little brother's head.

"Ahhh, that's what I'm talking about! Jam 'em Jerrell is back! So what's this buppy's name?"

Jerrell sighed. "Um, Kevin, I think. Middle…"

"Kevin Middleton? That dude who MC'd the ball the other night?" Sheldon wiped down and drank some water. "Yeah, I know that cat. Went to Harvard. He's not any average buppy. He's an above-average buppy, making real moves on the tech side. So you just gave up and let him have your girl?" Sheldon asked.

He really had hoped to use Jerrell and Maddy as an inroad to Chriselle, so they could get acquainted in a way that put her at ease.

"Man, I didn't give up. I don't need that shit right now," Jerrell said with a scowl. "My business and Gram are my only priorities."

"Now who's lying to whom? Your nose was wide open." Sheldon slapped the towel against his brother. "We all saw it. Especially when you and Maddy crossed each other Saturday. You were looking all hurt like you lost your puppy and shit."

"Man, forget you. I've got things to do."

"Call that girl and apologize. You can't be mad at her if she's got Kevin Middleton in the queue. You just need to get your weight up."

"Bye, Shel."

"Come with me tonight, to check out this Ivory spot. Introduce me to some of your new Poppin' Pauletta's patrons."

"Another nope, man. I'm running a business now, not working for one. If I don't go run it, it won't run." Jerrell held out his fist for a bump. "All the best, though, bruh. Stop being so scared of a married woman and handle that shit. Call your boy and tell me how it goes." Shel's little brother headed for the showers.

Sheldon heaved out mixed emotions on his way out. Jerrell was right. What was he so afraid of? What made Chriselle Mason any different from all the other women he'd dated?

Maybe the answer was simple. She'd told him no. Mrs. Mason had backbone. Now her sensuality wouldn't leave *his* bones.

CHRISSY VS. LANA

CHRISSY

"*Y*ou told him *what*? Are you alright?" Chrissy's cousin, Cher, asked as they sat in the hot tub at the Japanese spa that Monday morning, before their scheduled massages.

Chrissy rolled her eyes. "I said no. I'm a married woman."

"In name only, Chris," Cher pushed back.

"It doesn't matter!"

"Yes, it does," Cher hissed. "You're holding on to a sham. Something that is dead and was probably never alive. Road kill, boo. It's time for you to drive on."

"Alright, Cher, that's enough," their other cousin, Neera, intervened, giving Chrissy a much-needed assist. "We're supposed to be helping her relax."

"All I'm saying is stop worrying what people think. Or how it will look for your folks. Make yourself happy. Enjoy that fine-ass man," Cher pressed.

"Blake and I have multiple properties together. The kids. And now my clients," Chrissy shot back at Cher. "You don't get it. I worked hard for all that. To be Mrs. Mason. I can't just throw it all away for somebody with a nice smile." Even though Sheldon Rouse possessed a whole lot more than that.

Chrissy already feared the havoc Blake would wreak on her once she filed the divorce papers. How much would he flaunt his mistress in front of her, to extract his pound of flesh?

She was Mrs. Blake Mason, who had stayed home while he'd interned at CAA, rose from the mailroom to assistant on a desk, to an agent cutting deals, and now they were finally walking the Hollywood red carpet. Now she would simply give up her benefits for another woman to slide into her place?

"Let's change the subject." Neera cut into Chrissy's thoughts and brought her back to the pool. "The Ivory. Can you believe the Turners are selling it?"

Chrissy had heard the news over the weekend, and hearing it all over again deflated her holiday mood. So much of her childhood and teenage years had been forged at that restaurant.

"But why, though?"

"They're ready to retire. And word is, there are already several potential buyers," Neera reported and sipped champagne.

"Already?" Chrissy asked. That wasn't good. Competition. Outsiders. More invaders who could come in and tear apart their history.

"Mhmm," Neera answered.

"Who? Friends of ours?"

"Not exactly. You and your girls, Maddy and Adella, might have already crossed her," Neera said as her eyes narrowed while closing in on Chrissy.

"What are you talking about? Fill me in," Chrissy replied,

utterly confused now. "Who is thinking about buying The Ivory?"

Cher nodded toward the opposite end of the large hot pool. "Her."

Chrissy and Neera turned their heads at once.

Chrissy's mouth plummeted nearly to the bottom of the pool.

On the other end, a buxom woman their age stepped inside, along with an older woman who might have been her mother.

Unable to believe her eyes, Chrissy wiped them to ensure she hadn't gotten water in them.

Lana. Maddy's co-worker, and the person who was sleeping with her friend, Adella's, fiancé. "Aw, hell," Chrissy muttered.

"Who is that supposed to be?" Cher inquired. "Come on now. Give me the tea."

"A messy female who has no business here, and we'll just leave it at that." Chrissy's insides heated from more than the hot water. "She's got a lot of nerve."

"Why doesn't she belong here?" Cher asked.

Chrissy refused to put her friend, Del's, business in the street. Though Chrissy felt Del was crazy for staying engaged to a man who slept around on her, she would not humiliate or spread rumors involving someone she cared about. She was all too familiar with being on the receiving end of the rumor mill. "I can't say."

"Well, I can," Neera added. "The tea is that woman is messing with somebody's fiancé. She just came into the Hamptons and started parading her ass around."

Chrissy balked at Neera's big mouth. "So what makes you think she's buying the Ivory? How was that... *female* even aware The Ivory is up for sale, when we just found out a few days ago?"

"How does that broad have the money?" Cher asked. "How much would the Ivory go for? At least ten mil?"

Neera cut her eyes at the chick on the other side of the pool. "I guess we'll find out tonight at the open house. But no matter what, The Ivory shouldn't just go to strangers who are not one of us."

Cher shrugged. "Girl, you sure about that? Maybe strangers can do a better job than the locals. When do we ever come to Sag Harbor anymore? Chrissy lives in L.A. I'm in Virginia. And Neera, you're in the city but you're busy with the new promotion. We haven't really been around much the last few years. Have you checked out the Sag lately? Do you see how many outsiders have bought up property here? I hardly know half the folks here now. How easy is it to keep up a restaurant when a lot of us aren't around anymore? That's work. And this place must be lonely as hell during off-season."

"We'll start coming back more. We can't just take this lying down. This is history right here," Neera objected, a resentful look on her face as she rolled her eyes toward the opposite side of the pool.

Chrissy's gaze met Lana's at the other end, and Lana raised her champagne glass to Chrissy. "I won't wait until tonight. I'll pay her a visit now."

Chrissy waded to the other side.

"Chris! *Chris!*" Neera hissed behind her.

Remembering her poor childhood friend, Adella, Chrissy ignored her cousin and proceeded to Lana, where she and her mother soaked and munched on strawberries.

Lana's long eyelashes popped up. "Mrs…. What's your name again? Oh, that's right, Mason. Chrissy Mason—Maddy and Del's friend," Lana said in a slinky voice, throwing her curly weave over her shoulder.

"What are you still doing here?" Chrissy wasted no time. "Don't you work with Maddy? Maddy left New York yesterday. Shouldn't you have gone with her, since you came to the Hamptons as her guest?"

Lana snickered. "Wow, is that any way to greet somebody who might be your new neighbor?"

"I'll ask you again. Why are you here?"

"Not that it's any of your business, but I'm doing the same as you—relaxing. And looking into my future retirement prospects. Now, please excuse yourself. My mother and I would like to enjoy our spa day."

Chrissy lingered, to deliver a painfully clear mad-dog stare to Lana. "You don't belong here. And you need to understand that you're not wanted."

Lana snorted, her eyes narrowing until they formed knives that could have sliced meat. "Sweetie, that you came over here and gave me some of your valuable time, I take as a sign this is definitely where I belong. I'll consider your little visit as my welcome to Sag Harbor."

As she waded away, Chrissy planned to get on the phone with Maddy and Del to prepare them. She would need to start rallying all the political players and investors she could, and protect their heritage and identity from falling to destructive outsiders.

SEEING YOU SQUIRM

CHRISSY

The dying evening sunlight that sprayed into the Ivory's glass roof must have been an omen.

A long line of people filled the foyer from all walks of New York. This was definitely not the same Ivory. Any other time, Chrissy's family had always walked right in with premier reservations, and VIP treatment as one of the legacy families of Sag Harbor since the 1950s.

"Did you call up Mrs. Turner and ask her for a sit-down?" Chrissy asked her mother.

"Girl, no. Before this week, you haven't visited Sag Harbor in years. I still don't even understand why you dragged us out here into this freezing cold," her mother retorted.

Indeed, the frigid temperatures promised another coat of snow for New Year's, beyond what they'd gotten at Christmas.

"Oh, my God. This is crazy," Cher whispered. Some visitors spoke in Italian. Others spoke French. Yet more uttered languages they couldn't identify.

Champagne and snack trays flowed around the room.

Most people passed up food, too excited and eager as they made phone calls, lining up money and investors.

"Crazy isn't the word," Neera replied, her lips smacking her teeth. A hundred wide-eyed prospective buyers scanned the place. Greedy investors sized each other up, conducting Google searches to identify who was who.

"There she is," Cher whispered, and poked Chrissy in the ribs.

Chrissy turned to find Lana and her mother already surveying Chrissy and her group. They started heading toward Chrissy.

"Why is she coming over here?" Chrissy asked.

"Probably the same reason you went to her earlier today in the pool," Neera replied. "Whatever you do, just play it cool. We've never heard of her or her family. Not even my friends down in Texas know her. She couldn't possibly have the money or connections to compete here."

"Mrs. Mason, nice to see you again. This is my mother, Erlita," Lana said, with a competitive glint in her eye.

Steam curling around her chest, Chrissy delivered a warning glare to her new nemesis.

"Hello, how are you all doing?" Erlita asked, and ignored Chrissy to address Chrissy's mother, Mrs. Townsend.

"Wonderful, thanks. I'm Georgette. So, where are you ladies from? I don't believe I've seen you around here before," Chrissy's mother replied.

"Chile, that's because we're first-timers," Erlita explained in a deep Southern accent that dripped with plenty of barbecue, baked beans, and ribs. "My daughter was visiting here with her co-worker, Maddy, over Christmas. And she called me raving about this place Sag Harbor. I had no clue the Hamptons had black people in it, honey."

"So, Erlita, what brings you and Lana here to The Ivory?" Chrissy forced what felt too sugary of a fake smile.

"Well," Erlita started, and aimed a tense smile at Chrissy that was just as loaded, "I own a beauty salon back home, pretty successful, and I've been wanting to do something different."

"Oh, a beauty salon?" Chrissy asked while her eye twitched. "Do you have any clients here in New York? What will your clientele in Texas do? Follow you up North?"

"Chrissy, be polite, sweetie. I'm sure she can build up her clientele here, just like she's done before," Georgette said.

The woman sucked her teeth, tightening her gaze on Chrissy. "No, it's alright. I don't mind some pressure. I've certainly had more than my share of doubters in the past. They can be quite useful." Erlita's eyes danced around as if exploring for treasure.

Chrissy cringed at the audacity of these people. "I just can't help wondering why you are way up here, where you just said you are unfamiliar?"

Lana's eyes flared, and she pushed closer toward Chrissy, who did not budge an inch. "Oh, by the time we're done, you'll understand perfectly."

"You've got a lot of nerve," Chrissy muttered. "Flaunting your ass around here with a man who's not yours. We didn't make it clear to you last week that you're not welcome here?"

"Well, it's a damn good thing you don't own Sag Harbor, isn't it?" Lana replied, her grimace just as fierce.

"Excuse me, ladies, a Painkiller drink for you, my dear." A server butted in with a tray and forced himself between the two of them.

Painkiller? Irritated, Chrissy finally pulled her glare away from Lana and turned her ire to the server whom she knew from her trips to the restaurant. "Olivier, don't you see that we're—"

"The gentleman over there insisted that I quote, unquote, 'break up the girls on the playground', so would you like this drink or not, ma'am?" the server pressed.

Chrissy swung around. Slow, tortured drops of elation squeezed through the emotional faucet in her chest.

On the other side of the lobby, scrumptious and dressed down in jeans and a pullover sweater underneath a wool coat, sat a glass of enticing liquor. She froze. Why was he here?

With a brief salute, he shot her a sideways grin before pivoting and rejoining the conversation in his group.

The doors to the dining hall opened, and everyone proceeded forward. But Sheldon hung back, his eyes drinking her up once again.

"I must be your new fairy godfather or something," he said with a smirk. "How do I always pop up when you need help most?"

Chrissy laughed. "You're a stalker, maybe? I was doing fine. She and I were just having a friendly chat."

He snorted. "Is that what it was? Last I checked, that could have been a throwdown from my days on the Louisiana back roads. Like dusty feet were about to fly everywhere."

They chuckled, and now Chrissy's focus was shifting from Lana to the stunning man next to her. "So what are your dusty feet doing here?"

"Sweetheart, my feet aren't dusty. You need me to show you?" He bent over and slid off his ankle boot. "Don't let these fancy city clothes fool you. I'm a country boy at heart and I'll take these shoes off in a minute."

Chrissy burst out with a guffaw. "No. That's unnecessary.

Okay, okay, I believe you." She stopped him and struggled to control her amusement. "Why are you everywhere now?"

His gorgeous, smooth lips stretched into a smile, and through his long lashes, he peered down at her. "Yes, stalking is what I do. They don't give me enough hours at the bank, so my part-time gig is hunting down beautiful clients and breaking up fights, rescuing them from evil husbands, fighting off dragons… pulling them from burning buildings."

Joy rolled through Chrissy's belly. It felt so good to laugh, without worrying about her husband or children, even if just for a few minutes. "Aw, okay, that's a little exaggerated, don't you think? Dragons?"

"The way you two looked, somebody was about to set fire to something," he quipped.

"She was the one who would have needed rescuing," Chrissy snapped and sipped her drink with melancholy. Potential buyers fanned throughout the dining room where she'd held her Sweet Sixteen dinner. Where at age eighteen, she, Maddy, Del, and the other debutantes had their first luncheon to kick off deb week with The Madames' secret sorority. And later, where they crossed into the tight-knit Madames. No matter how long she stayed away, this place was part of their DNA.

"But really, why are you here?" Chrissy asked.

"I was hoping I would see you," Sheldon murmured. He walked close enough to her that he could nudge his elbow against her arm.

Her lungs grasped for the air that bolted from them and left her a little light-headed. When her brain did process oxygen again and reconnected to her senses, she inhaled his oceanic cologne with notes of wood. Lord, he smelled edible.

"Come on, Mr. Rouse. You've got better things to do than chase housewives around New York."

"Well, first off, you're not a housewife." His gaze danced around the dining room, checking it out. Before it landed back on Chrissy. "And second, what could be more tantalizing than pursuing a woman who won't give you a date?"

Another guffaw escaped her. "You make me sound harsh."

"You are harsh," he shot back. His beautiful teeth bit his bottom lip. "In a good way. It's one of the reasons you caught my attention."

A snort flew out, and she threw her hand over her mouth.

He continued, "But aside from that, I'm thinking about buying it."

That announcement whopped the smile right off her face. Her glare dug into him, and she waited for the follow-up "gotcha".

"You're kidding."

"Why would I kid you?" His eyes and lips were unsmiling.

"Because you're funny." Chrissy's mouth fell open.

His tongue swept over his lip again. It may as well have been sweeping her nipples. Mr. Rouse's hand squeezed her elbow, and his long eyelashes fell to her. "Thank you. I appreciate that. Please close your mouth. Don't tempt me."

Chrissy's jaw dropped lower. Her knees started knocking together, and a geyser of her blood shot into her ears.

"It's sweet real estate, Mrs. Mason. Check it out." He held out his drink, pointing around the room with his index finger. His eyes danced under the skylight. "Do you know what we could do with this? A nightclub that's jumping on the weekends. Doubles as a bar and restaurant during the week. We could even throw a game room in here, or a mini arcade."

Even as her lungs gasped for air, Chrissy shook her head.

"*No.* There are enough nightclubs in the Hamptons. Find one of those. We need to maintain heritage here. Make it a museum. Display artifacts and remnants that tell the story of what blacks have built here since the late 1800s. Keep the legacy alive and not let it die in some Chicks Gone Wild fantasy party."

His chuckling shook shoulders. "Um, okay, if you don't want it to earn much profit, sure. But throwing cash out the window isn't what I do. I love charitable projects and philanthropic work. But to spend money, one must make it. And I hate to break it to you, my dear, but this is just such a place to do so. Owners did a good job maintaining it. They are about to sell for a pretty penny."

Chrissy's heart sank. "And the new buyers will never understand the true gem they're getting—Black Sag Harbor. The bond and love we share around here."

"Help me understand then." His eyes turned serious, consuming her once more. "What's so special about this building?"

Her breaths tripped in her throat. Now it was her turn to gaze around the room, while she kicked her brain to gather a strong rebuttal. "Mr. Rouse, the first black people came here as settlers in the late 1800s. Their occupation was whaling. Former slaves sailed on the ocean, alongside white men, and—"

"No." He chided with a sweet grin, taking a step closer to her. "I don't mean recite all the history you've got in your head. I'm asking you to *show* me the Sag Harbor you love." His warm eyes glistened at her, clearing out the entire room, leaving just the two of them in it. And zero oxygen inside her.

Chrissy grappled for her right mind. "Will that convince

you to purchase it for something other than a nightclub?" she asked.

"No, probably not." He smiled. "But I can admire your lips, and watch your eyes while you think of reasons I shouldn't."

Chrissy's insides churned into grits, warm and mushy while sliding around in the core of her. What should a wife say? What would a responsible, fiercely independent woman who'd already been through a nightmare relationship do?

"If I can't change your mind, why do you need the tour?"

Sheldon closed in on her, bringing his lips to her head, where his breath kissed her skin. The aroma floating off his lean neck transported her to a private seaside villa.

"I don't need the tour. I just like seeing you squirm." His hand touched her arm again. "Mrs. Mason, you're married. Not enslaved. It's okay to take a walk with another guy. Who knows? An evening with a real man might help you… see your situation more clearly."

With a wicked smile on his mouth, he pulled away.

Was this really happening? It had been a long time since she had some feeling above her knees. Were her panties, dare she think it, *wet*? How long had it been since she'd felt that?

Chrissy's thoughts did cartwheels, while she figured out how to respond with coherent words.

He winked and walked away.

No! Where was he going? Had she offended him? What should she have said? He didn't turn back to wave or anything. Instead, he joined a group of guys who studied the dining room.

Downing the rest of her drink, Chrissy collected herself. Should she go to the bathroom and remove her underwear? Or just keep walking around the event wet?

She shouldn't have felt this excitement, or some trivial

crush. What would her mother think? Her grandmother? Both perfect, dutiful wives who'd held their families together with grace and class for decades. She needed to shake these thoughts from her head.

But first, what was her name? What was she doing here again?

"Girl," Neera whispered, surprising her. "Um, Earth to Chrissy. That fine-ass stallion just standing here... is he the guy who asked you out?"

"Yeah." Chrissy tapped the rim of her drink. "He was saying hi."

"No, boo, I think he was saying more than that." Neera's neck craned, and she served her cousin a suspicious side-eye. "Did he ask you out again?"

"No," Chrissy lied as her eye twitched.

"Yes, he did. It's all over you. *And* him." She stared across the room and back at Chrissy. "That man wants you."

Cher busted into Chrissy's conversation with Neera. "Don't look now, but guess who else just crawled in."

Bogarting the entrance, Kevin Middleton had appeared, waving like a celebrity on the red carpet greeting his fans.

"Oh, hell," Neera muttered.

"This might not be a bad thing. We can ask Kevin to meet with us about buying out The *Ivory* and saving it from these buzzards," Chrissy replied while assessing the possibility.

"I thought you hated him," Cher said.

"I do. But Kevin grew up here, just like we did. He is part of Sag Harbor. We should talk to him." Chrissy kept surveying the room. "I don't understand. Where are the Turners? Why wouldn't they come to their own open house?" She needed to speak with them about their plans for selecting buyers.

Neera sucked her teeth. "Probably because their rep told

them to clear out from all this, so we can't talk them down. They're going straight for the highest bidder. No playing favorites. Smart move."

"But damn, your girl over there certainly doesn't waste time," Cher said, and motioned in Lana's direction.

Once again, across the room, Lana and her mother had gone to work.

The Texan's hand slid over Sheldon's back. Her size double D chest pushed out, Lana said something, and the men surrounding her broke into laughter. One of them even got on his knee playfully, as if proposing. She may as well have sucked the energy from the event. In a tight, knitted wool dress and lace-up, peep-toe, leopard-print ankle boots, the woman clearly knew what she was doing.

Chrissy's head flipped away, as if she hadn't seen it. But a heated resentment rolled into her chest.

She called for another drink. "Well, if I didn't already feel like I was at the circus, I sure as hell am there now."

Her mother, Mrs. Townsend, came to join them. "Whew, child, these folks are breaking their necks to get this sale. If I was just a little younger, I'd try to jump in and start my clothier shop."

Chrissy turned to her. "But, Mom, you can. It's always been your dream."

"Oh, girl, no. I've lost that kind of energy now. I don't blame Odessa and Frank for walking away from this and enjoying their lives. I'm just worried about what breed we'll get in here next," Georgette said, and studied the eager bodies scouring the facility.

Chrissy left them all to head for her longtime nemesis, Kevin. She needed to round up a crew to stop this insanity. If she didn't, what kind of Sag Harbor would they return to later?

"Kevin, hey." She approached the group in which he stood.

He swerved around, and the big grin on his face faded.

Chrissy and Kevin had fought often when they were kids. Literally. While Maddy, Neera, Del, and other girls had fallen all over themselves for him, Chrissy had checked his arrogance on a few occasions. She'd never given him the chance to play pranks on her, or score points off of her, the way he had Maddy. His little ego may have still had a few burn marks on it.

"Oh, wow, Chrissy Townsend, or, uh, what is it? Mason now? I must have done something right in my life for you to come over here and bless me with your presence today," Kevin said with a tight jaw.

Chrissy thought fast. "Listen, we haven't always been on the best of terms, and I forgive you for your foolishness. I wanted to leave water under the bridge and see if we could discuss this place like adults. You know, team up together and stop the sale."

He sipped his drink. "And what makes you think I need your help for that?"

Keep your cool, Chris. "My family is as much a pillar of this community as yours. And because of your sparkling personality, there are still those around here—important people—who are not too fond of you. Officials on the village council who might shut you down. Couldn't you use hitters in your corner, like Maddy and me, to give you a softer touch and smooth over those rough patches for you?"

She stared down the young Silicon Valley tech mogul. "My ideas are solid enough that any politician in their right mind would be stupid as hell to pass them up. So I'm not worried about it, and besides, Chrissy, don't you have a slave-owner or somebody waiting for you out in L.A.?" he replied. "You're barely in the Sag anymore. I haven't seen you around here in years, so why do you care?"

Chrissy refused to back down or cower at the mention of Blake. She found her backbone and flipped the script.

"You know damn well the Turners loathe you. Hell, I loathe you. And the moment they get your bid—because I'm certain they will make the ultimate call—it's going in the trash. So, although we hate each other, we both love the Sag and wouldn't want it selling to strangers who can't appreciate what it is."

She watched him think as he sipped some more, peering over the rim of his glass, scanning the room of hungry entrepreneurs. Kevin's glare landed on Sheldon and his cohorts, who still talked up Lana and her mother.

Chrissy could have shucked corn with the knives of jealousy and competition she saw on Kevin's face. He sucked his teeth, and returned his focus to Chrissy.

"Alright. But get Maddy on the phone. Tonight. There's no way I'm dealing with you, unless she's involved."

"Why are you on Maddy's jock so hard now, after you tortured her as kids?" Chrissy asked.

"I liked her and couldn't say it. We were kids, okay? Besides, don't worry about it. Just get her on the phone and we can talk," he said.

"You weren't all that little. But whatever," Chrissy mumbled.

They both eyeballed the other side of the room, where it appeared their strongest competition was forming on Sheldon's side. Sheldon turned to catch them watching him, and he raised his glass. Kevin and Chrissy lifted their glasses in a mutual greeting.

"Chrissy, I swear to God," Kevin muttered, "if you're playing me, I will destroy you. I've got access to all the secret footage from your public fights with Blake—your driveway, the grocery store. Who do you think stopped them from going public? But for our Sag connection, your enemies could have screwed you."

The emergency lights of Chrissy's eyes blinked off and on. Heat twisted down her flesh and into her hands that shook so hard they splashed her cool drink. All these years she'd wondered what happened to the people who had recorded her and Blake on their cell phones. She had assumed the witnesses simply withheld it out of sympathy and respect.

Why would Kevin have helped her, without her knowing?

Seething, she reclaimed her voice. "Have you ever known me to play?"

"How do you know Sheldon Rouse? Why were you and him talking before you came over here to me?" Kevin scorched her with a conniving glare.

"He helped me with an issue at the bank a few days ago. I only met him last week. We were just speaking. He's a banker. Nothing else."

Chrissy never thought she'd see the day when she would explain a damn thing to Kevin Middleton. But now they needed each other.

"That had better be all." His arm reached, and she jumped as he surprised Chrissy by hugging her. "Either way, it's good to see you after all these years. You've really been strong out in L.A. Hopefully, with this deal, things will get better for you soon."

Their entire lives, from tug-of-war over the swings at the

playground to trading barbs at high school bonfires, they had never hugged.

Ever.

Now Chrissy stiffened at the shocking feel of his arms tightening around her. Perhaps in another lifetime, in a distant galaxy far, far away, she might have given him credit for a nice body. Very distant.

Before they parted, Kevin examined her with a long side-eye. Chrissy didn't flinch. Because she was telling the truth. Sheldon Rouse was nothing to her.

SHELDON

"I like it." Sheldon said, clapped. "Send me a write-up and I'll go over it with my team."

Lana and her mother, Erlita, squealed, hugging each other. "Well alright then, sir. We will do so. Expect to hear from us in the next day or two."

"Sounds good. Until then, you ladies take care." He shook each of their hands, holding them at arm's length as they tried to come in for hugs. Especially Lana, who casually tried to cop a feel of his wood.

Sheldon wasn't sure how he would approach this new path with his former college classmate, Brent. After all, they had been planning for a nightclub, and not a high-tech beauty spa. Complete with a hair salon, personalized music, food selections, and rooms available for small parties.

He turned Lana's idea over in his mind. Shel could revolutionize it with computerized options for wellness, weight, and health information. People could learn their cholesterol, blood pressure, if they were too stressed, or certain body parts that hadn't worked out enough, and the potential health risks that posed, all during one visit. That was just the begin-ning of his spontaneous brainstorming, without deeper thought.

As Chriselle had said herself, how many nightclubs did the Hamptons already have?

Reminded of Chriselle, he wondered what she and Kevin Middleton had discussed while scorching him from across the room.

Though Sheldon itched to go to her and vibe for a minute, he headed toward the exit. No goodbyes. He couldn't appear to be thirsty, or like he was beside himself. During this brief hour, he'd already ignored three women's phone calls asking what he was doing for New Year's.

"Sheldon!" Brent called out behind him. "What do you think of this place? I told you it was hot, didn't I?"

"And you were right on the money, my guy, but we should talk."

Brent's eyebrows linked in a question mark. "What have you got, dude? Hit me."

"A high-tech girls' club. Full services spa. Wellness and fitness."

Brent scoffed, leaning back on his heels. "Oh, no, man, don't tell me you came across a sweet piece of ass and now you're off your game?"

Not surprised at the blowback, Sheldon shook his head. "Nah, bruh, that's not it. I couldn't be thinking more clearly. I just finished talking to a chick who grew up here in Sag Harbor, who knows everybody, has tight connections. And she said the club scene is already saturated."

"But not if we do this right, my guy," Brent countered.

"Man, how many of them are there?" Sheldon pressed. "For the next few years, dude, the new joint is health and wellness. Wearables on your arm that tell your blood pressure. When you'll have a heart attack. Hiking. Relaxation. Meditation. Self-care. How often do you see the hashtag 'nightclub' nowadays? Everybody is all brunch-and-spa day. Even dudes. And if we could make that shit high-tech, you're talking subscriptions and memberships that continue to pay when folks aren't here. Nightclubs only work during the summer. This here would never shut down."

He could see Brent's mind turning over the concept, the way he would ponder which girls to leave the party with in their Brown University days. "Alright." He frowned. "Fine. So you make a little sense. I'll talk to the guys. When's the meeting?"

Before Sheldon marched to the car, he stopped and called Jerrell about this potential opportunity. He was in no mood for being stuck in traffic on the way out of Long Island, so he meandered down the side of the restaurant.

"Bruh, listen up. How do you feel about an ongoing deal that could get you and Gram more exposure?" He ran down the situation to Jerrell.

"Hmph," Jerrell said. "And if I want equity participation?" Little Brother was interested.

"I've got other people involved, but I'll work it out."

"That's tight. I'll talk to Gram and Aunt Rose, and you keep me plugged in."

Sheldon shut off the phone with new life coursing through his veins. He breathed in the invigorating winter air that blew from the ocean. The limitless potential of a nationwide black-owned beauty and wellness chain turned over in his mind.

"Yes, Maddy, that's right," a familiar voice spoke around the corner that stopped Sheldon in his tracks.

Chriselle. Insistent and hasty, she rambled.

"Yes, it's Lana. *And* her mama, both here in Sag Harbor. We found out the Turners are putting the Ivory up for sale, so I came to find out what was going on. This damn woman is actually here trying to buy this place for some beauty salon. Can you imagine the kind of people she'll bring in here with her?"

In a clipped tone, she continued, "I—*we*—have to do something. I've already started rounding up a squad, so we can all go to the Turners together and talk sense into them." Another pause. "Kevin wants to have a call with all of us tonight. Says he won't do this without you. N-no, Maddy. You brought that girl to Sag Harbor with you. Now you have to get back here and fix this. Yeah. Alright. I'll hit you in a couple hours."

Damn, she was coming. And Shel had accidentally eavesdropped. He couldn't just stay put. She would surely cross him when she walked perpendicular toward the cars and discovered him. He stepped from the shadows.

Chrissy's eyes flared. That lovely mouth plummeted.

"Wait—" Sheldon started.

"How dare you!" she spat.

The fight she'd deployed against the bank officers, now unleashed on Shel full throttle.

"No, not how dare me. This is a public area, I was out here having my call first, and you walked out of nowhere, already on the phone. I didn't know what to do because it would have been awkward either way," he said, holding up his long arms in a show of surrender. "Look, if it makes you feel better, I can share a little information from my side, and then we're even. We both walk away. No hard feelings. Cool?" he asked.

Goodness, her anger hardened his dick. For a snowflake of a moment, he wanted to see her use all that fury.

"I'll raise you. Forget about that." Chrissy's weight shifted, and it appeared her mind did too.. "Give us a chance to pitch you and persuade you to work with us. Drop whatever Lana and her mama are talking about and get in with the locals. *Then* there'll be no hard feelings."

Did she just counter him? Nice little surprise. "You want me to what?"

"You heard me. Lana is trouble. Not from around here. Knows nothing at all about us or how we operate. There's a vibe to Sag Harbor. We're quiet, behind-the-scenes. And our friends respect it. She doesn't. Whatever she's pitching, it's doomed. I'm going to make sure of it."

The sunset had activated the streetlights bouncing across her intentional face, which bounced across Shel's loins.

"How are you sure I've even picked a side? Or that I will take part in this sale at all? And when you say us, that includes you and who else?"

"Well, Kevin, myself, Maddy, probably our friend, Del, and a handful of other longtime residents I will line up," she answered. Her nails swept her hair back in the cold. Holiday-red lipstick staining her lips, eyes squinting against the winds and the fading sun, she set her jaw with purpose.

Sexy mutha...

"I don't know, Mrs. Mason. Lana's idea is timely and culturally relevant. Black natural beauty, when self-awareness and consciousness are exploding. A black-owned beauty bar with all the works. If it's rolled out properly, people up and down the East Coast will flock here by year's end. Folks from Atlanta and D.C. will file a line down the street. And in five years, I can predict chains across major cities in the U.S."

"You don't have the political connects to get the licenses and clearances," she shot back. "You'll also get stop signs from residents who refuse to deal with those *long lines* of intruders from Atlanta and D.C., day after day. And none of you have the history with the locals that we do."

He relished this light tête à tête. "But you forget I work for a bank. One of the major banks that services much of New England. We have connections and patron lists of our own, my dear. Including you. People who are just as grateful to us as you were a few days ago."

She was nothing short of stunning. How has she been cooped up for years?

"Sheldon…" Chriselle's chest rose, and her eyes bounced around. "I mean, Mr. Rouse—"

"Mm, Sheldon is perfect. And I love the way you say it. Go on," he said. It tickled him, how hard she fought not to smile.

"Mr. Rouse, you seem like a decent enough man. Maddy speaks highly of your family. And if your brother, Jerrell, is any sign, I'm sure you have firm principles." As she spoke, her phone lit up. A picture of a little boy popped onto her screen.

This time, Sheldon pivoted and backed away. "Go ahead. I'll wait. Out of earshot."

She murmured a few sentences in a mothering voice. "Oh, baby, that's awesome."

He walked further, checking a few text messages and emails for the next couple of minutes.

"Mr. Rouse."

He spun around, ready for part two. "Mrs. Mason."

"Thank you for your patience," Chrissy said, determined to finish making her case.

And Sheldon was here for that determination. He nodded, suppressing his humor and giving her his serious face.

"Where was I?" She wore the ultimate confused parent expression.

"My firm… principles," he reminded her, and tried not that hard to hide his amusement.

"Oh, yes. You wouldn't appreciate anyone invading your home that you love. All I ask is that you learn about Sag Harbor first, before you barge in, throwing around money." Her phone lit up again. She peeked at it and silenced it. "You and I just met. I don't want us to be opponents, or rivals, or anything like that."

"Why not? The people I respect most in the world are my opponents." Hands shoved in his pockets now, Sheldon eyed her.

She batted her eyes, apparently stunned at his nerve. Sheldon enjoyed observing her loss of words. Her hair continued to blow against her face.

Instinctively, Sheldon moved toward her, his arm shooting to help her out.

Immediately, she tensed up, lurching backward, as if Chrissy had expected him to… hit her.

Her eyes wild and glazed, she backed up, and Sheldon realized her terror.

"Whoa, hey… hey, hey." He lowered his hand. "I didn't mean to—"

"No. I had a little… shock there. You stunned me for a second," she replied, slightly scrambled, trying to laugh it off. But her chest rose and fell like she struggled for air.

"I apologize for startling you." Sheldon spoke in a soothing voice.

She shook her head. "You didn't. I just wasn't expecting you to…" Exhaling, she let out a nervous breath.

His hands moved slower this time. "May I?"

A newborn buck couldn't have trembled harder than Chrissy.

His gloved hand brushed aside the hair still whipping her face. "That's better." He stopped himself from soothing her with his mouth. "Now I can see you."

Her eyes focused harder on his. "Mr. Rouse, would you promise me you won't agree to anything with Lana until you've met with us?"

To hell with talking about business. He wanted those lips to tremble under him. And he would only do the kind of hitting she liked.

She was so determined to convince him of a lame idea from Kevin that she missed all that fierce energy she was serving.

"Only if you have dinner with me. And give me the tour I asked for."

A flurry of conflicting emotions tossed around on her young, wedded face. Sheldon was near certain he knew what half of them were. One couldn't become a divorced father by age thirty-nine and not relate to that anxiety of dating again.

While she thought of an answer, he had a suspicion. He whipped out his phone and opened up an app.

"Meet with us," she said. "And I'll come to dinner."

"Deal. I'll meet with you first. And if it's good, I'll meet with everyone else." He'd have to fight himself the entire night not to sop her up.

"But how do I know you'll take this seriously, and that you're not doing this just to hit on me?"

He remotely unlocked his Maybach. "I *am* doing this to hit on you." Hitting on her was the only reason he was really here. "But I'll try to listen... most of the time." Sheldon enjoyed one last glance at her.

Once again, she rolled those beautiful amber jewels she

called eyes. "Mr. Rouse, why are you even interested in buying The Ivory? There has to be more to you than just money."

"I guess you'll have to come to dinner and find out what." He turned his back to her. Again. "Call me with the time you'll be ready tomorrow, Chriselle."

Sheldon grimaced at what his app revealed to him. On his screen, two red dots appeared, signaling a large concern that unsettled him. But he wouldn't mention it now.

Behind him, she called, "I'm not some little girl with her nose wide open that you're going to lead around, Mr. Rouse."

Still not turning to face her, he continued strolling. "And what a disappointment you would be if you were."

Damn, her toughness turned him on.

Once inside his car, he watched through his rearview mirror to make sure she reached hers safely. He'd stopped short of walking her, opening her door, or making any overt moves. Too predictable. He wanted her to wonder why he didn't.

But there was also another, more grave reason he had not.

He recalled her shaken face, the way she'd almost leaped from her skin when he'd moved toward her. Why was she so jumpy? What had her husband done to make her that way? Sheldon could not imagine the hell she'd endured. If any man had treated one of his two sisters that way, they would not see light the next day.

He called up a hacker on the West Coast.

"Sheldon, buddy, Merry Christmas! What's up?" the voice answered on the other end.

"Jaycee, hey, same to you, lady. I need a favor. What can you get me on a guy named Blake Mason?"

CHRISSY

I wonder why he didn't walk you to your car." Cher wondered the next afternoon.

"Doesn't matter. I don't need him to." Chrissy tried on her fourth outfit, dissatisfied and taking it off. "Not what I'm after."

"Girl, what are you trying to do?" Cher asked. "Bore him to death? If there's a 'least sexiest outfit' award somewhere, you deserve a nomination."

As soon as Chrissy heard that, she decided her appearance was perfect. "That's the point," she replied.

Wrapped in an oversized blazer, bulky and unrevealing sweater, and tweed, wide-legged slacks, she smoothed her hair back into a tight bun at the nape of her neck.

No loose curls would fly tonight.

No red lipstick.

No bright colors, but browns and tans instead.

For makeup, she wore light foundation, minimal eye works, and Vaseline on her lips. To finish the look, she slid on flat, comfortable Mom boots for walking a tour and her thick-rimmed distance glasses underneath a felt fedora.

The disgust on Cher's face told Chrissy she was on the right trackl.

Last night's conference call with residents and longtime vacationers had encouraged Chrissy. Bids were due at the end of January. Then, the village council would hold a meeting to review the submissions and identify potential problems. A correction period would follow. Finally, after a vetting process by the town officials, the Turners could decide which of the approved businesses they would sell to.

Chrissy and the others were confident they could shut down these outsiders bringing in flashy parties and strobe lights.

"Honey," her mother started.

A preoccupied Chrissy reviewed her notes.

"Yeah, Mom?" she replied absently, making sure she had the pitch of Kevin's idea and the details correct.

"I know The Ivory means a lot to you. But..." Mrs. Townsend sighed.

"Spit it out, Mom," Chrissy said, already anticipating the next words.

"It's unnecessary to go to dinner with this man in order to make your point. You have a family, a husband, an entire life you've built for yourself in California. And with a little time apart, Blake will see... he'll come around and realize how much he needs you. They always do," her mother pleaded. "Don't mess all that up by taking a silly girl's road."

Chrissy didn't bother moving her gaze from her tablet. "And what makes you think I'll want Blake if he returns?"

Her mother's weight leaned against the back of Chrissy's chair. "Little girl, you look at me."

Chrissy glanced up at her mother's reflection in the mirror. They stared at one another through the vanity set. The pressure of her family's legacy bore down on her, as it always had.

"You want your children to have a father who is present and committed. Mistress or not. Family is your first priority."

"I know, Mom. You've said it enough times."

Over and over. Since the day she'd told her mother she was pregnant during her junior year at Spelman with a guy from Morehouse. And Georgette Townsend had insisted on calling Blake's mother, Mrs. Mason. Eight months later, they took a break from senior mid-terms on a chilly afternoon to hold a quick ceremony at the campus chapel. The following summer, she was traipsing after Blake to L.A., where Chrissy knew no one, save two or three classmates and distant relatives.

"As long as you don't forget it."

"How could I?" Chrissy replied. *You won't let me.* She didn't want an argument. This holiday trip had been going well so far. She remained silent.

She lowered her eyes to her iPad so her mother wouldn't see tears that stubbornly came despite her eyelids batting at them.

Her cousin, Neera, drove her to the Nightingale restaurant.

Seeing no sign of Mr. Rouse yet, she made a quick phone call to her children. In the background, she heard adults laughing and particularly, the shrill voice of a woman. Blake's friends must have joined them in Wyoming for New Year's, and he was flaunting his side piece in front of them all. She knew what Blake was doing—deliberately attempting to make her jealous so she would come running and cause a scene. But those days were long over.

Chrissy only cared now what example her daughter, Kara, would learn. And Little Blake who was already having behavioral issues at school.

Asking for her children, she bit her tongue and maintained her composure. Their voices, as they rattled off their play day, calmed her. They all promised to speak that night at bedtime.

"Relax," Neera said next to her.

"I am relaxed." The rippling through her stomach, and trembling of her hands, said otherwise.

"Cousin—"

"Neera," Chrissy half-whined, half-breathed. "If you're about to start up like Mama, then—"

"Chris, chill. I only wanted to say have a good time. Whatever happens, happens. You've been through a lot and if anybody deserves to get their back broken, it's you. I know how you are, Chris, overanalyzing every little thing that could go wrong. Stop worrying so hard about being the good wife. Tonight, handle your business. And then, just let shit flow. Alright?"

Neera always had Chrissy's back, and she was constantly on the lookout for Blake's crazy side. Chrissy had expected Neera to warn her about moving with caution.

So Neera's encouragement came as a small surprise that poured love and goodness all over Chrissy.

"I don't intend to let anything flow, but I appreciate you wanting my happiness. I love you, cousin."

"Love you too, boo. No matter what you 'accidentally' wind up doing tonight," Neera whispered and pulled back with a wink.

On the outside, Chrissy laughed, *all up in* her insides, she warred with her ten-year drought.

In the mirror, she checked her understated makeup before opening the door, and reassured herself that she had this under control. That she wasn't being a terrible wife or mother.

What if Blake found out? If nosey neighbors whispered? She had a mind to call Sheldon and cancel. But the Ivory was too important. If she could convince him to join her side, the team of her, Kevin, Maddy, and Sheldon would be unstoppable.

She got out and headed toward the Nightingale entrance.

A dapper gentleman immediately approached her. He held out an arm, as would an usher.

"Mrs. Mason, good evening, I'm driving you tonight."

"I'm sorry?" Chrissy asked. "I don't need a driver. We're already here. Where is Mr. Rouse?"

"Waiting for you, madam," he replied. He turned toward a taxiing Mercedes.

Chrissy protested, "The nerve of him. He never mentioned changing locations. Why didn't he ask me first?"

"He thought this might be a better option. And we're on a schedule, so we should take off. Shall we?" the driver insisted.

A better option? Annoyed that Sheldon had taken liberties without asking her permission (God, why were men so bad about that?), Chrissy moved toward the car and entered. A folded note awaited her on the backseat.

Sorry for the inconvenience, my dear, but after doing some homework of my own, I do believe these extra steps are best.

Her heartbeat pumped into her throat on the twenty-minute ride, while Chrissy watched every turn through the tinted windows. Finally, after she'd sat in suspense and questioned why this was necessary, the driver delivered her to a nearby private helicopter landing pad.

Among high winds, with Chrissy mashing her hat down on her head to keep it from blowing off, she marched toward the waiting helicopter, its propellers spinning. The pilot offered a hand to help her on.

Chrissy hesitated. "This is the right place? Sheldon Rouse?" she asked a polite woman at the stairs.

"Yes, ma'am, you bet," the middle-aged pilot yelled over the running engine and propellers. "Just hop on and I'll get you to Alpine in a heartbeat."

"*Alpine?*" Chrissy asked, stunned. *"New Jersey?"*

She boarded. Inside, Sheldon sat with a studious look. His gaze roamed over her matronly outfit, and amusement animated his face, as if he immediately picked up on what she was trying to convey.

His leather-gloved hands patted the seat next to him. "Mrs. Mason."

Chrissy sat and buckled up. "You want to tell me what this is about?"

"Yes. When the time is appropriate, I have an explanation for the change of plans. In the meantime, I'm going to ask you for your cell phone."

He delivered a firm gaze with no humor.

"What?"

"And your coat, please. You can borrow mine."

She sat in shock, numerous doubts storming her brain. Specifically if she should even be here, let alone making incognito moves. Who the hell did he think he was?

"No. We barely know each other. Besides, there's no need to—"

"I'm afraid I have it on good authority that there *is* a need.

Trust me." His gaze deepened. "I won't hurt you. Or your marriage. I promise."

A quick fight-or-flight urge to bolt rushed over her. This had already gone too far. And yet something was nailing her feet to stay put.

"M-my children, what if they—"

"I got you," Sheldon said. His chiseled jaw came toward her. The helicopter propellers may as well have been spinning in Chrissy's chest. He took off his leather glove and opened the palm of his bare hand. "Has your fairy godfather steered you wrong yet?"

Chrissy's life flashed behind her eyelids that fell to her wedding bands.

They rose to meet Sheldon's eyes again. Serious and unflinching, he awaited her.

Seconds ticked in which she had to choose. Blake's words suddenly echoed through her mind. *Come home with me. It's not too late. And I'll forgive you for thinking you could make a decent life without me.*

She already knew what lay behind door number one.

Her hands shaking, she turned over the phone. Sheldon's hand closed over hers and took it.

ALPINE

CHRISSY

In a few quick moves, Sheldon went through her settings, sliding off options and turning on others. He passed her phone to an assistant waiting outside the helicopter door.

Chrissy unbuckled the seatbelt and took off her coat. Sheldon took it and also handed it to the assistant.

He removed his own coat and placed it around her shoulders.

"There. You should be good until we get back."

Utterly confused, Chrissy snuggled inside it, shielding herself from the cold and inhaling his sensual, mahogany-and-oak scent.

She was glad she'd worn her thickest clothes, so he couldn't see her heart gallop or the changes in her other body parts.

"How often do you do this?" she asked him as they looked out the window at miles of coastline below.

"Do what?"

"Sweep up women and fly them away so you can distract them?"

"Distract? Is that what I'm doing to you with a simple helicopter ride?" His grin slid over his face. Relaxed and in his element, he was clearly unperturbed by her suspicion of him. "You shouldn't be so easily impressed, Mrs. Mason. Besides, everyone else gets first class overseas."

Chrissy erupted into laughter that she couldn't hold in.

He leaned back, continuing, "And if you were really special, you would have gotten a jet."

Easy and disarming, he didn't think too hard. She struggled against his cavalier humor. His smile was infectious, and no matter how hard she tried, she could not suppress hers that bubbled up from her insides.

Responsibilities, she remembered. The face of her mother looming over her in the mirror, and the faces of all the other women in her family who came before and had never experienced divorce.

As they flew across New York pointing out landmarks they recognized below, she told him funny stories about her childhood. Getting in trouble and having fun in various places.

Sheldon cracked up, slapping his leg at her memories of taking a subway by herself to find a lost doll at age eight, her and Neera sneaking into nightclubs at age seventeen, and crashing her new car after a DMX concert while pursuing his entourage.

Recalling all those free-wheeling adventures reminded Chrissy of her old self, and tiny twinges of sadness twisted her chest.

Sheldon must have picked up on her somber energy,

because he gave her hand a gentle squeeze. Once again, she was swimming in his eyes. Not sexual, or overbearing, but like he understood. A protective, brotherly vibe emanated from him.

Forty-five minutes had flown by. After landing, they walked to a classic 1960s model Porsche. No chauffeur stood by, and now it was just the two of them.

This time, he opened her car door and held it. His walnut-colored eyes studied her once more.

"There's a great, quiet spot not too far away, and we should get there shortly," he stated, starting the vehicle. He operated the gears and antique knobs like he had an intimacy with this vehicle. "The heat should kick on here in a moment. This old girl likes to take her sweet time."

"Is this… your car?" Taking off her gloves, she explored the tan leather seats with red trim.

"Yes. We go way back, about ten years."

"She's beautiful. Does she have a name?"

"Luscious."

Chrissy burst out laughing again. What was wrong with her tonight?

"Girl, why are you laughing? That was the name of my first bike," he said with mock defensiveness as they took off.

Sheldon drove through the beautifully manicured neighborhoods of Alpine, New Jersey, and he pointed out the homes of key figures who lived in the city—politicians, CEOs, and a couple of celebrities. The car entered a gated community tucked among tree-lined streets that curled around woodsy, snowy hills. The attendant waved and opened the gate before they drove inside. The quietude and intimate homes were breathtaking. Snow from Christmas still salted many yards, giving the slopes a perfect holiday vibe from a greeting card. The New York snow Chrissy missed most while living in warm Southern California.

He drove up the hilltops until they arrived at a tiny restaurant shaped like a log cabin called the Firewood Village Inn. Reaching in his backseat, he grabbed another coat for himself and came around to open her door.

Inside the cozy, dark establishment, Sheldon placed his hand at the small of her back as the server escorted them to a corner against a bay window. Rolling, snow-capped hills stretched around them for miles before meeting decorative lights and the city skyline in the distance.

"This is gorgeous." She sighed out a slow, wishful breath.

"Yes, it is. Not a day goes by that I don't give thanks." He held out her chair. "Wine? Champagne?"

"Oh, no, it'll be tea," she said to the server. Her nerves still rattled slightly, and the last thing Chrissy wanted was to wind up in a compromising situation. More specifically, tipsy and weak.

Sheldon smiled, clasping his hands over the table, eyes twinkling over the light of a small candle. "Of course, it will be."

"So," she started, and whipped out her tablet. "The bids."

"Yes," he said, his expression switching gears. His finger pointed directly at her. "My eyeglasses. You have them in that jacket pocket."

"Oh." She handed them over, their hands brushing in the exchange, and she watched him slide them on.

He stunned her with thick eyeglasses that were as nerdy as hers. He'd matched her studious appearance. Chrissy batted away an urge to cackle again.

No amusement colored his face this time. "You were about to say."

His jaw set, he was fine as the pricey liquor he drank. Now, with him giving her his undivided attention, Chrissy was more than a little uneasy.

Damn.

She proposed Kids Tech Layer, an idea of Kevin's that she thought would work well in Sag Harbor. A family-oriented computer and space exploration site where kids could go to build and explore. She'd read about it a couple of years before and had liked it. She was okay with pushing the project now, and so were the other longtime residents who wanted to keep Sag Harbor private and sane.

He scrolled through the photos on her tablet. "So you're talking about a children's playroom with AI, VR, and space games, instead of arcades and a ball jumper."

"Yes, a place where children go while parents shop, relax at the beach, head to a spa, or out to eat, or where summer birthday parties can be held," Chrissy suggested, watching his eyes absorb figures that Kevin had provided to her.

Sheldon's strong jawbone curved into a muscular neck that escaped inside a black turtleneck. She realized that she stared, and Chrissy diverted her gaze out the panoramic windows.

"And what will you do during off-season?" he asked bluntly.

"Specialized learning year round. For students struggling in school, or those who want college prep, test prep courses, conferences, and conventions," she answered, glad the group had discussed that question the night before.

A wrinkled nose was his first response. "I'm not so sure. Christmastime. Winter. Even if they need tutoring, most kids are hitting the slopes, having fun, and aren't thinking of the

Hamptons." He sipped more wine before his head tilted curiously. "Does Kevin know you're here talking to me?"

She slid her tongue across her teeth, remembering Kevin's literal meltdown about Sheldon the day before. "Yes."

"Hmph," he said. "And he agreed to that?"

She grinned and sipped her tea. "I wouldn't go that far."

That brought laughter back to Sheldon's face. "I figured as much."

"What is the rub between you and him?"

Sheldon shifted in his seat, his calm eyes settled over the candlelight. "I didn't hire him for a job when he first left college. It was an on-campus hiring affair and, you know, there weren't too many brothers in tech at that point. So he and I were two of about five men of color in a room of hundreds. I think he assumed he had it in the bag. The other three guys I hired went out of their way to show they actually wanted the job. Kevin didn't take it seriously, and it showed. He never got over it."

He returned Chrissy's tablet to her.

"Kevin is a very smart guy, and he's already gone far. He cranks out some solid ideas, but he hasn't produced the money one yet."

Chrissy placed her device inside her purse. "So are you penalizing Black Sag Harbor because of Kevin?"

"Of course not," he said, removing his glasses, his broad back covering the entire chair. "Besides, I'm not the ultimate judge. And you have home court advantage here. The village council or the Turners might choose you. I'd say you're in a far better position than Lana at this point. As long as you keep doing all the talking, and lock up Kevin's colossal head somewhere, you just might get the sale."

She nodded, acknowledging the truth of Kevin's arrogance. "Alright, that's fair."

The server brought their food. A simple steak for him, and a salmon salad for her. No fancy spreads or foreign delicacies. They both seemed content with an understated meeting where the focus could be conversation.

"Now, I must say, I'm a little surprised," he noted.

"At?" She tried her dish that tasted scrumptious with the seasonings.

"I expected to hear about actresses. Singers. Possibly a theater and playhouse. An art school. College kids traveling to a cool beach town, so they can have experiences and exposure they don't normally get." He dropped her a few hints in his raised eyebrow over his steak.

He had researched her career moves. Shallow breaths sprinted through her airways. Chrissy had not prepared for that. "Well, I'm just starting out. I have to make a name for myself and prove my skill. That I have a nose for this."

"Karema Jackson is a very promising talent. I read she's already secured two tent-pole projects coming up. I've seen her on stage here in New York. That was all you?"

Now Chrissy's lungs had contracted as if clapping with glee. "Yes. All me."

"Hat tip to you. So you don't think you could've used that building to, perhaps, build *your* brand?" he asked.

"Well, as you lightly put it, facilities cost dough. I'd have to develop my clientele first, to keep the money flowing all year, or else it would always be winter for me," she cracked.

He chuckled. "I'm sure you'll do it. You're certainly off to a strong start. Impressive, and I can't wait to see who you find next."

"Thank you. So what about you? Why aren't you

presenting any ideas of your own, Mr. High-Tech Smart Guy?"

He shrugged, cutting more steak. "I don't want to throw out just anything. I want to create an asset the world needs. A gadget or system no one expects but can't live without. I tinker around sometimes, but I'll admit, I'm not too inspired these days." A hint of a scowl crossed his face as Sheldon practically stabbed his dinner.

"What about your family? Did you say you have a son also? Does he help you?" Chrissy asked to change the tempo.

"He's in Chicago with his mother. Divorced three years. She got primary custody." He took a sip of wine.

Chrissy stopped herself from asking the most obvious question.

But he seemed to read it on her.

"Now you want to know why it ended. I was traveling too much for the job. Setting up systems and overseeing operations all over the world. I thought she would wait for me to settle in with my career as long as I was bringing the money in. But she is a daddy's girl, comes from a big family, and hated being in New York alone. By the time I finally transferred to a desk role that would keep me in the city..." he said, pausing for a deep inhale, "... she'd jetted."

Sheldon's massive shoulders had fallen almost onto his plate.

"I'm sorry to hear that."

"Don't be. What's done is done." A hint of sadness flickered in his eyes.

"You really loved her," Chrissy concluded from the traces of pain she saw.

He swallowed as if the food was gasoline. "I did."

There was once a time when Chrissy would have given

anything for Blake to feel that way about her. "Go back to Chicago and get her."

A thin smile playing at his lips, Sheldon shook his head.

"Not an option. To tell you the truth, I wouldn't do anything different now. I love my life, and my career. It's my passion. My ex didn't want to compete with my ambition. She thought she should have been enough, that my appetite was insatiable. And maybe it was. Still is. She wanted a simple existence. I wanted it bigger and better. And yada, yada. Sorry to bore you. How did this become about me?"

"Probably because you're the one flying women around in helicopters." She tried adding a light touch back to the conversation.

He chuckled. "Is that what it is?"

Right then, he pulled out his phone, which was buzzing, and handed it to her. On his screen was a number she recognized—Blake's.

Now Chrissy understood his earlier moves.

Sheldon had kept her phone in the Hamptons so the location technology would display a signal from there. Meanwhile, he'd forwarded her calls to his phone in New Jersey. This way, Blake would not know she had left Sag Harbor.

And Sheldon had taken her away to some place secluded, so that prying eyes and ears could stay out of her business.

To top it off, he hadn't been at her side when she entered a chauffeured car in Sag Harbor, so it appeared she was leaving alone. He had literally covered her outing from start to finish.

While she talked, he headed to the restroom to give her privacy.

When she finished settling the children's dispute over who could play the video game first, she handed Sheldon his phone. "Thank you. Really."

"You're welcome. Really." He ordered dessert, and a stronger drink.

"And for the lady?" the server inquired.

"Hot chocolate," Chrissy answered, determined to maintain her discipline.

Sheldon's expression had turned cryptic. His mood had dimmed some. Now, she struggled to make out what was on his mind.

"Why did you do all this for me?" she asked.

His long finger extended up his jawline while he observed her. Chrissy suspected he needed to say something but couldn't decide if he would disclose it.

His fingers linked over his chest. Big inhale.

"Because if a psychopath was tracking one of my sisters everywhere she went, I would want someone to do the same for her," Sheldon finally answered. He pulled out his phone again.

When Chrissy stared at it, she saw several red dots. "What is this?"

"Listening devices on your coat and purse," he replied.

Chrissy's breath clung to her ribs, arrested in its cage. Appalled, she could only direct her fury out the window, so she didn't break down into a humiliated mess in her seat. "Oh, my God."

"Any of these could pass through an airport scanner if he turns it off and reactivates it when you've landed."

She rubbed her convulsing chest that seemed crushed under Blake's hand.

Sheldon continued, "When I saw how you reacted last night, I had a suspicion, so I scanned you. Today, we removed two of these bugs, but be careful. Later, before you head back to L.A., I'll show you this app and how to use it, so you can keep an eye out…" He cut his eyes to his drink, "… while you decide how you'll handle it."

Unable to stop shaking, Chrissy managed a nod.

He passed her the harder liquor. "I ordered that for you. The good news is you're only thirty-one. Plenty of time to fix those decisions we made before we grew up." Now, his smile was not slick or humorous but sympathetic.

With no hesitation now, Chrissy took the drink.

"If I had bugs on me, that means Blake may have heard you asking me out. And getting on your helicopter," Chrissy thought aloud.

"Maybe. Maybe not. The propellers were so loud, it may not have been decipherable," he replied.

Fear of what might happen next transported Chrissy out of her body, to an unknown future that terrified her.

"This could kill my life," she muttered.

"Or maybe your life's been dead." He stared at her like he knew other secrets she didn't. "And learning this could give you new life. Finally. There's a bright side to everything."

The candle between them danced, illuminating the softness of his stare. Illuminating Chrissy's fear.

He'd ordered Cherries Jubilee. "Two spoons, please."

As Chrissy sank her worries inside the brandy, he reached out to her with ice cream and confection. He waved it in front of her mouth. "Come on. Your fairy godfather wants you to open up."

A reluctant grin pushed through her melancholy. "What am I? Five?" She parted her lips so he could slide in warm, dripping dessert.

"Yep, I feed hungry women everywhere," he laughed, intentionally letting some sauce glide over her lip. "Uh-oh."

She sputtered, laughing and trying to lick it off. The liquor was settling into her, softening her muscles, and the whole effort was sloppy.

Suddenly, in a moment too fast for her to react, Sheldon got up from his chair. He leaned over the table and sucked the cream from her mouth.

Wet, liquor-laced, his tongue played at the corners of her lips. Patient fingers touched the exposed skin above her turtleneck.

The skin over her cheekbone reacted to his thumb's caress by telegraphing the inside of her panties. Tortured, sweet, and hot, his kiss fell like rain on Chrissy's desert that hadn't seen water in years. The parched earth inside her begged for moisture.

She buried the tiny voice in her head and kissed him back. Their tongues danced an exhilarating waltz. Deeper and wetter, she forgot herself in warm passion so foreign to her.

Until he pulled away.

His chest rose and fell like it was lifting a heavy weight. That kiss had clearly rocked him too. "I can't say I'm sorry for that. But I did promise you I wouldn't hurt your vows. If you want me to take you back to the helicopter, now's the time. We should go so you can get back, and I'll give you some tips on how to protect yourself." He signaled for the check.

"What if I don't want you to?"

Was she speaking the words coming out of her mouth?

Sheldon stared back at her across the candlelight.

"Sweetheart, you didn't want to come here," Sheldon said, and appeared as remorseful as a kid who'd eaten too many cookies. "I did all this without asking."

The scorched earth inside Chrissy pleaded for water. "Now I don't want to leave."

He paused a moment. She saw the wheels of his mind

turning, likely conducting the same analysis as she. All the ways this could go wrong, how their reputations were on the line, that they barely knew each other, how people got murdered over extramarital affairs.

"Stay with me for New Year's," he whispered. "I can't say what else happens after that. But I do know what happens for the next forty-eight hours that you're with me."

In her head was Blake's voice. *Come to your senses, baby. And stop this independent woman bullshit you running. It won't work.*

Chrissy knew the real reason she'd gotten on that helicopter. And left her phone behind.

LET ME LIGHT YOU A FIRE

SHELDON

Inside Sheldon's house, Chrissy set down her purse. He took her coat and shoes she'd kicked off.

Even if this went nowhere and they did nothing, her presence felt too good. Sheldon wasn't ready to leave her.

"Let me light you a fire," he said at seeing her shudder in the walls of his two-story home that sat cold many days. He hadn't used his fireplace in forever, but fortunately, the housekeepers had left good, dry firewood.

After he handed her his oversized football jersey and some basketball shorts, she went to his bathroom and changed.

"I have bottled water and beer," he said with an embarrassed laugh once she got back. "Because I honestly wasn't planning on company." He really had arranged to send her back to Sag Harbor and had to call off the helicopter.

She laughed with him, her eyelashes skipping in every direction. "I'll take the beer."

He brought it back to her and joined her on his sheepskin fur rug where she leaned against his sofa. Leaving two feet of distance between them, Sheldon didn't want her to feel pressure.

"So may I ask why you're in this big ole house all by your lonesome?"

He shook his head, not wanting to discuss one of the most sensitive issues of his adulthood. "Not tonight. I'd rather talk about the kind of movies you like."

Her giggle erupted, and she snorted the beer.

So goddamn cute. He resisted the nagging urge to grab her again. Because damn, if she didn't look like the perfect, sexy little NFL wifey in Sheldon's football jersey. Her thick, muscular calves slid out of his basketball shorts, which fell back when she lifted her legs and laughed, revealing her meaty thighs. They boasted nice, toned hamstrings, like she was well-fed but still worked out. In his head, Sheldon was already grabbing and flipping her ass cheeks. *Shit.*

He redirected his eyes around his living room, to reclaim his thoughts real quick, so they didn't stray too far.

"Well, first off," she started, the back of her hand wiping beer from her mouth. She was obviously too tipsy to notice Sheldon checking her out. "What kind of movie person do I *cross* you as? Let's finish that convo."

Entertained enjoying the way she tossed subjects back at him, he slinked down on his rug and crossed his legs. He liked this vibe between them and easily recalled their playful conversation at the debutante ball.

He thought of her fierceness at the bank, how she'd confronted Lana, and laid out her case to him—she was a stealth warrior.

"You're the *Captain Marvel, Sarah Connors, Lara Croft: Tomb Raider* type. Fierce. Intense. Ready to whip somebody's ass at the drop of a dime. Yeah, you try to act all soft and gentle. But you are definitely not mushy, Hallmark channel." He loved watching her mouth spread over all thirty-two of her teeth. "I might even give you *Terminator*. You've got a little edge under those pricey suits you wear. So am I right, or am I right?"

Chrissy turned up the beer, giddiness still riding on those lips. She held up her index finger and thumb, separated by half an inch.

"You might be a teeny bit right."

"I'm a lot right." He tickled her side until she snorted laughing again.

"Sappy doesn't suit me. Never did. Give me *Aliens* and thrillers. DMX, Trina, and Eve anytime. Then you're talking my language." Chrissy's gaze needled him. "You were also going to tell me what motivates you besides money."

Sheldon's eyebrow cocked up playfully. "I was?"

She nodded. "You said if I came to dinner… well, I came. Now you can tell me if there's more to you than dollar signs."

A spot in Sheldon's chest fluttered at seeing her genuine interest to know. Damn, now that was hot. She remembered. And it didn't feel like she was making polite conversation. In her eyes, she actually waited, as if ready to analyze the truthfulness and sincerity of what came out of his mouth.

"Technology. Innovation," he answered honestly. "Making things work. Creating software and programs that improve people's lives in a way they didn't know they needed."

"Hm," she said as her lovely eyes rolled around, "so then, what are you doing helping me at a bank?"

Sipping his beer, Sheldon reflected back to his teenage conversations with his elder brother, Roland. How Roland had convinced him to avoid their father's wrath by dropping his dreams of software development.

"Our dad steered us all into finance. It was a condition of

him paying for our educations. So all five of us studied money. He felt like it was the surest way to be successful in life. To always have money, we had to *know* money," he repeated a refrain his father often said. "So I minored in computer engineering. Me being the head of technology for a bank is my way of preserving a little piece of myself."

"Do you ever see yourself quitting, the way your brother, Jerrell, did, and going for what really makes you happy?" she asked.

The question dug at a part of Sheldon he'd tried to keep buried. The part of him that was still not satisfied and very bored with his life. He was kind of jealous of Jerrell leaving the assigned family career path. Even though Sheldon was no longer chained to a desk, fixing other people's problems all day was a well-paid level of hell. The money and perks were fabulous, sex and adulation plentiful, high-level networking endless, but it was all getting old for Sheldon.

"I think about it. All the time. But the pieces would have to be in place. I couldn't just trash a career and connections I've spent almost two decades building." He thought of his exit plan he'd been tossing around in his head for years. "I'd need a winning hand to play with first."

Chriselle seemed to want nothing from him. When she'd entered his house, her eyes didn't dart all over the place, as if she calculated a path to move in. If they didn't do anything tonight, even though he was more than ready, Sheldon would have been perfectly okay just watching her eyes flutter and her tongue wet up her lips.

"There is no perfect time to take the leap," she said with a smile. It deepened when she pointed her beer at him. "Take it from a housewife who knows firsthand."

"You've got a career now. There's nothing wrong with being a housewife, but you are now thriving as a new agent."

She waved her bottle at him again. "Yes, I am, because I took the leap of faith you're too scared of… scaredy cat."

Laughter rocked him as he rolled around on his rug. She'd called him out.

Chrissy kept waving her beer bottle at him. "You opened yourself up to that one!"

Nodding from the floor, Sheldon agreed. "I did open it right up."

She had relaxed more, and he was glad he'd put her at ease. Her laughter rang from her chest with hearty gusto, the way his grandmother's did. He caught hints of her real personality that was energetic, fun, and witty. Alongside the firelight, her smooth face gleamed, looking ready to be kissed. Licked. Sucked.

He was fighting to keep his distance, and Sheldon tried to focus on her cute humor instead.

But her beer bottle tapped the marble floor where she set it down. In a breezy state, she lay next to him, the back of her hand touching his, and stared at his high ceiling. Chrissy released her bun at the nape of her neck and swept her shoulder-length hair aside, exposing the valley above her collarbone that Sheldon resisted the urge to suck.

"You said it gets easier. When?" she asked.

Sheldon immediately sensed she was referring to her breakup. He'd told her at the debutante ball that it got easier with time. Now he thought about that, remembering the end of him and Genie.

"When you stop thinking it's your job to suffer." His voice was as low as the crackling flames.

That must have resonated, because she laced her fingers through his.

The fire cast a radiant glow over Chriselle. In her eyes that searched him, he saw so many more conversations he wanted to have, many of them in silence.

"I'm glad you're here," he said. "I enjoy you."

"Let's see. I could either go back home to my annoying mother, or hang out with you," she replied honestly, with a tipsy smile. "Thank you for saving me."

Again, Sheldon's gut shook at her humor. "Thanks for that, I think." Several hours had passed that he was in her company, and he hadn't reached for his phone once. That was huge.

"I'm glad you invited me. I've never done this before. It's nice." Chrissy's thumb caressed his hand. Their fingers played together, and so began the little game of who would light up the night.

"Never done what?"

"Been with another man."

This time it was Sheldon's eyelids that beat back his surprise. "You've never cheated?"

No words, she shook her head.

Wow. After the way her husband mistreated her, she had been faithful all those years? He wasn't buying it, or that a woman so loyal would come home with him—a stranger— after just one week. What made Sheldon so special? "Why should I believe that's true?"

The flames danced inside her eyes that didn't flinch. "Because I'm not here to convince you."

Nor did she rush to try to explain or justify herself. Chrissy seemed just fine with her truth. And didn't need him to validate it.

The solid weight of her gaze may have even told him she was at the threshold where married people were truly done.

He could have sworn her eyes stared at him like they were waiting. So he hoped she wasn't offended at what he did next.

Sheldon lifted her hand to his lips and laid an open-mouthed kiss on it. The tip of his tongue tasted her skin. "I've wanted to do that since I first laid eyes on you."

She parted her sensuous lips that revealed her wet, glistening tongue. "And I was praying you would."

Then, Chrissy raised his hand and kissed it in turn. His flesh relished the warmth of Chrissy's satin lips. The skin on his hand melted under her tongue sliding across his fingers, sending his dick into overdrive.

"Damn, Chriselle, you're trying to start—"

"Yes. I am trying to start." Along the floor, her fingers found his face, stroking it. Not with lust but curiosity. Maybe both. "Don't make me second-guess myself. Not right now. I'll do plenty of that later."

Her mouth open, face content and relaxed, it called to Sheldon. Even fresh out of a bun, her auburn, silken hair feathered around her face and onto his rug. With her shoulders peeping out of his oversized jersey, she seemed like a Christmas painting. He couldn't get enough of this portrait.

Come to your senses, Rouse.

"Your marriage…"

"Is over. We've been living apart for months." Chrissy's eyes were tentative, questioning as they penetrated him. Those seductive lips spread into a half-grin. "But you knew that when you brought me here. Or you wouldn't have brought me."

A corner of his lips curled up. "I did."

They no longer needed the fireplace to heat them. Her supple, smooth thighs fired him up enough.

He couldn't be the gentleman anymore. Sheldon drew her to him. His tongue met Chrissy's again, and he needed to know if she really was as delectable as she looked.

A sexy moan left her throat, like she'd been wondering the same. Mrs. Mason surprised him when she beat him to the sucking. He received her curiosity and eagerness that spilled into his mouth.

They kissed long and deep, at first tasting, and then, their saliva and tongues began their own get-to-know-you session. Her daring energy intoxicated him.

He slid his hand under her jersey. She had left off her bra earlier, and the softness of her breasts fell into his palm. Sheldon's hunger followed his fingers as he nibbled on hardened nipples that popped against his tongue.

Chrissy's curves were everything he'd imagined since he'd first seen her in the bank. Squeezing her hips, he nipped her with his teeth, swirling her belly button with his tongue, while his fingers massaged tantalizingly close to her womanhood. Sheldon could bite on her forever and hear her chest contract and little breaths skip from her mouth. Her hands scraped his chest, shooting hot sparks of electricity in every spot on him she touched. Her soft skin smelled like Thanksgiving dessert —like cinnamon sprinkled on baked apples.

He pulled his basketball shorts off her, and fighting to control his trembling hands, he explored her dripping slit.

"Aaah," Chrissy whined.

Fuck. Why was she so wet?

Eyelids fluttering, her raw desire triggered his dick to start its own happy dance toward her shiny pussy.

Wait. *Hold up, Rouse. You're a grown-ass man.* He'd had a lot of sex, and he needed to get himself under control. But Chriselle was so ready, and damn, he was too.

He dipped his finger in her core and dragged her juice up her slit, through her folds.

Chrissy stiffened. "Mm…" She responded to him as if she had never been touched. "Shit," escaped her lips, so small and low he'd barely heard it. "Sheldon, please don't torture me."

"Why not?" he whispered. "When was the last time you were tortured?" Loving how she twitched for him, Sheldon slid two fingers inside her pink heat that creamed. *Grrr…* She was tight. How were those muscles clenching so hard? She had kids.

"Baby, your pussy is soaking. I want to taste her."

Chrissy rode his fingers that massaged her walls. He pushed in and out, and she gyrated her hips in rhythm with his motions, losing herself while her perfect breasts thrust toward the ceiling.

"You like that?" Sheldon murmured. Shit, *he* liked it. He lowered his face, nuzzling his nose in her wet folds, dipping it in her creases. "I can't hear you," he said, moving his lips against her clit, watching it shimmer as her flesh shook.

"Aaaahhh, yeeesss… please," she gasped.

"Yes, please what?" She was so thick and scrumptious. But despite his longing to munch her ass up, and his dick beating his thigh, he needed to know how much she wanted him.

Her mouth dropped, back arched, and her fingers clenched his head. Chrissy's eyelids squeezed tight, as if she couldn't bear it. Moaning, she scooted away. He pulled her back to him, his fingers still kneading her walls, not letting up from her G-spot.

Her response was a whimper. "Shel…"

"Chriselle." He loved saying her name. And goddamn, her

canal burned in response to his voice. He blew softly against the creamy pearl that was her clit. "Yes, please what?" He purposely moved his mouth against her nub, taunting her more.

She was on the verge of coming.

"*Please*, eat me," she whined.

Sheldon lowered his tongue, slow, intentional, tasting her jewel and its succulence. "Mmm…" he hummed, so she could feel the vibration from his vocal cords.

On impact, she screamed. The amazing sound actually formed lovely notes that carried across his high ceilings.

"Sh… ahh…" Her ass shot off the floor, and Chrissy convulsed. She gripped the fibers of the rug, her cream dripping onto his face, in his mouth, and down his fingers. He pressed her G-spot again, prolonging her ecstasy. She scooted more, and he followed her.

Sheldon loved watching her reactions so much, his hard dick exploded, and he came in his sweats.

"*Fuck*," he growled, his entire body shuddering.

That hadn't happened in a while. At least a decade. He needed a minute to come down from his own high.

"Are you alright?" he asked, kissing her thighs.

She swallowed. "No." Another gorgeous, open-mouthed smile. "Not until I have a lot more of that."

Sheldon laughed, resting his head between her legs. "You act like you've never had it before."

"I haven't."

Again, another revelation that blew him away. "Chrissy, you've got kids."

She was smiling, but her eyes were serious. "That was my first orgasm."

"*Ever?*"

"Ever." She kissed his hand, and her glistening eyes still gave up tears. From the gratitude shining through them, she wasn't lying. "Thank you."

A speechless Sheldon stared back at her. What the hell had she been through? He had so many questions. Where did he start? "You... *how?*"

Chrissy's index finger pressed his lips, shooting tiny sparks all over him. "Like you said earlier, no tough subjects tonight." Her fingers brushed his neck, her irises burning under the flames, supercharging his hunger for her.

Laid out in front of the fire, she was so incredibly serene and beautiful. As if she'd had numerous conversations with herself and was now at peace. Sheldon lowered his face between her legs again. Chrissy's hand stopped his head.

"No."

He bit one of her thighs. "I want to taste you."

"And I want you inside me." Her eyes didn't waver. "Condom?"

He brought one back, prepared to cover himself, but Chrissy held out her hand to take it. Her hands were a little shaky as she eyed his length.

Sheldon grinned. "It won't bite you."

"But it might do something else," she cracked with a little fear on her face. Still, she managed to sheath him.

Lying over her, he held her face that somehow appeared both naughty and nice. "I'll make sure he only does what you want him to."

His instincts told him Chrissy didn't need any rough stuff, not right now, not until he heard more of her story.

Even after he made that decision, Sheldon paused at the entrance to her.

Another man's wife. This had seemed like a far better idea back at the restaurant.

Underneath him, Chrissy's eyes still held flashes of vulnerability. Her war with her vows couldn't have been clearer in her irises.

"Are you sure?" he asked, staring into them.

Two inches from his lips, hers curved upward. "No."

They both laughed in the easy way that was intensifying his attraction to her.

Goodness, his heart pounded so hard. Why was *he* so nervous? As if Chrissy could sense it, she slid her hand to his chest and rubbed it, strumming his growing feelings for her. This was becoming more than lust.

What he was about to say next, Sheldon had never said to any woman before in his life. "I don't want a one-night stand with you. Maybe we should wait. And get to know each other."

Chrissy's smile was lazy, easy. Her innocent, fire-lit golden eyes stared up at Sheldon with expectation. "I don't want a one-night stand with you either. Maybe we should do it. And get to know each other," she said with a wide grin.

Yet again, they were back to giggling like teenagers.

"Seriously," he said. "Why do I feel like… I'm taking something from you?"

A tear slid down her temple, wetting his finger that rested there. Her nervous breaths mingled with his own.

"Because you are. And I'm okay with it." Her fingers slid inside his. "Please."

He had no clue what awaited them on the other side of this decision. But he'd never known a woman so confident and yet scared, who seemed to possess many layers he wanted to unpack. And every moment that Sheldon couldn't made him ache. He took one last look at the bird underneath him.

Her determined eyes asked him to.

Sheldon entered her.

Ohh, shit, she really is tight. How was she married with kids and this tight? When was the last time her husband had touched her? He swept all the questions aside.

Her body welcomed him, and Chrissy's tongue grazed her teeth again. Tears danced from her eyes. Seeing and feeling Chrissy's wonderment was like watching a person who'd never experienced snow.

With her every surprised gasp and twitch, Sheldon opened a doorway to a new world. She arched, reached her hands around his waist, and clung to his ass. Sheldon filled her up, loving to feel her shudder in his arms.

"Aaah…" she whimpered.

Shit. Her walls contracted around him, while his dick swayed in ecstasy and he fought not to come.

Nibbling her cheek, he whispered against her mouth, "Chriselle, open your eyes. I want to see you."

She did as he told her. Pushing his manhood deeper into her, Sheldon wanted to see all of Chrissy's vulnerability, all her fear, her every secret stripped bare.

"Pump your hips toward mine," he instructed, diving in her plush muscles.

He sensed her husband had never taught her.

Underneath him, Chrissy formed a rhythm with his thrusts, throwing her pelvis to meet his. Sliding his hand under her ass, he guided her.

They moved in unison now.

Exhilaration struck her face, and he saw how she felt the difference. "Oh, God!"

"Yes, baby… that's it," he murmured against her forehead. another wave of her juices gushed over him. *Umph. Goddamn.* He'd better not come in just a couple of minutes his first time with this woman. Not while he was having an out-of-body experience.

He slowed down to enjoy her satin walls that caressed him like flower petals, and to collect his head. Both of them.

Trying to stay strong, he slowed whenever her walls grew hot, halting her orgasm. Her mouth hung open and she panted for his next stroke.

Chrissy trembled, and her breaths tripped out of her throat. "Aaah…"

Her mouth and eyes opened wider. He gazed past them, and into *her*.

"Chriselle, baby." He cradled her head and rolling his hips. Shit, her pussy was burning. "Come for me."

Her gorgeous eyes stared into him. Her next word was a whine. "Sheld—"

Dammit, don't whine like that, girl.

"Yes." His tongue snaked across her lips, while she gripped his ass, pulling him into her wetness. He needed to release. "Come, baby."

Her shriek echoed through his house. Pressing her fist into his chest, Chrissy scooted. Sheldon gripped her, longing for every one of the tremors rolling through her.

Her orgasm was long and intense while her valley hugged his wood. Her wet walls contracted around him, sucking him into her, rocking Sheldon.

Their foreheads touching, her cream flooding over his dick, he lost himself.

"Haaah," he half grunted, half moaned. The sensation

tortured him. She felt so damn good this could have been *his* first orgasm.

"Mm," she moaned, still trembling while tearing at his back.

Sheldon kissed her temple, checking her eyes for signs of buyer's remorse. "You okay? Talk to me."

Shit, this was going to be a problem.

Satisfied eyes beamed back at him. "Mhmm. You?"

Chuckling, he kissed her forehead. "Perfect now." He was so glad she was alright.

But he wasn't.

The thirty-nine-year-old serial dater was feeling things he shouldn't. His mind was entertaining questions it shouldn't. Like how often he'd be able to clear his schedule and fly to L.A.

"You're incredible," Chrissy whispered.

"And you're stunning," he whispered back, lying next to her.

She snuggled against him, and Sheldon opened his arm for her to lie against him, fitting so naturally it seemed she belonged there.

"Wow, you're still here and haven't run for the hills."

"You thought I would regret it."

"Mm, not really." A devilish grin spread over his lips. "I knew all that pretending you weren't interested was just an act."

Grinning, she poked him. "When did I say I was interested?"

Laughing, Sheldon replied into her hair, "When you told me you didn't want to leave. When you said you didn't want a one-night stand." He looked down at her, searching her eyes. "Or were you lying to me?"

The contentment on her face answered before her mouth did. "No. Sheldon." Her eyes were certain and yet uncertain. "I wasn't lying to you."

The soft seriousness on her face pried open parts of him he'd closed a long time ago. After Genie. He brushed Chrissy's lips with his, his touch as light as air, and he whispered, "Are you scared?"

Her chest shuddered, but her gaze didn't leave his. She nodded. "Yes."

Slow, intentional, he brushed his lips over her nose, her forehead, before his nose swept hers and their lips caressed. Sheldon inhaled her essence while he nibbled the plush skin on her neck.

It was cute when Chrissy nibbled him back, on his shoulder, gripping his flesh, sucking hard until her lips finally let go.

"Are you trying to brand me, Ma?" he smiled.

She offered a one-shoulder shrug. "And if I was?"

"I come at a high price. You'll need to work a little harder than that," he murmured, sliding down her body, his tongue leaving behind a trail.

"And if I'm up to the task?" she replied, her wide, jewel-like eyes daring him.

"I'll be the judge of that."

In the next heartbeats, Sheldon was tasting her again, delighting in her whimpers. Now, he wanted to show her everything her husband clearly hadn't.

Chriselle moaned and whined until sunlight broke. And damn, if she wasn't the sunlight breaking into him.

❄

Every rule in Sheldon's playbook, he'd broken it.

No special treatment until later. Broken.

No kissing the first night. Broken.

No more one-night stands. Broken.

No married women. Broken.

Especially those with baggage. Broken.

And kids. Broken.

Chrissy had enthralled Sheldon the moment he'd seen her trying her hardest to repel him with those thick-ass glasses and enough layers of clothes to cover the Northern hemisphere. The longer she'd tried to fight an attraction to him—ordering her teas and hot chocolate and "safe," unsexy food like salad—the more her little antics had aroused him.

What attracted him most—she wasn't thirsty. Chriselle already wore a rock on her hand. Already had the houses and prestige. She hadn't batted an eye when she'd entered his mansion. All the typical materialism that bled a woman's motives hadn't displayed itself once with her. She'd had no other motive than trying to escape Sheldon.

Only when he woke up did the doubts haunt him. She'd slept with him in the eye of a marital storm, and her night with him might have just been revenge or liberation sex.

There was also the issue of her husband. Sheldon had avoided drama his entire life, and damn sure hadn't brought it under his roof. This situation of a spouse tracking her had trouble stamped all over it.

Yet his doubts sank like sand to the bottom of his ocean when she appeared under his dining room archway in his button-down shirt. He had takeout sitting on the long table as he did some work remotely.

"Good afternoon, Sleeping Beauty." He pulled off his

glasses, stretching out his hand and welcoming her to his long, twenty-person dinner setting. "How do you feel?"

A groggy smile still on her face, she entered. "Mm, drained. Hungry. Sore. Have my children called?" She opened a box of food.

"They have not. Make yourself comfortable. I ordered both lunch and breakfast. I wasn't sure what you'd be in the mood for. Kitchen is back here. I ordered up some drinks too, so there's juice and soda if you're into that."

She stared at him from the other end of his spacious dining room. "This is a long table for just one guy. I hope you don't dine in here by yourself all the time." She popped a grape into her mouth.

"No, I usually eat in my office or the living room on the couch. I rarely come in here, actually. But I wanted you to have quiet and get rest."

"So it's not nighttime anymore. Can I finally know why you're in this big house?"

He smiled a schemer's grin, having expected her to bring that up again. And she was correct; he'd told her he didn't want to discuss it last night, and now it's afternoon. Smartass. "Sure, if I can ask you a few questions of my own."

He eyed her to see if she would play.

A daring gleam in her eye, Chriselle's head slowly nodded, a smile on her lips as she took the furthest seat from his.

Ha, creating distance. She's teeing up.

"I bought this house as a surprise for Genie, four years ago, to show her how serious I was about still wanting our large family. And to reassure her the traveling wouldn't last much longer. But after I returned from China, she had left with our son. I had already signed the papers to this place. So I moved in here alone. Genie's never stepped foot in here."

Even now, it stung for him to say it.

"You wanted a bigger family."

"I did. I do. I come from a good-sized one. We have fun. Never a dull moment. Lots of noise and laughter and fights and debates. Everybody's always got each other's backs, us against the world. The complete opposite of what you see in here. My punishment for wanting too much."

"And nobody's showed up in three years that made you want to try again?" she asked, her eyes dropping to the shrimp she now picked at.

A chuckle escaped him. "You're not slick."

She shrugged and feigned innocence. "It's just conversation."

"Okay. Sure, amazing women cross my path all the time. I'm still bored." He refused to give her what she hunted, a peek at his feelings for her. Whether last night had only been a fluke or maybe the birth of something real. He already had the answer, but she would wait.

"And Lana?" she asked. "You and her are familiar?"

"Jealous? So soon?" He grinned.

Her nose wrinkled with clear disdain. "No."

"What's the rub there, between you two?" he inquired this time.

"It's not between her and me, but her and my friend. She is Maddy's co-worker from Capitol Hill, whom Maddy brought here for Christmas holiday. And ever since that girl arrived, it's been one hot mess after another. Now we can't get rid of her. And if you go forward with her project, she may never leave," Chrissy spoke as if drinking vinegar.

Hmph, Capitol Hill. Helpful info. "So I should decide how to spend my money based on somebody's personal life?"

"No, I want you to decide based on your decency," she replied, still eating.

Sheldon's eyebrow cocked up. "So you're not decent because you're working with Kevin Middleton?"

She released a stubborn grin, and her index finger shot up. "It's not the same. Kevin brings value—he's got successful start-ups and a long list of powerful connections. Lana has not proven her value."

"She works on Capitol Hill and brings a different value set that you Hamptons folks don't give enough credit until a direct dollar sign is attached."

"Dollars make the world go around, not laws and political gridlock, and you of all people know that." She dipped another shrimp and nibbled it.

"Laws protect your dollars, but okay."

"Laws are not real, because the people with dollars bend and break them, Mr. Wall Street Tech Guy. You know this firsthand because someone froze me from my account despite the *law* telling them not to. But okay," she clapped back with gloriously wide eyes.

Sheldon burst out laughing, his gut shaking. "Okay. Alright. Fine. That's fair. Now my turn." He examined her. "Why haven't you ever had an orgasm?"

Her gaze floated from her plate to Sheldon, slowing down the fast-paced tempo of conversation. "Because I never loved Blake. He never loved me."

Her icy face was a glacier that could have scraped the *Titanic*.

For every question she answered, he had so many more fucking questions…

"Then why did you—?"

"Our parents made us. We slept together our junior year.

He was the hot boy on campus, throwing parties and bringing in rap groups. I was a sheltered girl who was infatuated, with stars in my eyes, until we did it. Doing the deed with that Negro was nothing like my fantasy…"

Her gaze sailed low enough to have hidden under her plate. As if the experience must have been dark.

"When I found out I was pregnant, I told my mom I wanted to keep it. I didn't want Blake. But I did want the baby. Of course, my mother called his…and she took over the whole situation the way she tends to do. She made it very clear that a child out of wedlock wasn't an option if I wanted my inheritance and for her and Dad to keep helping me."

Sharp chest pains twisted Sheldon as her story ripped through him.

"You gave him two children."

She shifted. "The first three or four years, we tried. And we had decent moments here and there. We could tolerate each other, even with the cheating and his temper. But every time we did it, I was disgusted. Sometimes I faked it so he would just get it over with." She paused, staring out the window, seeming to reflect. "And I guess I was also trying to be my mother—grace under fire and all that—putting up a good front. She always says there is no such thing as a perfect man."

"Has he hit…" Sheldon stopped himself, unsure if that might have been too invasive.

"Yes."

"And you stayed."

"Are you judging?"

"Only wondering."

"I was young. Alone in L.A. No family there with me or support. For a long time, Blake was my life. I had never been with anyone else. And I didn't know what leaving would look like."

Sheldon sat up. "No one? You mean, I'm your second?"

She nodded, peering at him from those round, pecan-shaped eyes.

Well, damn. If he'd known she was *that* pure, he may not have touched her with a ten-foot pole.

"You say that like I have cancer or something," she muttered. "I didn't know it was a crime to be a good wife."

He sighed. "No, I say that like I have a good wife sitting in my house, and she is not mine. Whose man is going to eventually realize she is never coming back. And that's when all hell really will break loose. A woman who is damn near a virgin, and a diamond in her community and whom I'd hate to taint."

Chrissy scowled. "You didn't think about all that before you asked me out?"

He had. And he had already taken some protective security measures on his house, office, and car to ensure he didn't receive any unwanted gifts from California.

"Yes, I thought about it a lot actually. And I was feeling you enough that I wanted to take the risk. I still want you. Still want to reach every corner of that... *why* are you still sitting way down there?"

She hesitated, her posture stiffening as she pulled her arms closer to herself. As if in defensive mode.

"I see." He removed his glasses and closed his laptop, before getting up and padding over the floor. He took the seat next to her and held out his palm.

Hesitant, Chrissy placed her hand inside his—her ring hand. Sheldon's thumb glided across it while he thought of the right words.

"How long have you and him been living apart?"

"Six months, since June. Before the kids went back to school. I didn't want them adjusting to two separate homes in the middle of a school year."

"How's it been? By yourself?" he asked.

"Hard. Uncertain. But peaceful. And a little liberating." She smiled. "Okay, a lot liberating. I don't have to get all anxious in the evenings. I no longer question if he'll show up, or how the night will go if he does. I'm living my life for me and not for insanity."

Sheldon's fingers touched her wedding rings. He placed her finger in his mouth, moisturizing it, sliding his tongue around it, enjoying the tender ecstasy of her surprised eyes blinking. Then Sheldon slid her finger out. And slid off the bands.

"If you're so happy alone, why haven't you removed these?"

Sheldon knew the answer, but he wanted to hear her say it. He needed to check if he was developing feelings for a girl or a woman.

Chrissy swallowed, her focus falling to the rings on the table. "For pretense. To keep up appearances."

An A+. No long, delusional explanations about being confused.

"And if he shows up saying all the right things, humbled and restored? And he promises you a whole new life?"

She shook her head with a smirk. "There is nothing more for us, if there ever was."

Sheldon pulled drew her onto his lap. "Are you sure this isn't too much? Intimacy with another man so soon?"

She shrugged, a snappy glimmer in her eye. "When was the

last time you had another woman? Last week? Are you sure it's not too soon for you?"

He grinned. "I've been single for a while, and I'm used to… variety."

Both of them burst into chuckles. Shit, she had a gorgeous, musical laugh.

"Oh, is that what we're calling it?" she asked, still giggling. "Well… when was the last time you were with another woman?" Her brow lifted.

"Last week," he answered frankly.

Aghast, she dropped her jaw. "Ew!" Chrissy said in disgust. "So you're a male thot!"

He shook his head. "I have high sexual energy, Miss Lady, but not a thot."

"Was she sitting in this seat? Was she on the rug?"

"Yep," Sheldon lied just to watch her melt into appall. "We did it here." He pointed to the table. "There." His finger aimed at the doorway. "And definitely there." He pointed to the bottom of the staircase.

All lies.

No woman had entered his house in months, not even Darian. But he wanted to see Chrissy's mouth fall open and display all those teeth in horror.

"Good thing we used protection," she replied.

"Yeah, because there's no telling where that husband of yours and his little yoga instructor have been," Sheldon shot back. He'd for sure done his homework.

Again, Chrissy's mouth gaped in shock that he was so insightful.

He continued, "I've had a couple yoga instructors myself, it's kind of fun."

"Ugh," she sneered and tried to bolt.

Sheldon snatched her back down, his arms circling around her. "It was a long time ago. You are not just a number." He turned her toward him. "You are definitely not that."

When she relaxed and stopped worrying about her husband and what other people thought, her shining eyes told him she was happy to be with him.

Chrissy's face hovered inches from his. "How do I know you're not some deadbeat dad who was cheating all over the place and refused to bond with his son? And now you like to spit that house-buying story to every woman you bring here," she challenged.

His mouth spread into amusement. That clapback. "I guess time will tell."

"I'm sure it will."

The late afternoon sun dipped over the woods in his backyard. The yellow-orange light settled over the dining room, illuminating their faces.

"You're beautiful." He rubbed her hip. "I wanted you from the moment I first saw you."

Chrissy's breath deepened, and her chest rose like his words added to her oxygen. Her ringless fingers skated along his bare collarbone, arousing Sheldon.

"And I wanted you. I probably even needed you. Thank you. Really."

Her searching eyes were scanning his again.

Sheldon shook his head. "The pleasure is mine. Really."

Setting aside his laptop and her wedding rings, he lifted her onto his dining room table.

Chrissy's face relaxed with ecstasy when his finger penetrated her wet valley. Enjoying her startled expression, he leaned her back until she lay on his table. He propped up her thick legs so her naked ass was facing him.

He licked her folds, slow and tormenting, snapping her back into an arch.

"Mmm." In his hands, Chrissy's thighs shook. "Aah," flowed from her throat at the feel of his finger sliding inside her.

He damn near lost control watching her juice glisten on his hands.

His tongue taunted her clit, sucking, swirling, as her screams echoed all over his house. Chrissy's energy brought him home to life, after it had sat quiet over the years. After his devastation. And she'd brought Sheldon back to life.

He held her hand while she yelped.

Not sure where this was going, or if it would last, he wouldn't overthink one of the best moments he'd had in a long time. He was happy to take Chrissy on a new adventure, and the excitement in his chest was a new trip for him too.

WONDERFULLY CRAZY

CHRISSY

Her marital shackles. Gone.

Sheldon had indeed taken them.

A complete stranger to Chrissy had penetrated her on the first date.

Sheldon's big six-foot, three-inch frame formed a mountain, gently sloping over her. And Chrissy took the journey up. His tender hands caressed and cupped, strokes burrowing, mouth insisting, giving her one of the greatest gifts besides her children.

Layer by layer, Sheldon had unwrapped her. Older, more experienced, patient, he explored her body like she was virgin terrain.

Unable to control her shaking at times, she could only fall back against his arms.

His unflinching eyes seemed to take seriously what he was doing to her. For her. Inside her. Chrissy hung on to him, while his manhood massaged her G-spot.

"Mm," she moaned when she started to climax, the sensations arching her back, widening her legs. He lifted her and drove deeper.

As midnight struck New Year's, Sheldon's neighborhood streets were not the only site of fireworks popping.

He didn't half-step. Careful and attentive, he ensured every touch and kiss was an experience. The risk had been worth taking, and then some.

Later, she lay curled between his legs, ringing in a New Year she wouldn't have imagined possible.

"I'd like to see you again." He bit her ear. "Before you head back to L.A."

Her heart all but floated from her chest. Chrissy was already falling for him. It was a feeling so foreign. To be with a man and actually *like* it.

But Blake.

She'd just had an affair! No, she was not technically with her husband, but the rest of the world didn't know that yet.

How would she pull off a real date without sparking rumors? Without all of Sag Harbor knowing about it? Something her mother and grandmother had never done.

"Don't jump for joy now," he said, maybe even sounding a little hurt.

"No," she said, turning to face him. "Can I think about it?"

"Ouch." Sheldon laughed. "I've never gotten that response before."

Chrissy stroked his face, a large smile spreading over her. "I would love to hang out with you, but I can't exactly do what I want right now. There's a lot to consider."

He nodded, kissing her hand. "Of course. Forgive me. I understand, Mrs. Mason."

"It's Ms. Townsend. No more of that Mrs. Mason stuff. Chriselle Townsend now."

In the tight space between them, she offered her hand, and he took it. They shook.

"Yes, ma'am. Nice to meet you, Miss Townsend," he replied with a grin.

She kissed him, too happy to suck his lips and feel all the giddiness bubbling inside her for the first time since college. Sheldon returned her attraction, kissing her deeper and longer while he cradled her head. Her heart rate pitter-pattered so fast she thought her chest might explode.

Oh, goodness, how would she manage this?

She hadn't counted on a man who drilled holes through her with his eyes, like he saw things about Chrissy that she couldn't. As if he were introducing her to more of herself.

The drive back to the helicopter that afternoon was tougher than she'd expected. How could she be so attached after just two nights? Even if it was magical and heavenly, they'd been brief.

Sheldon stood alongside the stairs, turning her to face him in the crisp air. He tightened his coat around her shoulders, lifting the collar to her ears and snapping it, until Chrissy was a well-nested bird. Concern creased at his eyes.

"I know you're a grown woman," he started, shoving his hands in his pockets, averting his eyes, as if trying to accept a lot of things that lay outside his control. "And it's not my job to worry about you, but would you call when you arrive? So your safety is not on my mind."

She nodded. His protectiveness touched her, most likely because it was so foreign. "I already thanked you, but..."

His glove slid underneath her chin. "But I never thanked you." He slipped something inside the pocket of his coat that she wore. "It's another phone. Secured encrypted line. If you need anything, just press '3'. That's speed dial to an unknown number I have. When you call, I won't speak until I hear your voice. In case someone else finds it and dials. Don't contact anyone else on this but me."

More concern darkened his face. Chrissy nodded.

Tremors flew across her arm as he gave it a final, supportive squeeze, and then Sheldon stepped back.

She hadn't realized how protected and safe she'd felt until he was no longer at her side.

This warmth that had engulfed her for the past two days disappeared, and Chrissy's body turned cold again.

The pilot closed the door between them.

Still, Sheldon remained, standing watch while she took off. And Chrissy didn't stop peering out the window, until he became a dot, and then disappeared. Now she flew alone to face the decisions ahead.

"Oh, my God," Cher muttered no sooner than Chrissy walked through the door. Cher's mouth dropped with one look at Chrissy's messy hair bun and wearing the same clothes she was wearing when she'd left. "Oh!"

But then came the face Chrissy hated seeing most.

"Young lady, where are your wedding rings?" her mother hissed.

Meanwhile, Chrissy's two aunts hid their loaded smiles and sipped their coffee, playing cards.

She'd already practiced what she would say, and the force with which she would say it. But at first sight of her mother's gall, the rehearsed words flew out of Chrissy's harried (and still a little delirious) mind. "Mom, I just took 'em off for a minute."

Cher chortled. "A minute, huh?" She shot a glance at Chrissy's naked hand. "Mr. Wall Street banged you right out of them rings, huh? That must've been one long minute."

"Cher, mind your own business," Neera said, and rolled her eyes back to Chris. "So how was your outing with your college classmates, girl?"

"It was fine. We hung out through New Year's, that's all."

"Where did you guys go?" Cher asked, obviously testing Chrissy.

"Jazz restaurant, a club, Times Square, usual stuff," Chrissy hung up her coat that Sheldon's assistant had returned to her upon exiting the helicopter.

"And what did *he* eat?" Cher threw her a curve ball.

Ignoring her, Chrissy started up the stairs to the room she and her cousins had shared as children. With all of them still visiting at the same time through Sunday, they were all sleeping in cramped quarters while sharing space. So Chrissy wouldn't have much privacy to think and reflect on all that had just transpired. And the road ahead.

The road that involved leaving Blake.

How would she do it exactly? When? How would she keep Blake calm in the meantime so he didn't feel more threatened, which would certainly lead him to become more dangerous? But she had to go. It was not an option now.

She almost saw Sheldon's appearance at this crossroads as a sign. Whether or not they wound up in a relationship, Chrissy had tasted the possibilities. Now the thought of Sheldon's tongue sliding down her chest kept a constant curve on her lips. And in her chest. How could she return to California and keep tormenting herself now?

"So why did you have to pull off your wedding rings?"

came her mother again once Chrissy exited the shower and changed.

She would assert some backbone this time. "Mom, that's not really for you to worry about."

"Since we're paying for the apartment you're living in, now that you've moved out of your marital home, I'd say it is my business. You know your husband called here this weekend."

Chrissy's focus floated to where her mother stood in the doorway. "Yeah? What did you tell him?"

"I told him you were using this time without the kids to enjoy your friends. Don't worry. I covered." She sighed. "Fine, Chris, I get it. We all go through hard times. There were a few occasions I thought about leaving your daddy. But return to reality now. You have a good life."

"A husband, a house, and an unlimited credit card are not a good life, Mom. It's window dressing."

"So you're going to ride off into the sunset, to a perfect new world? With some dude who just tapped you for a weekend and sent you back here? Did he put a new ring on you to replace Blake's? A commitment? A house? Did he give you the keys already? Did he at least honor your children by asking you for a second date?"

"Yes!" Chrissy's blood ran hot. She was sick of always biting her tongue to avoid an argument. "Actually, he did."

Georgette Townsend's eyes flared. "You will *not*!"

"When will you be happy, Mom? When Blake has done something I can't cover with makeup? Just how much wrong can Blake do before you stop cheerleading for him? When I'm dead?" Chrissy snapped.

"Girl, that man is not doing anything to you. All men get hot. They all sleep around. If you've got some fantasy in your head that this new one won't do it too, you are fooling yourself."

Chrissy's pulse beat in her ears, partly from her upset with her mother's rules, partly from her exhilaration at finally breaking them.

"Mom, it is *not* your life. You have made more than enough decisions for me these last ten years. But *not* this time. I appreciate you and Dad helping me, and I will inform you of what I decide. You ought to be proud of a daughter who is asserting her right to be happy."

Her mother's anger shook in her clenched hands. "Put those rings back on so people won't talk. Be grateful you've got rings. A lot of women don't."

Chrissy rolled her eyes.

Mrs. Townsend started out of the bedroom door before she stopped. "And Kevin dropped by."

"When?" Chrissy asked as her heart rate sped up.

"A couple days ago. Not long after you left. Wanted to know when you would be here, and I thought you were coming home Wednesday night. That's what I told him," Mrs. Townsend said, exiting with a heavy gait, as if the conversation had weighed her down.

She picked up her phone to call Kevin, but before she hit the button, Neera entered.

Neera closed the door, and their fingers found each other. Her expression matched those they'd shared as teenagers, before Chrissy had married, when she still knew how it felt to live.

"Oh, my God, your face," Neera murmured.

"I'm trying to hide it," Chrissy bubbled.

Neera's gaze danced across the ecstatic woman in front of

her. "Girl, you can't hide this. Any more than a fiend can hide being high."

So much joy formed a river flooding Chrissy, that it spilled from her eyes in happy tears. "Neera, I haven't ever... not even Blake..."

"I know. Oh, Chrissy, I am so excited for you." Neera grabbed her, clinging to her tightly, her voice no higher than a breeze. "So, so excited."

"What am I going to do? Because this man is... haaah... he wants to see me again."

Neera wagged her head up and down. "You have to do this. Even if it doesn't work and you two go your separate ways, accept this joy. You more than deserve it."

Chrissy's joyous river hit a big dam once reality settled in. She had to return to L.A. in two days. The kids.

"But Blake. And Mom."

"No!" Neera hissed. "You've lived for them long enough, and you can't—"

Buzzing interrupted them from somewhere on the bed. But her phone lay in front of her, pitch-black.

Neera's eyebrows scrunched in confusion, before her eyes widened. Chrissy's cousin covered a broad smile once she realized Chrissy had another phone now. Chrissy's index finger snapped to her lips. Neera nodded, agreeing not to tell the others as she snuck out.

Chrissy found the buzzing now inside her purse. The encrypted phone Sheldon had given her. Her heart pounded through the roof, no matter how she tried to quell it.

"Wasn't I the one who was supposed to call you?" she asked, unable to suppress the bubbles in her stomach.

"I thought so too," Sheldon's sultry smoothness replied.

"You were going to make me send a search team, to confirm someone else hadn't stolen you?"

She chuckled. "Because you're the only one who's allowed to steal me?"

"You learn quickly. And I wish I could steal you again. My rug misses you."

She pressed her eyes shut. How she missed his rug. She'd only met this man a week prior. How was this glee even possible?

"Glad to hear you made it back safely," Sheldon murmured.

God, his voice...

Her mother's voice echoed right behind it, snapping her out of the daydream.

"So am I." She swallowed needles. "Good thing my children aren't here to know this phone exists," she said, hinting at the coming dangers if she carried on with this nonsense.

"I won't call it again. Just wanted to confirm you were safe and I hadn't screwed up somewhere. That the jewel was returned to the vault."

The needles ripped her chest and throat. Sure, she was going to board the plane in two days, for a one-way ticket back to hell and Blake. Easy.

"You certainly made me feel like one."

"May I make you feel that again? Tomorrow evening? I'll come and meet you in Southampton. At a friend's home. I can send a car."

An instant "yes" almost flew off her tongue, but she stopped.

She was somebody's mama. No longer in college, or able to pick up all the pieces of her life where she'd dropped them ten years ago.

"Sheldon, I can't do a fling… or a tryst or… or hell, I've been married so long I'm lost on what they're called now."

"Good thing I'm not asking for any of that. I'm aware you haven't known me as long as your husband. And that puts me at a slight disadvantage. But Chris… Chriselle, give me the chance to show you in just a day what he can't show you in a lifetime."

Lower lip sliding under her teeth, eyes shutting tight once again, she whispered, "You haven't already shown me?"

"Haven't even begun," he replied, without skipping a beat.

Her heart skipped several.

Chrissy pressed the phone against her chest. His easy, relaxed smile, gentle touch, sensual voice in her ear, she hungered for him to be all over her again.

But all the no's, every no, any imaginable no entered her brain. Her mother was right.

Even if she divorced Blake, of which she had every intention, was she really about to stake her reputation and family name on a playboy? How did Chrissy know Sheldon hadn't sucked every other woman's thighs, made them laugh from the bottom of their gut, and put them in his jacuzzi before massaging them with oil? This was crazy. Deliciously, wonderfully crazy. But still, she had a responsibility to end this. She couldn't be sideshow entertainment, and her head needed to be in one piece when she touched down in L.A. to deal with Blake again.

"I can't, Sheldon. I'm sorry. You take care of yourself."

The core of her descended to the seventh level of Hell.

Long pause, during which she could have sworn she heard a suppressed sigh on the other end. "Of course. Understood. Forgive me for hoping."

Her conflicting emotions twisted her into a knot as she

ended the call. Now the world felt like something had thrown a black shroud over it. How did she feel this way about a man she had known only a week?

Right before she called Kevin, a text popped up from Maddy.

We have a solution. Toss Kevin's Kid's Layer. Racquel, Miss Emma's eldest granddaughter, will move back, and she has an online fashion company. Wants to use the Ivory as a storefront.

Chrissy's heart lifted. Good news, finally. She would rid herself of Kevin and join up with a promising business that would eliminate Lana. She remembered Racquel from childhood, a few years older but a chill, drama-free person who would keep the traditions and vibe of Black Sag.

Visions of her two nights still fresh in her mind, Chrissy started to call Maddy—somebody not in her immediate family, with whom she could share her joy. Maddy had also vibed with Sheldon's brother, Jerrell, over the Christmas holiday, and Chrissy had seen the change in Maddy's mood. She wanted so badly to tell someone. Maddy was a mature friend who could relate to years of being responsible and prudent at the expense of genuine love. They'd just talked over Christmas about putting men on the back burner, and it was Chrissy who'd argued hard for avoiding romance. She'd been totally convinced that her situation with Blake was typical of all men.

But Sheldon had blindsided her. And now she needed an outlet for her elation.

Chrissy, stop. You're a grown woman, and in forty-eight hours this will be over.

She knocked the delusions from her thoughts, refocusing on Racquel's company, pulling up information on her laptop.

But Neera peeped through the doorway. "Okay, so are you seeing him again before you leave?"

With determination, Chrissy shoved the secret phone inside her purse and her thrill into a mental lockbox.

"No."

TO THE MOON

SHELDON

"So we have a deal then?" Lana's mother, Erlita, batted those wings she called eyelashes at Sheldon for the millionth time the day after New Year's.

All I ask is that you learn about Sag Harbor first, before you barge in, throwing around money. Chrissy's words, a few nights before, now rang through his head. Among his sexier flashbacks of Chrissy.

"Um," he stammered, his thoughts far away on the afternoon he should have been relishing with Chriselle. "It means I have a lot to consider with my fellow investors."

"Well, what more is there to discuss?" Erlita crossed her legs wrapped in tight leggings and knee-high leather boots. Her long, ruby fingernails hung over her thighs, and she rubbed her V-neck bosom once again, right where the cleavage peeped out.

Sheldon tried not to gag. As good as Lana's idea was, he did not look forward to her mother's claws "accidentally" scraping his arm and back for years to come.

"As I'm sure you know, funding and investments are difficult. Drawing up contracts for ownership shares and participation, voting and control, who'll sit on the board alongside you. And what you're offering us versus… other options we're considering."

"Well, just remember, Sheldon, that there are no other opportunities as good as this one. Black beauty is a billion-dollar industry. And these rich people *will* want a piece of that. Don't sleep on us too long, sir. My daughter and I have other funding pathways besides you," the older woman replied with a clever glint in her eye.

"Understood, ma'am." Sheldon maintained his professionalism, despite it being much harder today. When he had so many other issues irritating him, or primarily two—he hadn't spoken to his son since Christmas day, and tomorrow, a titillating woman was boarding a plane for the opposite coast. "Give us a few days and we'll get back to—"

Right then, Sheldon's pocket buzzed. But his primary phone sat on the table.

It was the other phone.

Sheldon practically jumped from his skin.

"I have to get going. Got another fire to put out."

"I'll bet you do. Just don't forget about the fire my daughter's bringing." Erlita winked under her super long, black curtains for eyelashes.

He couldn't lose this call. His wooden chair scraped the floor as he stood from the table. "Y-yes, I look forward to—"

Already his feet made their way toward the exit of his brother, Jerrell's, NYC dessert shop.

"Chris," he breathed, so grateful she'd changed her mind and he could squeeze her waist again, wrap her softness in his coat. There was so much he wanted to do with her in the short time they had left. "Baby, you have no idea how—"

"No," another voice said. "Not Chrissy. But if you meet us somewhere, I'll make sure she's there."

"Who is this? How did you get this phone?" *Shit!* What had Chrissy done? Sheldon's hand shot to his head, and the world began to spin.

"I'm her closest cousin. The one who dropped her off at Nightingale. And you and I are on the same side. If you go to the Nightingale this afternoon, she'll be there."

"Same side? I'm nobody." *Damn.* How was this not a trap? He had been dumb, ignoring his own rule and speaking first, giving away his presence.

"She likes you. I haven't seen my cousin this happy since college. Where do I bring her?"

Was somebody setting him up?

Jerrell. Jerrell would be in Sag Harbor today at his pop-up shop. Sheldon would have Jerrell approach Chrissy first and feel things out. He didn't trust this so-called "cousin," but he did trust his brother.

"The Firehouse. Go there. One o'clock," Sheldon said, before immediately clicking off the call. Had he made a mistake expecting Chrissy to keep discretion? Was he being a big fool for thinking with the wrong head, as his father had always warned him and his brothers not to do? *You can't un-stupid yourself once you've already done it.* Charles Rouse's words reverberated through his head now.

But his doubts didn't stop Sheldon from calling Jerrell to secure his help, and then making the two-hour drive across Long Island.

"Dude, you know Pop and Roland will take a bite out of your ass for thinking with the wrong head, right?" Jerrell asked from the other end of the phone.

"Man, you're not one to talk after Maddy! Forget about

Pop and Roland and just go greet her. Keep it casual, ask how Maddy is doing or something so you're not too obvious," Sheldon insisted, tamping down his irritation. "If everything feels cool and you don't get any crazy vibes about people lurking, bring her to Southampton and I'll take it from there."

"And how do I get her in my vehicle?"

"Improvise, negro! Tell her you want her to consider your business for investment in this bid thing, and it's a quick ride to show her some new product."

The Sag Harbor Hills Firehouse was the social hub of Black Sag Harbor. Everyone hung out there for cards, dominoes, drinks, and small community events. Chrissy could not enter the vehicle of another man anywhere near there, not without starting rumors. But the members of that community trusted Jerrell now, so Sheldon needed for his little brother to convincingly pull this off.

Once Jerrell laughed him off the phone, Sheldon drove with his stomach in knots for the next ninety minutes.

After texting Jerrell his location, in a dark parking garage next to a bank, Sheldon waited, along with his nerves. If anyone saw them, he could form a credible excuse.

1:11 p.m. No sign of them. *A trap*, Sheldon huffed. His lungs gripped his air from escaping, and he started to call Jerrell and make sure his brother was okay. Had someone mistaken the two of them and done something to J? He would kill anybody who tried to hurt his brother.

1:14 p.m. *Damn, how stupid could a man be?* What the hell was he doing out here at age thirty-nine? Waiting outside like a high school young buck sending his boys to do his bidding for him?

1:18 p.m. *Bad goddamn idea.* Sheldon rang Jerrell's phone.

"Patience, Negro, please," Jerrell said, answering. "She's in the bank, the way you wanted. You owe me."

Sheldon exited the car, carrying a surprise gift he'd gotten her, nearly tripping down the stairs. Before walking into the building, he paused a moment to watch her confusion and irritation. When she whipped around to question Jerrell, her eyes widened to find Sheldon at her back.

"Hi."

"Shel—"

"I know. Before you fuss—"

Chrissy's demeanor toughened. "We cannot do this. I have things to do before I leave here. Research for this bid, interviews, a showcase to attend tonight. You took a huge risk. What if somebody *sees*?"

"We came far enough away from Sag Harbor Hills. I wanted to surprise you." Sheldon could only stare at the fear in her eyes. "Don't look at me like I'm Satan."

Her chest rose and fell like it was groping for the same oxygen as he.

"Outside," she muttered.

Through the backdoor, and into an alleyway they walked, away from backdoors of local restaurants and shops. She scanned for people she might know. They moved to the darkness of the parking garage, where he'd already ensured there were no cameras and few cars parked.

"So how did you arrange this? Was my cousin in on this?" she asked, scrolling through the secret phone he'd given her. "I see an outgoing call she made at 10:45 this morning. I'll talk to Neera about getting into my business. She knows better."

Her nervousness rattled her hands and voice.

"It's not her fault. It's mine."

"Neither one of you had any right."

Gusts of condensation drifted in heavy breaths through her mouth. He could feel how the frigid temperatures had frozen her since the day before. Sheldon wondered who in Chrissy's life had sucked the joy from her in the last twenty-four hours. He wanted to find that person and bury them.

"Please calm down. Nobody's trying to hurt you here. Apparently, I'm not the only one catching feelings. You're into me too, or your family wouldn't have called me. Come on, Chriselle."

"So, you have no respect for my wishes," Chrissy pressed, her eyes targeting him in that way she could. Only this time, he wasn't turned on but concerned for her.

Sheldon kept his tone even, reassuring. "I have every respect for your wishes. For your dreams. For who you are. And out of respect for all that you are, you would never have heard from me again if your cousin hadn't called me. But is that really your wish?" He paused. "Or is that somebody else's wish for you?"

He waited for her answer. The bones of his rib cage quaked so hard under the pounding of his heart, the vibrations touched his knees.

She hesitated, cutting her eyes away. "No, Sheldon. That's not what I wish. And you know that. It's just—"

Damn, was he glad to hear that. He walked toward her, taking off his gloves and reaching to cup her neck and face. "So you're just being a scaredy cat."

Chrissy's tongue responded to his the way fire responded to gasoline. One spark was enough to send them back into hot ecstasy. Even in the thirty-degree cold. Her hands discovering his chest again, meandering to his neck, her fingertips caressing his jawline… all hardened Sheldon's dick and softened his heart.

Catching their breaths while they still nipped and bit one another's lips, his forehead fell onto hers. He inhaled her sweet holiday apple-cinnamon scent like she was cocaine.

Snow flurries wafted around them.

"You feel so good," she whispered into his neck. "But I shouldn't be doing this. Especially not in public."

"I apologize. I'm not trying to be disrespectful," he said, savoring her nearness to him. Sheldon agreed. They shouldn't have been doing this, but…. "Hurting you, or crowding your space, or stepping on your freedom is… the last thing I intended. But I'm feeling you, Chriselle." He would be honest with her, because he was a grown-ass man and didn't have time for anything else.

Chrissy tilted up her mouth, and he caught her kisses, grazing her lips slowly while he stared in her eyes and fought off the strong urge to sex her in the garage.

"Mmm," they both released.

"It's been a long time since any woman has done this to me."

"What am I doing to you?" she asked in a breathy voice.

The party in Sheldon's heart answered for him. "All the things I don't let women do to me."

Sheldon's dragged his fingers down her neck and underneath the collar of her coat, clinching it while he kissed her. He needed more, as much of her as he could get, before she boarded her plane back to L.A. the next day.

She moaned. "Nooo, don't say that. It's so much easier for me to turn you away if I believe you're a womanizer who'll humiliate me."

Once again, his laughter at her flowed out of him. He kissed her temple. "Humiliate you, huh? The man who flew you out of town to keep your business private? The banker who's sleeping with the wife of a Hollywood agent? Whose career could be ruined if this goes wrong." Sheldon kept chuckling. "*Me* humiliate *you*. Tell me, what else did your imagination cook up in the last twenty-four hours?"

She burst out laughing as they walked. "Well, when you put it that way…"

"Thank you," he shot back.

"But, Sheldon," she started, her penetrating eyes staring into him, "I have no shortage of people in my life trying to make decisions for me. Planning out my next moves like I have no goals of my own. I already have one controlling man to escape. Let's talk about plans next time?"

He admired her even as she put her foot down. "Yes, ma'am. Understood."

Chrissy's jumpy eyes conducted another sweep. "Speaking of privacy, we should probably get out of here." She swung her hair behind her ear, but it kept whirling around her face in the wind. "But I don't have much time. Maybe a couple of hours, three max, and then I've got to hit a showcase and a dinner."

Fightng off his inkling to touch her hair, he smiled at her drive that first attracted him—fiery Chrissy was on a mission. With time limitations, her own life she was pursuing, and goals for her hustle…

Sheldon nodded. "I can work with that. I got you a surprise."

She beamed. "What is it?"

"You have to come see." Why did he feel like an elated kid who wanted to show her everything? Ignoring the urge to take her hand, he shoved his in his pocket. Within a few minutes, they stood outside an old movie theater.

Chrissy's mouth dropped open, and the grin on her face grew broader. "Oh, my God."

Terminator Marathon was on the marquee.

He pulled two tickets out of his pocket. A thirty-two-teeth smile, accompanied by the revived light in her eyes, was his reward.

Minutes later, he had bought her almost the entire snack counter. She sat with popcorn, gummy bears, junior mints, and Hi-C punch. They took turns feeding each other.

"Don't sign up to be a caretaker anytime soon," Sheldon teased. "You can't even get the popcorn near my mouth."

She giggled, throwing a kernel at him. "I am doing a fantastic job. Stop yapping and the popcorn will get in there."

"Me yapping has nothing to do with it. You're so bad at this," he teased as her hand shoved a large cluster at his mouth. Popcorn fell everywhere, and only two or three kernels got inside. They burst out laughing, their shared goofiness tickling parts of Sheldon he hadn't felt for years.

With her next attempt, he finally bit her elegant fingers, licking the butter off every one of them until they were back to kissing like horny teenagers. Even in the dark, he could feel her happy, open-mouthed grin that he licked.

She bit his lip, sucking it and driving him nuts, before Chrissy let it go. She surveyed the empty movie theater, before landing on him. "Why are we the only people in this theater?"

Again, he chuckled once it dawned on her what he'd done. "Somebody—I won't say any names—may have bought out the theater. You know, privacy and all that…"

With her in the crook of his arm, her mouth and fingers gave him the sweetest thanks.

"Can we go somewhere else?" she whispered against his mouth.

Hell, Sheldon would have taken her to the moon.

"Of course," he replied, wasting no time getting up.

Within the hour, arriving separately, at separate times, and using separate entrances, they entered the five-star Water Lily luxury hotel in Southampton. And Sheldon didn't care about paying $1100 for a suite to get just an hour and a half more with her.

Once she joined him inside the hotel room, she closed the door and leaned against it. For a moment, time stood still while they stared in disbelief that this second meeting was really happening. They studied one another like two teenagers nervous before their first time.

Chrissy's bottom lip slid inside her mouth. Her chest ratcheted her breasts up and down, with her sucking in deep breaths. The mix of nervousness and wonder in her eyes told Sheldon all he needed to know. He hadn't made a mistake bringing her into his home. Possibly even into his heart.

"Come here." Walking backward, he reached out his hand, taking hers, and led her into the room.

She started to remove her coat.

"No." Sheldon wanted to undress her. The thought had crossed his mind numerous times over the last twenty-four hours. "Let me unwrap you."

Because she was indeed a gift.

Seeing her eyes go wide erected a statue between his legs. Her wonderment was Sheldon's rocket fuel.

He'd been lonely during the holidays for years.

But this week Chrissy's laughter had broken the quietude in his house that often formed Sheldon's jail bars. He hadn't been trapped with memories of what he had lost, or how he'd failed.

Right now, her hanging jaw urged him to keep prodding, to keep exploring the classy, put-together Chriselle. Despite her pricey makeup and all of her classy exterior screaming "I'm somebody's wife," her facade dissipated once Sheldon touched her nipple through her bra.

The woman had been married for ten years to someone who wasn't loving her. And in her bewildered expressions, Sheldon sensed he was every bit a gift to her as she was to him.

Staring at her now, he continued his real Christmas celebration, and unwrapped the present in front of him.

THE SECOND CHRISTMAS

CHRISSY

*E*very move Sheldon made so expertly was a first for Chrissy. The way he left her sweater to linger over her head, while she felt his tongue drag over her breasts.

"Mm," she moaned, arms in the air, folded over her head and still entangled in cashmere.

Trailing his hot breath across her stomach while he unfastened her slacks, letting them drop to the floor. Removing her panties with his teeth, he dived into her womanly core with his fingers.

"Shit, Chriselle," he gasped.

Sheldon's rich, smooth voice triggered thoughts she'd never imagined with Blake. Too many times she'd wondered if the day would ever come when she would actually enjoy sex.

Now, here she stood, blindfolded, anticipating where his tongue would torture her next as each article of her clothes fell to the floor.

Surprising Chrissy, he finally lifted her by the butt cheeks and carried her to the bed. He pulled off the sweater, and once her vision was restored, she saw that he hovered naked in front of her. That glorious body.

"I wanted to undress you," she whispered.

"You can make up for it." He towered over her.

"And I will," she said, surprising him as she eased down the mattress. She stopped directly in front of his thick, long dick that stood ready to do the job it had done two nights ago. Chrissy had never given oral, no matter how many times Blake had laid his shaft on her face first thing in the morning and demanded it.

But now, she took Sheldon's length in her hands and laid kisses along his massive erection. Though a pleased expression crossed his face, he also had a slight look of concern.

"If you've never done this, Chriselle, you don't have to—"

Curling her tongue under his shaft, letting saliva gather around her lips and wet him up, she stared in his eyes, letting him know she was ready for him. Sheldon's stomach tensed, and his mouth fell, eyes becoming hooded while the breaths from his chest grew shallow.

She slid out her moist tongue, stroked along his balls and licked up, before she circled his head.

Chrissy was really going through with this. When she returned to L.A., she wanted Sheldon to look at every woman and wish for her.

Never taking her eyes off his, she inserted his length through her lips.

Letting her mouth get wetter, she pulled him in deeper and bobbed her head. She laid her dripping tongue on his wood and sucked while his tip hit the back of her throat. Chrissy's saliva gurgled.

Sheldon's mouth fell, eyes becoming hooded. His sexy, chiseled torso loomed over her, and he must have been the most beautiful man she'd ever seen. Just the sight of him slicked up her thighs with squirts of her cream. She readied herself to worship him. As they formed a rhythm, she slid her hands around to his firm butt—one of her favorite spots on him—and pressed him forward. He gently thrust into her, his hands gripping her head.

"Fuck, Chris. You're a real fucking fast learner," he muttered, biting his lip. "I don't want to nut in your throat, baby. Get up."

Ignoring him, she clutched his butt cheeks and kept going. He was so fucking fine and god-like to watch. His chest muscles rose over her head, his stomach muscles contracting, like he'd stepped out of an African painting. The pleasureful facial expressions crossing his face pushed her to keep slurping, gagging, and bobbing. He kept his thrusts small but sped up.

The act excited her valley that throbbed and creamed. When Sheldon gritted his teeth and shot his warm seed into her throat, Chrissy climaxed at the same time.

She didn't know what the hell she was doing, or where they went from here, but she'd barely slept for thinking about him all night. And though she was trying to be smart and discreet about this affair, the truth was she wanted to scream her giddiness from the rooftops.

Moments later, he lay next to her, in shock.

"You had an orgasm just from sucking on me?" he asked.

Still swallowing his seed, she stayed silent, only wiping her mouth. She didn't want him to think the worst of her, that maybe she'd gone too far or been too forward. When Chrissy only gazed at him, Sheldon felt around her. The comforter was wet, as were her thighs, confirming that she'd indeed climaxed. Her breath caught in her windpipe as the doubts crept through her. But he seemed to process the depth of her attraction to him, pulling her to him, sucking her gaze into his.

"I think you and I are in trouble," he murmured against her lips.

Chrissy stroked his neck. "You're the kind of trouble I never thought would find me."

Sheldon licked her neck, up her jawbone, to her lips, before kissing her with his eyes open. "I want to show you everything."

Still trying to believe this amazement was even happening, she welcomed his tongue against hers. "And I want to feel all of it."

Chrissy's giddy head was still spinning when she rushed into an Uber.

Biting down on her smile, fighting it, it fought her back. Her legs still wobbled. Chest still clanged.

"Southampton Theater Company. Plymouth Street," she said to the driver.

Get it together, Chris. It was time to focus on the real world, on her career, and making a new life for herself without Blake.

She was late when the driver arrived at the theater house.

"Mrs. Mason!" someone called.

She whipped around. A young actress popped into view, forcing Chrissy out of her stupor.

"You came. I'm Saneel, friends with Karema Jackson. She said you were in town and I should introduce myself to you."

The young woman's eager eyes were an extra shot of caffeine in Chrissy's already hyped veins.

"Hi. I'm certainly glad you did. Good to meet you," Chrissy said with extra energy.

"Here's my card, and my reel," Saneel said, proudly presenting a packet.

"Awesome," Chrissy said, still searching for a hole somewhere inside herself to bury these new emotions. "What kind of work do you prefer?" She would throw herself into what she had wanted for a long time—a career. What she'd always seen Blake do—be the powerful dealmaker in the room. She wasn't there yet, but this step took her in the right direction.

"Drama theater and comedy. So far I've done six off-Broadway productions, one of them leads. I was Marguerite in *I Know Why the Caged Bird Sings*. And a supporting role in *Grapes of Wrath* on Broadway."

"Last live performance?" Chrissy flipped through Saneel's packet. The actress had graduated college four years prior, which would make her twenty-six, a mere five years behind Chrissy.

"Last month."

Chrissy looked up and into her eyes. "What are you doing for work between shows?"

Saneel's face lost some energy upon being asked one of the tougher questions of show business. "Part-time dental assistant."

Chrissy smiled, reassuring her. "Good on you for staying at it. We all have to start somewhere. Myself included. So where would you like my help?"

A combination of bashfulness and hope flitted across the actress's face. Saneel emitted anticipation that Chrissy wished she could place in a bottle. More girls approached, introducing themselves, handing her their folders and offering their hands to shake.

"It's so nice to see a woman here," one of the young men said, a nineteen-year-old from Tuscaloosa, Alabama. "I'm Jody, and I've been doing commercial work here and there. This is my folder."

"I recognize your face. Didn't I see you in a commercial for Glow? I love that toothpaste?" Chrissy asked.

"Yep, that's it." He laughed proudly.

"So why aren't you represented already?"

"I am. It's just," his eyes fell, "I'm queer and…"

Chrissy's insides heated. "You don't think your agent is working hard enough to find you better work."

His lips pursed. "Exactly. Just bit jobs here and there because I have a pretty face. But I'm practicing my craft, and I'm ready to try for television parts."

She finally felt she was home. Near the stage and performance.

Only she was no longer a starry-eyed college theater major, swooning over the charms of a young Blake producing B-list movies and music videos.

Chrissy stared into the young man's wishful eyes that seemed to reflect her own sleeping dreams. "Let's see how we can help each other."

Their performances resonated with Chrissy's desire she'd lost, snuffed out by the last ten years of mothering, dinner parties, and propping up Blake. Their faces aflame with determination, these actors reminded Chrissy of all the determination she'd surrendered. At points, she had sat on edge of her seat, so engaged she didn't feel her own nostalgic tears.

"I forgot," she said over dinner a few hours later with

Neera and Cher. "They're everything I wanted to be. They just haven't gotten their chance."

"Everything you *will* be," Neera insisted. "No, you didn't forget. You simply put it on hold. You thought you and Blake were going to build something together."

"And we have. It just…"

"*He* has built a life for himself," Cher snapped.

Chrissy's indignation flared. "With *my* help. His agency would not be what it is without me. Those girls he represents, they're coming over to me now. I have every right to stay married to him and use his name and connections while I build my own thing."

Chrissy just needed a little more time, to put up the front and pretend everything was perfect while she picked off his clients.

On his road from parlaying his Atlanta producer moves into a Hollywood agent career, Blake had treated women like products instead of people. Most of them tolerated it. Some might have even liked it. But with four of the actresses, he had gone too far. It was Chrissy who had stepped in and helped when they didn't want to go to police.

"How long do you think that will last?" Cher drove a jackhammer through Chrissy's calculating. "Blake won't let you keep picking off his clients, especially while you still wear his name. You may as well serve Blake with divorce papers now. And move on with your life. With this banker dude."

"No," Chrissy replied. No matter how wonderfully intoxicating Sheldon was, Chrissy needed to stay focused and wring every benefit from her marriage that she could before she ended it.

"She's right," Neera muttered. "Divorce papers right now will set Blake off."

"It'll set Blake off whenever she does it. Especially when he finds out about the banker," Cher replied. "Get it over with and file. In fact, why don't you ask the banker to help you. He could probably take care of all this quickly."

"No." Chrissy gave them both a threatening eye. "Blake won't find out about anything, because there is nothing with *any*one."

And she would not ask Sheldon for help, because Blake was her problem and not his. He had already done enough.

Neera sipped her wine. "What you need is an ace in the hole that Blake will never see coming. A way to bury his ass, so no matter how mad he gets, he can never come for you."

"Right. Some sort of leverage forcing him to accept it's over and move on," Chrissy thought aloud, her mind turning over his baggage. "No parents. No revenge. No mess."

She needed a smoking gun to shut him down.

Without putting his young clients in jeopardy.

If word got out that they'd complained of assault against a talent agent, whether or not their complaints were righteous, other agencies would blacklist them as "difficult to work with." The entertainment industry was still very much male-dominated, and while new attention on gender equality was slowly bringing changes, a snitch was still a snitch.

The warmth of red merlot slid down Chrissy's throat. She pondered her next steps over her last dinner in the Hamptons.

"Chriselle." A voice behind her whipped her around in her seat. A familiar face stared down at her. Kevin. "I'm glad I caught you before you boarded the plane back to L.A." He sat in the fourth seat, and poured himself a glass of merlot.

"Where did you come from? How did you know we were here?" Chrissy asked.

She stared at her two cousins, and Cher's face seemed… uncharacteristically innocent.

"Why haven't you returned any of my phone calls?" Kevin asked. "I'm sure your moms told you I dropped by."

"I planned to hit you up before I left," Chrissy lied. "I've just been busy."

He smelled the wine, spinning it around, holding it up to observe its consistency against the glass. "I'll bet you have. Busy in Alpine maybe?" His eyes swung from the glass to Chrissy.

Her pulse beat outside of her. Either that, or the floor fell from beneath her, dropping her body and leaving her vital organs suspended.

She hardened. Conjuring up her best poker face, she asked, "Alpine? I've been in the city with the girls."

"So your girls put you on a helicopter and convinced you to leave your phone behind?" The barrels of Kevin's glare narrowed, his gunsight closing in on Chrissy. "They were sophisticated enough to do that? Tell me. When were you in the city? Before or after Alpine?"

"Wait a minute. You got a hell of a lot of nerve," Neera spat.

Swatting off Neera like a fly, he stayed focused squarely on her cousin. "And *you've* got a lot of nerve thinking you would skip out of New York without at least saying goodbye to me first. I hope you and Maddy don't expect to jump ship so suddenly, before we even get started," Kevin replied, not blinking an eye. "Especially not to Sheldon Rouse's raft."

Chrissy tried to swallow the clanging of every function inside her. "I'm not in anybody's lifeboat. There are no deals. We haven't signed anything. I don't understand why you're tripping."

"Because you slept with Sheldon Rouse. After you said he

was nothing to you. And I guess you didn't know he signed a deal with Lana and her mama this morning." Kevin sipped before smacking the wine off his lips.

The revelation dropped Chrissy into space. *How could he?* He hadn't breathed a word to her about this. She had only seen him four hours ago.

Another spark fired in Kevin's eye as he brought down the hammer. "I guess he didn't tell you that when the two of you were fucking around at the Water Lily."

How had he known? About this? The same way he'd known about hers and Blake's fights.

Chrissy's boiling pot overflowed. "How dare you!"

"Easily. One of us was actually working while you were fucking," her childhood nemesis shot back. He was slamming the basketball against her arm all over again, just like when they were kids.

Finally, she managed, through her clenched jaw, "What do you want?"

"You gave me a good idea. For once. I like the thought of you and Maddy walking the Kids' Tech Layer into Sag Harbor City Council. That would work. I would like to be allies, all of us. As you said, saving Black Sag Harbor. I won't hold it against you that you banged Rouse."

The appall crisscrossing the table couldn't have bounced any harder. Chrissy's sharp fingernail stiffened in his face, and she hunted for her voice.

"Like I said, we have made *zero* decisions about who we will support. Yet. We will inform you, in a few days." It was a lie, but she needed him out of her face.

His glass of wine moved Chrissy's hand aside, bringing him close enough that she smelled his cologne's attempt at making him sexy.

"And like *I* said, allies. You need them now, more than ever. Because I would *hate* for your husband to receive the passenger bookings for Joanna's Private Helicopter Service that show one Chriselle Mason took a flight from the Hamptons to Alpine, New Jersey. At the same time her phone signal stayed in one location—the helicopter landing port. For two days. And that she was at the Water Lily. With the guy from Alpine, one day later. We could all use an ally to help us out when we need them most, no?"

Whipping from his coat a stack of photos, he tossed them on the table. Large, 11 x 8 inch images of her entering the hotel, and Sheldon entering minutes later, stared back at her.

Kevin slurped more wine.

A roasting Chrissy cooked in the oven of Kevin's scheming. "What do you want?"

"That's more like it. I'll send you the paperwork. You send it to Maddy. Let's conference it middle of next week?" Setting down the wine, he got up. Giving Chrissy a rough pat on the shoulder, he added, "Safe travels back to the Golden State."

A LITTLE PRESSURE

SHELDON

Hard knocking at Jerrell's door raised Sheldon from the dining room table. His brother was still out working his business, and Sheldon was going over the particulars for *Escapade by Erlita*.

He opened it to find Chrissy standing in front of him. Winded, eyes wide, staring at him like she was ready for action, this incredible late-night surprise supercharged the synapses in his brain.

"Baby, damn, I know I just saw you, but you're *still* scrumptious as fuck. To what do I owe this—"

Chrissy's hand bolted into his chest.

He stumbled backward, not from her force, but his shock at what he now guessed was anger. "Chris, what is—"

"Did you sign with Lana and not tell me? Were you distracting me today—these last three *fucking* days—so your boys could sign her? Were you using me?" Fury jacked her chest in and out. "Is that all you wanted with me? Not to partner up. Not to take me seriously. But only to *fuck* me and use my hope that you would?"

Now Sheldon realized what was happening.

"Chris, no… That's not… I was not…." He took a breath, so his brain could sort out her frustration. "Yes, Brent and the others called and left a message while I was with you, that they were okaying Erlita's project. I called them back after I left you. When you and I were together, I didn't know this."

Her mouth trembling, chin shaking, she shot bullet holes through him. "I asked you to hold off."

"Chriselle, this is business. Whatever you think about Lana personally, her mother has a solid concept. But that has *nothing* to do with us. Or how I feel about you. I told you the entire time. And I never gave you any impression that I was into Kevin's thing."

"So you left me to find out about this from Kevin. *Middleton.*" The boulders of her words tumbled out as if she'd had to lift them.

They fell onto Sheldon.

"Chrissy, even if I wanted to tell you once I found out, how would I? We agreed I can't call you and would wait for you to call me. It's what you wanted. This is not personal. So stop treating me like I've betrayed you." He watched her shudder with hurt that he very much wished he could take from her. "Baby, come here."

"No." She wiped her eyes. A complete contrast to the happy-go-lucky woman who'd waved beer at him just three nights before.

Without another word, she turned away from him, taking a bigger part of Sheldon with her than he thought he had to give.

"Chriselle." Not the least bit worried about a coat, in his t-shirt and sweats, he followed her into the freezing oceanside cold, out of Jerrell's rental, to her car.

She opened her door, and Sheldon reached around her, pulling her against him. "It's a good idea. And you know it, Chris. That's why you're working so hard to defeat it."

"She is an awful person, and you ought not want to do business with people like that. It comes back to bite you."

"Really? Then how do you explain your doing business with Kevin? Or you being married to Blake for ten years, despite his shady business practices that toe the legal line. We've run background on Erlita, and she might be drama, but her shop is pretty popular down in Texas."

She pushed his hands away before getting in her car. "Bye, Sheldon."

The way his jones for her was ballooning inside him, Chriselle might have been driving off with his dick.

An hour later, once Jerrell got home, Sheldon moaned to his little brother. "What did I do so wrong?"

Brandy in one hand, his phone in the other, Sheldon sipped his third glass of the night. He took another peek at his encrypted phone to make sure he hadn't missed a notification since the last time he'd looked five minutes ago.

In case Chrissy wanted to talk.

"You're a greedy Wall Street jerk who's only out for money," Jerrell answered with a chuckle. He sat at his tiny dining room table, covered in papers as he calculated expenses for his pastry business.

Sheldon threw a couch pillow at him. "Forget you, man."

"Dude, she's new to the game of business deals. What did you expect?"

"For her to act like a grown-up," Sheldon huffed.

"You. Have. Been. Terminated." Jerrell laughed while reciting a refrain from a video game they'd played as teenagers, and sometimes still played.

Sheldon's heavy chest let out a couple of chuckles.

"Ya'll had a good roll. And if you hit it just right, she won't be able to shake you when she gets back to Cali. That's all you can ask. You made your move, and the ball is in her court."

"If she ever plays ball with me again. So now I go back to being bored."

"No," Jerrell replied on his way over to Shel. He slapped Shel's shoulder. "You've always got me. So, moving on to Lana, what's up with her and her mama and this beauty spa, or salon, or what is it?"

"All the above. How many black-owned spas do you know of? That could be worth something."

Jerrell nodded. "So we're competing against Kevin Middleton's project?"

"Yes. And didn't you say Kevin is seeing Maddy now?" Sheldon asked.

"Yep."

"Damn," Sheldon sighed. He calculated the competition in his head. "So it's you, me, and Lana versus Kevin, Maddy, and Chrissy."

"Maddy probably asked Chrissy to join up with her and Kevin. That dude's got Maddy's nose so wide open," Jerrell fumed. "She would jump off a cliff if that fool told her to."

Sheldon sipped his drink, letting the liquid burn his air pipes, hoping it would numb the agitation Chrissy had left behind.

"I'm not so sure about that. Chrissy is the one pushing this, bringing everybody together against us. Chrissy does not want outsiders taking over their Sag Harbor."

Jerrell poured himself a drink. "These legacy residents have been around for decades, and they're aiming guns at you.

This might become a war. And if so, you might kiss any chances of you and Chrissy goodbye."

The new streams of excitement pumping through Sheldon's veins stopped their flow. He had just found her. He wanted so badly to check in and ensure she was okay.

"Don't turn into a softy now, dude," Jerrell said. "You've always been a businessman."

Until Sheldon's hunger and ambition had ruined his marriage.

Now it was happening again. He suspected Chrissy was stronger than a little competition.

Sheldon looked to the youngest Rouse man. "How do you feel about moving against Maddy?"

Jerrell's jaws ground together. "Screw Maddy. And her pretty punk Kevin Middleton. She blew me off for that shiny negro, because she thinks all I am is some cookie salesman."

Sheldon chuckled. "But you *are* a damn cookie salesman. You are in your feelings about that girl."

"And you're not in your feelings about Chriselle?" Jerrell shot back.

Sheldon thought about that. His brother was right.

"I know how to keep my cool. But can *you,* though?" Sheldon asked, pointing his drink at Jerrell. "A hundred percent professional. No beating Kevin's head in or nothing like that. Because one blowup—and I mean *one*—and I'll drop your ass. And our old man will not be mad at me. He'll be pissed at you."

"I'm good, bruh. Let's go to work and get this money." Jerrell raised his glass for a toast.

Sheldon lifted the weight of the world to raise his arm.

He hadn't felt so shitty since coming home to find Genie and Hadar gone. But he had powered through it. It's why the finance world now respected the name Sheldon Rouse. And if Chrissy fell apart under the slightest pressure, then she wasn't the woman he'd thought.

"They're about to get a taste of these Rouse boys then."

LONGTIME RESIDENTS of Sag Harbor gave Sheldon a hard side-eye.

"Have you discussed your idea with legacy families like the Townsends, the Middletons, or the Pages?" one neighbor asked.

"Yes, we have, and we differ on the Ivory's potential—they want a kids' technological playroom, which is a valiant concept. But that will not bring in the income or foot traffic Black Sag Harbor needs if you want to keep it black," Sheldon pressed.

Inside Sharon's Seascape Restaurant, Jerrell, Sheldon, Brent, Erlita, Lana, and the rest of their team worked every local customer they could.

Erlita had provided beauty gift boxes.

Complimentary massages were being given, body tension evaluations, and Jerrell's new store manager had worked with their grandmother to create treats just for *Escapade Beauty & Wellness by Erlita.* Curled and molded chocolate sticks swinging around succulent cake towers, filled with warm fruit and cream, got people's attention. Eyes rolling into the back of their heads and lips licking up cream sealed the deal.

By week's end, Brent and his team would build a model on Eastville Avenue for neighbors to tour and get visuals.

"But Sag Harbor is quiet. Low-key. Relaxing," one black resident said, licking up the chocolate orange delight. "I don't want to come in from my boat and see piles of strangers staring at my house. We've already got enough carpetbaggers busting in here. If I wanted my peace disturbed, I would've moved to some celebrity neighborhood in Atlanta, but I didn't. So I like the kids' idea better."

"Sir, all these crowds you're expecting, won't happen. This is still the Hamptons. It's only affordable for a tiny tier of people to enjoy, so the price point will keep away the..." Sheldon swallowed, "... rowdier types you're concerned about."

The man thought it over a moment. "Nah, no, it won't. I've been around too long. Business brings noise. And traffic, like you said. And yes, we should consider income. But we should find cash without chaos," the resident declared. "Thank you for the dessert. I'm sure my wife will enjoy putting all this beauty stuff under her sink."

Sheldon and the others all reconvened in frustration a few hours later. "These uppity folks around here are no joke."

"Not uppity. Just protective," Jerrell said between munches of lunch. "I've spent some time here getting to know them. Understanding this Hamptons energy. These folks worked generations for this, and for the past few years, outsiders like you have started barging in." He glared at Erlita. "Go to the Firehouse, and the Whaling Museum, and The Ivory, and the Episcopalian church. Learn what makes them tick. It's wealth with community, *not just* wealth. That generational bond is sacred to them."

Sheldon smiled, truly proud of his brother for making this much headway in the Hamptons community so soon. Many of the neighbors and their kids knew Jerrell by name, and he even walked their dogs, did yard work, or dropped off groceries.

"Maddy spent a lot of time drilling it into my brain," Jerrell added.

"And that's good. We need that knowledge on this team. You should be the one making these pitches and not me," Sheldon suggested.

"Nah, I'm working too hard for them to trust me. Going to them with some outsider shit, not the way to do it."

Sheldon rolled his eyes. "You mean Maddy would be mad at you for hustling her friends."

"Maddy will already be mad when she finds out I'm siding with you and Lana. Part of the reason I'm doing this is to shut down her and Middleton. But the people around here are a different issue. I am not trying to piss *them* off."

"Maddy pissed about Lana? They're co-workers," Erlita said. "For the last five years. The only reason they're on the outs now is Maddy put her nose where it didn't belong."

Sheldon sighed, rubbing his head. "Well, Ms. Erlita, you should tell Lana to calm down and tend to her own business, instead of some other woman's. From what I hear, Adella is much loved around here. And if the neighbors who love her learn you are not only opening a business that threatens them, but your daughter is sleeping with Del's man, you might finish us before we start."

Jerrell went a step further, wrapping up Gram's gourmet sandwich he'd been eating. "May I ask why you want to come here, instead of doing this in your hometown, back in Texas?"

Erlita's back straightened in her seat, her long gold nails dusting crumbs off her electric-blue pants. "Not that I have to explain myself to you, but I like this place. Who doesn't want to be in the Hamptons? I've got a good idea, and it deserves the very best."

Jerrell's own shoulders squared, and Sheldon could feel his

brother's notorious temper flaring. "You don't have to explain yourself to me, but you and Lana will have to explain yourselves to these residents. This isn't like being down home in the South where folks are itching for new business in the 'hood. These folks moved here to get *away* from the masses."

"He's right," yet a fourth voice intervened.

They all turned to see a beautiful, tall woman gazing—or more like glaring—down at them all. The woman's stare flashed like lightning, as if she practiced it in the mirror. Sheldon wondered who this person was that arose from nowhere.

"Mrs. Page," Jerrell said, immediately shooting up, wiping off his hands and reaching out to hug her. His anger dissolved, and Sheldon watched his tone and body motions become respectful.

Sheldon sat stupefied at how somebody could have so much sway over Jerrell Rouse. Who was this person?

"Jerrell," the woman muttered, her face remaining stiff and unwelcoming as she pulled from Jerrell's hug. Her guns pointed at Erlita.

"And this must be Lana's mother."

Erlita stood, and the two older matriarchs faced off. "And you are Maddy's mother, who kicked my daughter out of your home."

Both of them clutching their bags like steel swords ready to fly, the two did not shake hands.

"I am. Your daughter was starting trouble in my house. I thought she would have gotten the message and left Sag Harbor by now. But she brings her mother here to spread trouble over our neighborhood," Mrs. Page replied.

Now Sheldon understood. *Oh, shit.* Maddy's mother hated Lana's mother.

Erlita sucked her teeth. "Now, what kind of welcome is that? Here we are trying to make your boring little streets better, and you're complaining?"

"Protecting its integrity from troublemakers trying to destroy it. You must be lost. This isn't Texas. We don't need cowboy hats, shiny tassels, and rodeos here." Mrs. Page turned to Jerrell. "So it's true then? What Maddy is telling me? That you and your brother are taking part in this foolishness? Jerrell, my husband brought you into this community and trusted you."

"Mrs. Page," Jerrell started, shocking Sheldon with his humble tone. The man truly had come a long way from his days of telling a person where they could go for questioning him. "I know what it looks like, but this is a good idea that could multiply your husband's investment."

"We wanted your grandmother's pastries. Not a beauty salon," the beautiful but firm woman asserted.

"I understand that, ma'am. I'm only asking you to keep an open mind for the possibilities. This is a wonderful opportunity for black business to come together in the Hamptons. It could be special, particularly right now, when you're about to lose one of your iconic cornerstones in the Ivory," Jerrell nearly pleaded.

"I can't make any promises, other than Maddy and I will push as hard against this as we can," Mrs. Page said. "And we will inform your parents of this issue." Her stare dropped from Erlita's head to her feet, dismissing the woman as if she were diseased. "Gentlemen." With that, she was off.

Damn. The parents? "She knows our parents?"

"Yes," Jerrell replied, rolling his eyes. "They weekend together at the country club."

Erlita's face had soured. "Well, isn't that lovely. House negroes who don't like the field negroes."

Sheldon eyed his brother. "We can't do this without someone from this community."

They desperately needed to find an ally.

"For us to do that, you need to tweak your business mission," Jerrell fussed. "Stop talking about bringing in partners from all over the country and start with the ones right here. Tailor your service just for Sag Harbor. Involve their dogs and cats. Offer some home visits and beauty parties."

That night, Sheldon scoured the lists of bank clients in the areas of Ninevah, Sag Harbor Hills, and Azurest—all predominantly black. He searched their careers, their children's colleges and careers; he was especially on the hunt for the entrepreneurs, open-minded types more amenable to progress.

He worked to put together a short list of Sag Harbor community members he could approach, and while scanning, one name stood out to him. A socialite who moved in all the right circles, was a member of the Madames' secret sorority, had graced the covers of fashion magazines and had owned her share of clothing boutiques over the years. An older woman whose social media photos showed her hobnobbing with all the players in Black Hamptons.

There was just one catch. His using this person would be controversial. And definitely divisive. But his team of investors was low on options, and he had to give this person a shot. She had a long history of throwing Hamptons parties for international celebrities and diplomats, which told him her mindset was broader than local politics. She could be convinced. He had to do it. But it could jeopardize another phenomenal opportunity now lying in front of Sheldon.

Buzzing somewhere in the room broke up his thoughts. Not from his main cell phone.

Sheldon's heart could have thumped out of his chest as his legs scattered for the extra phone.

His nerves on edge, praying he could find the right words, he activated the call.

Saying nothing, he waited for her this time, holding the phone while staring out of Jerrell's panoramic window at the endless night.

If the two of them didn't speak the whole time, just listening to her breathe would have been enough. It reminded him of her panting in his ear while trembling beneath him.

Sheldon's breath waited in his windpipe. *Baby, please talk to me.*

"So you're winning at getting the neighbors to hate you," she finally said.

Sheldon laughed, relieved and elated to hear that singsong, smart-ass voice.

"I was thinking this call wouldn't come."

"It probably wouldn't have. But you are invading my favorite community."

He smiled from his insides, leaning his head against the cool window. "If it was your favorite community, it wouldn't have taken you five years to get back here."

"If it wasn't my favorite community, I wouldn't have been there in the first place… and then we wouldn't have met."

The grin in his heart valve deepened. "Thank God it's your favorite community." He inhaled. "But I was hoping this call was about more than that."

"Sorry to disappoint you."

"Maddy must have called you, after her mother obviously contacted her."

"I've known Mrs. Page my whole life. She called me herself. And you're still not letting this go."

"What can I say? I know a winner when I see one." In his head, all over again, he reimagined her lush curves. "And feel one. And hold one."

A tiny sigh entered his ears from the other end. Sheldon sensed she had so much more to say.

"Then you'll know this winner won't rest until your little child's play with Lana Gilley is a bad memory."

Shit. Fierce, feisty Chrissy was back. He reached between his legs and rearranged his erection. "I wouldn't expect anything less."

Finally, a woman who could handle his drive. *So* damn attractive.

"Good then. We understand each other."

Did they. The jet engine in his dick was pointed straight at the West Coast. He needed to understand her in person. Skin to skin. Until sunrise.

"I want to come and see you, baby."

Silence.

But he didn't think it was a bad silence. More like shocked. From her winded breathing, and the tiny sucking sounds that came across the phone, it seemed she was stunned. And that she might be anticipating the delicious details of his visit.

"Sheldon, you know I can't—"

"Tell me yuour pussy's not throbbing for me, Chriselle, and I won't ask again."

Silence. Another gasp.

He grinned. As did his manhood.

"I would love nothing more, Shel." She'd lowered her voice to a sultry hush. "I can't stop thinking about you either. You're *all* I think about."

He closed his eyes against the window, almost able to feel his dick slipping into her warmth now.

"I can be there by tomorrow morning."

On the other end, her heavy, excited breaths answered before she could create an excuse. "That's not a good idea. I need to handle some things here. Before I come back East to handle your ass. And Lana's."

Humor pushed across his face, even as his disappointment cratered him. "I can't wait for you to come handle me."

"Careful what you wish for, sir. Goodnight."

"Goodnight, Chriselle."

But the night could have been so much better.

Calm down, Rouse.

Chrissy had made herself clear. But Shel was very much aware of all she hadn't said.

AN EVEN MORE GORGEOUS VIEW

CHRISSY

*B*ack at her condo in L.A., her hands shaking, heart racing, Chrissy lowered the secret phone to her chest.

At her dining room table, she recalled how Sheldon had filled her up and pleasured her, for two delirious days. The best sex she'd never had.

As pissed as she was at Sheldon for signing on to Lana's project, he wasn't Blake.

The thirty-nine-year-old banker hadn't been cold-hearted in how he'd handled her. No snickering, taunting, or threats awaited her when she'd gone to him upset. His calm energy made it hard to loathe him.

"Mommy, I'm finished!" Little Blake called out from the bathtub.

"Okay, don't get out. I'll come to help you," she said, collecting her thoughts.

After bathing her children and getting them ready for school the next day, she sat at her dining room table.

Sprawled before her was all her hard work since returning

to California days before. Three piles of to-do lists lay before her: a list of talent on the East Coast, all the neighbors in Sag Harbor to organize against Sheldon and Lana, and her strategy for breaking away from Blake.

Neera was right. Chrissy needed a loaded gun ready to fire at Blake when she filed divorce papers. A way to check his itch to retaliate.

Surprisingly, she hadn't heard a peep from him since she'd gotten back. During the pickup and exchange of the children, his girlfriend, Giselle, had been the one who appeared. Chrissy knew he was trying to get a rise out of her, but she was actually relieved. Without facing him directly or talking to him, she could avoid his quizzes about her plans and how she was surviving on her own. At remembering Sheldon's comments about yoga instructors, she had to stop herself from cracking up in front of Giselle.

And even though Sheldon irritated her with his Lana deal, their lovemaking still ran on instant replay through her mind. So Giselle could have Blake, and Chrissy didn't give two squats if she was now sleeping in their marital home. When he got hit with the paperwork for division of assets and alimony in a few weeks, she wondered how much yoga Giselle would stick around and do in the bedroom then.

For now, she readied for two wars—the one against Sheldon, and the one against Blake.

Names of Blake's associates and contacts dating back to college sat in front of her, all who he'd vacationed with at the All-Star basketball games, whose videos he produced, and whom she suspected had unsavory histories. The kind of histories that included assaulting and abusing women. She'd heard the rumors over the years, of wild industry parties that bordered on illegal, where drugs flowed freely and some aspiring actresses were tricked into sex.

The same guys who had helped Blake ascend in Hollywood were the kinds of seedy people with connections to freeze Chrissy from hers and Blake's joint account.

Chrissy printed off bank statements that included questionable deposits from unidentifiable sources. She'd always wondered how Blake had gotten into the building on pricey Wilshire Boulevard so quickly. After only two years of being an agent, when he was still so new. She reviewed numbers and deposit entries spanning back to their early days when she'd helped him open his office.

Almost a lifetime ago, Chrissy stopped going to her own acting auditions and gave up a supporting role on a B-level show to help Blake when he stressed out most. With Little Blake on her hip, she set up Blake's computers, administrative system, held lunches and showcases to bring in talent, and hired his office manager, who was now loyal to Chrissy. Their efforts had paid off, with three current offices in Beverly Hills, Oakland, and Las Vegas.

Though they'd made some good deals here and there, the money still had not always added up. And she suspected Blake received cash infusions from somewhere else. A side hustle. Or a deep pocket, who was not operating under the table.

But since the birth of their daughter, Kara, Chrissy had largely been out of the loop.

And for the past two years, Chrissy had returned her attention to her own ambitions, checking out on Blake. Which escalated his irritation from pushing and threats to hitting.

Now she gathered all her information, and organized it in spreadsheets of neat columns and rows that displayed dates, associates, and Blake's large cash deposits. She only needed someone to help her connect the dots.

The next morning, she called the number scribbled in Sheldon's poor handwriting from their first encounter. A divorce lawyer.

After dropping off the children at school, she headed to the lawyer's office in Santa Monica.

"And you're certain you're ready to do this?" Attorney Afua Nelson peered at Chrissy across the desk. "I've heard of this man before. Blake Mason. Friends with quite a few rappers and street types. Good things, and not so good. You've been together a long time. Since before graduating college. Two young children."

Chrissy wondered if she had made a mistake coming to this person, and why Sheldon had recommended someone who second-guessed her. "Yes, I am absolutely sure. But perhaps I should consider someone else, who will be more supportive."

"Mrs. Mason—"

"Chriselle." She got tired of people using her married name to handcuff her. "Townsend."

The woman's face remained as smooth and unbothered as the endless Southern California blue sky outside.

"I've done this a long time. Long enough to know most women start the divorce process but won't finish it. Especially when he finds out how much you'll walk away with, and he starts begging, promising to act right, and offering the sun, moon, and stars. Then the children cry and break your heart, and suddenly, you're back in his bed."

At the biting truth of her words, Chrissy's eyes fled out the panoramic windows. How many times had she already left and gone back?

"Back to suppressing your own happiness for the good of everybody else. It's just what we do. So please don't take offense at my questions, Mrs.… Chriselle. I'm only giving you a chance to check in with yourself before we proceed."

Chrissy stared out the window at the Pacific Ocean, a few steps beyond the door of the building. On merely the sixth day of January, California's pristine beaches glistened under the bright sun. At first glance, the state appeared so liberating and free. But for all of California's warmth and beauty, the entire ten years had felt like Chrissy's gilded cage.

She would have given anything to be back on the frigid East Coast, in her family's home on Eastville Avenue. There, she could sip hot toddies with Maddy again, and even Adella, whose innocent naïveté often annoyed her. At least on the East Coast, what one saw was what they got. No mirages. No lovely facades to cover up the vicious backstabbing required to survive.

Her phone rang. Maddy. She excused herself to take the call.

"So when are we breaking the news to Kevin? That we're not going with his project?" she asked.

Chrissy squirmed, remembering his lethal face days before. And his threat.

I swear to God, I will destroy you.

She still wondered how he'd found out about Sheldon. Her upcoming plans could mean literal life and death. If she broke the news to Kevin and set him off, he would go to Blake. That couldn't happen until she had leverage against Blake. "I'm ironing out that part."

"Girl, we don't have long to iron. The wrinkles should be straight by now. This proposal is due in a week, and then there's the city council meeting for all the projects. We have to line up all our ducks in the next day or so."

"I got you and I'll handle it. Conference call with Racquel this evening?" Chrissy asked.

"Alright then. We'll talk," Maddy answered.

Chrissy started to hang up when her childhood friend spoke again.

"Chris?"

"Yeah?" Chrissy responded.

"Are you sure you're okay out there? You sound a little more… tense now, than when you were here last weekend."

Chrissy swallowed, already knowing what she'd have to do. "Stop worrying, girl. Everything is fine."

She reentered the lawyer's office and gave a nod. "Yes, I want to do this. I'm sure."

"Good then."

Chrissy readied up to leave, but a weird smile spread across her lawyer's face. Puzzled, Chrissy stared. "What's funny?"

Attorney Nelson chuckled, and her eyes fell to her desk. The lawyer shook her head, like there was a joke Chrissy wasn't getting. When the woman looked up again, she stared *past* Chrissy.

Which compelled her client to turn around and see what was so amusing.

Chrissy's heart dropped, along with her breathing. Right outside the glass door was an even more gorgeous view than the sparkling ocean.

Holding a fistful of long-stemmed tulips in his gloved hands, a gigantic, boyish smile spread across his face…

… stood a tall, elegant Sheldon.

NOT JUST SEX

CHRISSY

Chrissy moaned, her toes curling, eyes open, her fingers digging into his taut back. His pelvis tapped against hers, gentle, slow, as Sheldon's fingers pressed her clit.

His manhood teased her softly, barely, with her feet draped over his shoulders, him bearing down between her thighs. He kissed and sucked her legs. "I couldn't lay in my bed one more night imagining your pussy wrapped around my dick."

"Mmm…" Her insides heated from his strokes, his words, her feet bobbing over her head.

"Keep your legs open. Don't close 'em."

"Sheld…" The tingling in her creamy canal traveled up her insides, seeming to shock her vocal cords until she could hardly speak.

"Chriselle."

When he whispered her name… The way it glided off his tongue… While his gaze dug into her, and his waist pumped into her at the same time.

His steel massaged, cajoled, gently commanded her inner

muscles until they convulsed. At a private, oceanside home in Malibu, tucked among the hills and away from prying eyes, she could scream as loud as she needed.

Like now. When she screamed his name during her crazy release.

They'd already gone for a walk on a private beach, with the cool night sand under their feet. Holding hands, kissing, sucking, he'd brought the romance to her.

And even though Chrissy had a ton of tasks to knock off her to-do list, she'd delayed it all for the day. This magic of being swept off her feet was too foreign, felt too good in the center of her chest, for Chrissy to ignore it or even get mad. Especially not when, every *single* time she turned to him, Sheldon's eyes were undressing her like he would self-destruct if she didn't put out his fuse.

Thankfully, Little Blake and Kara were already with Blake's parents, which saved Chrissy the suspicion she would no doubt draw if she asked for a babysitter out of the blue.

"You're going to get me in so much trouble." Now after a full day that included yachting, privately catered seafood, and custom desserts, she turned in his arms to face him.

"I'm sorry, baby, but you were sounding too damn good on the phone." He parted his legs so she could slide hers between them.

"You're not sorry." She laughed against his lips.

Smiling, he stared down at her. "Okay, maybe not, but don't I get brownie points for at least saying it?"

She sucked her teeth, half grinning but half serious. "No. I don't need to be patronized. You flew out here to get in my guts when I asked you not to."

"Well, yes, but I also want you to not be mad, since you

wanted me in your guts too. And that's not the only reason I came here."

She drew back a little. "It's not?"

"No," he said, looking over at her. His finger swiped down her face. "I also came to offer you support. In case your husband tries anything, I want you to know I'm here for you if you need me. For anything. Not just sex. And I mean it. I know you're taking a risk, and I feel partly responsible."

His words touched Chrissy. The tender way he gazed at her told her he meant every word.

But hanging over them was reality. As incredible as this felt, she had to keep the situation with Blake in check until her lawyer had filed the divorce papers. Even though Blake cheated openly, and Chrissy had every right to enjoy happiness of her own, he held a lot of the cards with accounts, properties, and other assets. Chrissy did not want any drama or conflict that would set him off—that might cause him to start hiding assets, filing for custody, using his connections to ruin her budding business. She was trying to avoid an unnecessary war that would complicate her next moves. It could prolong her main move. Back to New York.

Another thought entered her head while she lay against Sheldon. Chrissy squinted, and raised a suspicious eyebrow. "Did you really come here, and find me at my lawyer's office, so you could check up on my divorce?"

Sheldon rolled his eyes and faked being offended. "Girl, nah."

Chrissy poked him in his side. "The truth, Mr. Rouse."

"Okay, in my defense, I actually came because your pussy was crying out to me through the phone last night. You were saying no, but she and I were having a whole other conversation without you."

Chrissy's sides shook from laughter she couldn't stop.

Sheldon broke into a high-pitched female voice. "Your pussy was like, *Sheldon, baby, if you don't get your ass on that plane, Imma be so wet I'll flood all of California. All these damn wildfires, my wet ass will put out every one of 'em—2300 square miles, 1.5 million acres, the Caldor Fire, the Dixie Fire, San Francisco, Greenville, you name it, I'm soaking it. Noah's flood won't have nothing on me. You better bring that dick on here before I drench the West Coast.* So, baby, as much as I want to save the planet and shit, pussies need saving too. And my dick was like, we really do need to get our asses out there and help her out, before California has a different kind of problem."

Her nose wrinkled, and she pursed her lips. "Pussies need saving?"

"Yes, ma'am, absolutely." He bit his lip, and his gaze dropped to her thighs. "Especially this one. And I think I'm pretty good at coming to her rescue. If you almost blowing my eardrums out a few minutes ago is any proof."

Chrissy scoffed. "Gee, you sure are humble."

His gaze traveled around while he thought. "Mm, more like honest. And then, second, I really do mean it when I say I'm here for you. You didn't ask me to be here, and I know you actually asked me not to, but I stepped into your marriage. Kind of inserted myself into your... life. Literally." Sheldon grinned. "In case your *ex* tries any shit with you while you're here handling your business, I'm still here for you. I won't leave you holding that bag on your own."

Still in disbelief at this man she'd met not even two weeks before, she stared. Sheldon's eyes did not waver. As if he would jump from the bed right now and go whip somebody's ass if he needed to. This level of caring and protection, from somebody besides her parents or longtime friends, would take some getting used to.

He continued, "And then, yes, my last priority—not really a *priority*, so much as an *inquiry*—was checking for how things were moving along with you leaving his ass." The two of them laughed now that he was finally admitting it. "Because... you know..." Sheldon stopped and kissed her hand. "I would kind of like to see where this goes. And if you're not crazy, maybe... see where this goes some more."

Chrissy chuckled. "Hm, but I'm not the one showing up at your meetings unannounced in the middle of the day. So what if *you* turn out to be crazy?"

He smiled that gorgeous heartbreaker she couldn't get enough of. "Oh, I'm letting you know now. I *am* a little crazy. But I think you are a little bit too. Since you go off on folks at open houses, go off on people in banks, and then come to my house and wave your beer in my face."

"I don't think that's crazy. It's interesting."

"Aah," he replied. "So *that's* what we're calling it."

"No, that's what it is," she said with a grin.

She watched Sheldon's sexy mouth move toward hers, feeling the flutter along her heart muscles when his lips sucked hers slowly. Released a moan from the depths of her brain when his hand rested along her jaw. It slid down her neck, to her chest, where her skin simmered under his touch.

His tongue penetrated more than her lips, caressed more than her taste buds.

Hot, intentional, prodding, it was making a point.

As if his flying out to the opposite coast hadn't already made one.

And when he drew away, his eyes still on her, the warm spot he'd touched on her flesh now cooled in the air. And that's how Chrissy was starting to feel just thinking about his leaving her again the next day. Warmth taken away from her. Heat on her body, and through her chest, that would now leave part of her cold with his departure.

Settling back against the pillow, Chrissy was indeed considering the crazy notion of entering a relationship before she was even divorced.

"What's going on in this head?" he finally asked, placing his index finger over her lips.

"Since you really are crazy, and not just interesting, should I be running from you?"

"Probably," he replied before they laughed.

He slipped from underneath her, and they both turned until they lay on their sides, sheets covering only their waists, their naked upper bodies exposed. Outside, in the distance, ocean night tides crashed against large boulders, forming what was becoming their soundtrack. His smooth hand rested in the groove of her neck, where his thumb stroked the base of her throat.

"But you're not going to run anywhere. And we both know why."

Chrissy had no retort when he told no lies.

There was no question of what these escapades with Sheldon were doing to her. Hell, even before she'd made the fateful decision to go to his home, Chrissy had already started imagining her life if she'd done things different. If she'd only waited to marry a man like Sheldon, instead of Blake.

From the night they'd met each other again at the debutante ball, the moment she'd rejected his dinner invitation, her mind hadn't stopped toying with the question. *What if...?*

Sure, she understood the grass was never greener on the

other side. That Sheldon had an ex-wife himself, so he likely had his own issues.

Still.

No matter how hard she tried, the machinations of her love-starved mind hadn't stopped zooming a hundred miles an hour. And it was simply too hard to recollect her common sense when the man showed up in L.A., holding tulips, sailing her on yachts, and making private accommodations in advance.

"So who's trying to claim who now?" Chrissy asked.

"Not trying. I did… already claim you. Do you want me to inform that other guy?" He smiled, with a grin that indicated he was more than ready.

Again, Chrissy's blood pumped through her heart like those ocean waves were crashing against her ribs. She brought Sheldon's fingers to her lips.

"I can't tell you what you've done for me. For my heart. In just this short time I've known you. You've reinforced the joy waiting for me on the other side. Reminded me of all I haven't gotten and certainly deserve. And that's all I can ask." She inhaled. "But the rest of it, I need to do for myself. Every part. Blake and I have been together a long time. And after all he's put me through, he needs to get his just deserts, straight from me. And me only."

Sheldon's eyes glimmered with what might have been warm admiration. "Alright then, woman of steel, but you let me know if you need an assist with any part of that." His mouth on the inside of her hand, he licked her palm, and kissed it.

"I absolutely will." Chrissy settled further into his arms, where they kissed and caressed each other on the glistening ocean, through the wee hours.

"You sure you don't need me to stay a little longer?" Sheldon asked, turning to her. Outside in the driveway, a chauffeured car waited to take him to the airport. But on his way out the door of their rental, his arms slid around Chrissy. "Sure you don't need my rock-hard… protection?"

He smiled down at her, and she almost melted.

"What I need is to destroy you at the Village Council meeting coming up. And I need to get started, Mr. Rouse." Still, she sucked his lips.

Sheldon kissed her back, taking her bottom lip with him when he came up for air. "But if you need me to help you destroy anything besides me, like that fool's nuts, I can make time."

"You've destroyed enough meat over the last twenty-four hours, sir. And she's still missing you already." Chrissy was certain he knew what she was talking about.

He finally forced his long legs to back away. Like lovesick kids, they blew each other kisses even as his car pulled off.

Once Sheldon flew out and Chrissy cleared out of Malibu, her next stops were to visit the small crew of actresses she was representing. And to give them a heads-up about Blake's potential wrath.

Once Blake got word of a divorce filing, and that Chrissy truly was not returning to him, she fully expected he would take it out on whoever he could—including his former clients whom Chrissy now represented.

He possessed information about their past lives the actresses did not want released. Details about how they'd gotten their starts, sometimes at private homes, and with money they'd borrowed to send home to their families.

"You promise? He won't touch me, and he can't say anything?" Karema Jackson asked, her eyes brimming with tears.

Chrissy grabbed her hand. "I am doing everything I can so he doesn't mess with you at all."

"May I ask why you're dropping me? Did I do something wrong?" Karema mumbled.

The younger woman's sadness blanketed Chrissy's chest.

"Of course not. You are perfection. Girl, I hope every client I ever get is as talented and awesome as you. It's been my pleasure to advocate for you. But you need to be separated from mine and Blake's mess. A clean break, and not to have this cloud over your head. So you can focus totally on you. The agent I'm referring you to will do just that."

"Forgive me for being selfish, but I wish you wouldn't. I want us to keep working together," Karema said, throwing her arms around Chrissy's neck.

Chrissy pulled the younger woman into her arms, and they clasped one another.

Karema half laughed, half cried. "Nobody's ever fought for me before. When I'm listening to you talk about me to those casting people, I wonder who on earth are you talking about. You make me sound like some kind of supernatural force."

She drew from her first client ever and looked into Karema's anxious face. "Don't lie to yourself, girl. You know exactly who I'm talking about. And never forget it."

Inside her, uncertainty also shook Chrissy's nerves.

She was breaking up her family, risking the upset of Little Blake, the ongoing interrogations of her mother, walking away from three homes and three business offices, and growing money and exposure as Blake's wife—this may have very well been a catastrophe in the making.

Picking her children up from school, Chrissy braced herself. Every interaction, teacher conversation, and parent meeting, she maintained her cool and stayed on guard.

At night, while the kids ate dinner and read, Chrissy, Maddy, and Racquel worked via conference call, on a surprise proposal that no one would see coming.

Two days later, she heard from Attorney Nelson.

"You were right. I'm confirming your suspicions. He's got another source of income out of Atlanta that will be devastating if word was to get out."

Chrissy's heart could have somersaulted into the Pacific, and she let out a ten-years-long breath she hadn't realized she'd been holding. So overjoyed, she had to plop into a seat and cover her mouth with her hands. She whispered, "Thank you."

Attorney Nelson replied from the other end, "Thank yourself. Now begins the hard part. When do you want to file?"

Her rib cage clanging, Chrissy thought of her strategy. "Wait."

With a deep breath, she got off the call with the lawyer and called Maddy. "I'm ready."

"I'm worried," Maddy responded.

"Don't be," Chrissy said.

Now that she had Blake where she wanted him, there was no reason to fear his wrath. Or Kevin Middleton provoking it.

She and Maddy dialed Kevin to deliver the bad news.

"Chrissy, I thought we had a deal. You remember what we discussed, right? Is this really how you want to do things?" he asked, dropping a veiled threat.

His ire could have blown flames through the phone. And fiery gasoline could have flowed through her veins. An explosion for all of Sag Harbor to see.

But Chrissy would risk it. For her to do anything other than reject him, would mean going from one man's crucible to another's.

She could no longer live that life.

"What is he talking about? What deal?" Maddy pressed on the conference call.

Chrissy inhaled, knowing already what to expect.

"Yes, Kevin, I'm sure this is how I want to proceed. I thank you in advance for understanding."

After they got off the phone with him, Maddy called her back. "What is going on between the two of you? You hate Kevin. Always have. So what is this with you two making deals suddenly?"

"There was never any deal, Maddy. It's just Kevin trying to flex."

As bad as Chrissy wanted to tell it all to her longtime friend, she simply couldn't. Maddy would go after Kevin, and it could have spilled into a public fight while they should have been focusing on Sheldon and Lana. The fewer people who knew, the better. Chrissy needed all her plans to run smoothly. No interference from anyone else. No matter the risk.

"You seem nervous, and that's how you've sounded all week. What does Kevin have on you? Does it involve Blake?" Maddy asked.

Chrissy pressed her head so it wouldn't start hurting. "Look, I need you to just lay low. Don't call my folks or do anything, and I'll see you in a few days at the meeting."

Her breaths swung wildly through her windpipe as her focus fell to the next task—a piece of paper her lawyer had given her with a contact number. Hands shaking, unsure if she should, Chrissy reached through her terror, and dialed.

CHICAGO

SHELDON

asketball sneakers screeched up and down the gymnasium court. Parents yelled at the top of their lungs. Pom-poms waved, and the scoreboard reflected a two-point jumper Sheldon's son had just made. His calves sprang him to his feet as the proud dad pumped his fist.

"Yes, Hadar! That's what I'm talking about!" he screamed.

The bitter Chicago air cut deeper than temperatures in New York. But the surprise on Hadar's face when Sheldon appeared in his classroom, right before lunch that day —priceless.

He hadn't mentioned the trip to his ex-wife, Eugenia, in advance. She would only have tossed him excuses for why he shouldn't come, or why she couldn't arrange it, or why Hadar didn't have time.

Score after score, his son's excellent game bolstered Sheldon's spirits. And he'd needed it.

In the two and a half weeks since he'd returned to New York after surprising Chriselle in Cali, he'd grown sick of the barren walls of his house.

He missed her in a way that stunned him. They'd only spent a few precious days together, and yet, that small period felt so easy and natural he was craving more of them. For more of her.

He had hoped she would call him, ask him to come back. But Chrissy hadn't. And she'd insisted that she needed this time.

Sheldon could not call her or hear her voice. So he'd been left with this void, in which her sudden appearance and disappearance in his life had left him reeling.

To keep from going nuts with missing Chrissy, work, and the *Escapade* project, he'd hopped a plane to see one of the few other people who could light up his heart.

At only halftime, his little eight-year-old had already put thirteen points on the board. When he looked around, Genie was still missing. After the game, pizzas, root beer, and ice cream flowed plentifully when Sheldon took Hadar and all his teammates out to celebrate a big win. It gave Sheldon a chance to do what Genie had taken from him —parent.

He caught up with the coach, heard the goofy stories of Hadar turning over the ball, tripping over each other, and a sprained ankle Sheldon hadn't heard about. Over his son's lopsided smile, his hand resting on Hadar's head, Sheldon talked with other parents. And longed for all he'd missed.

"So, is this a regular thing that happens where Genie's not here for some games?" Sheldon asked another parent.

"Oh, well, we all carpool and trade off. Some of us work late, others pick up the slack. Then we switch the next week. We're all in this together, supporting each other," one mother explained.

Sheldon looked down at Hadar. "What are you doing when

you go home to Granny's house? Is it just you and Mario playing video games all night?"

"Dad, no. I do homework and do chores. I only get one hour of game time or television."

"Is that right? And what do you boys do on the weekends?"

Hadar hesitated and shrugged. Sheldon slid his finger under Hadar's chin, turning him so they faced each other.

"Movies," his son finally said.

"And where else?" Sheldon pressed.

"To Shawn's house," Hadar replied, his eyes falling.

"And how long has that been happening?"

"A few months, since summer."

"He treats you alright?" Sheldon asked, holding his breath as if that would help him hear the answer better.

Hadar nodded, looking away. "Yes, sir. But he's not you."

Sheldon laughed. "Of course not. That's impossible. I'm That Guy, and nobody can replace That Guy."

Hadar chuckled. "Why can't you be here with Mom and me, so we do this all the time?"

Sheldon reflected on the proper answer. One that wouldn't place blame on Genie for leaving. "You remember that robot toy that talked, you used to take it to bed with you every night? What was it called?"

"Oh, yeah! My iBot!" Hadar's eyes lit up.

"Yeah, that's it. iBot. No matter what, you dragged it with you at all times. You loved that iBot so much. You got on our nerves with that thing," Sheldon recounted, as Hadar laughed. "Do you still sleep with that? You'd better not!"

"No!" Hadar replied, his face scrunching up.

"Where is it now?" Sheldon asked. He knew exactly where his son's old toy was. Back in his room at Sheldon's New Jersey home.

Hadar shrugged. "I don't know. It's for babies, and I'm on my PlayStation."

"Exactly," Sheldon said. "That's how grown-ups can be sometimes. We love that one person so much and can't be without them, but later, we grow up and we realize we were only babies. You still care about that person. You still like them, but you grow into other things, and you don't get so excited about them anymore. Same as with your iBot."

Right then, Sheldon's phone rang with a number he'd never seen before.

"This is Sheldon." He rose from the table.

"Sheldon, this is Madison Page."

Madison Page... Madison Page.... For a moment, confusion gripped him. He didn't know a Madison Page. "Wait. Maddy?"

"That's me. I got your number from your dad," she said.

Why was Jerrell's woman calling him? "Um, yes, I heard you were close with my folks. Actually, my son is with me. What do you need? Look, if this is about the Village Council meeting in a couple of days, I've said all I had to say to you, Kevin, and your mother. It is what it is. We'll just let this thing play out."

"Actually, it's about Chrissy. I'm concerned."

At the mention of her name, tremors ran through his chest. They hadn't spoken in two weeks, and as badly as he yearned to hear her voice, he refused to call the secret phone. Chrissy had made him promise.

"Is she alright?"

"I don't know. A part of me wants to go to California and check. She hasn't sounded good. Her conversation is... different. Not as relaxed or happy as she seemed at Christmas. Something is wrong."

He remembered Chrissy's face that afternoon they'd spent

together, when he'd first surprised her. She was conflicted, like she struggled with which direction to take. And her words still rang through Sheldon's ears as clearly as if she'd just spoken them. *I have no shortage of people in my life trying to make decisions for me. Thinking they know better than me. Planning out my next moves like I have no goals, judgment, or destination of my own.*

As he held the phone, remembering his incredible time with Chrissy, his ex-wife, Eugenia, walked through the doors of the pizza restaurant.

Even with panic on her face and hands jammed inside her coat pockets, she looked as beautiful as she ever had. How had he arrived in this exact situation twice in his life? The sight of his ex-wife made all the old lessons painfully new again.

I already have a man whose control I need to escape.

"Sheldon?" Maddy asked on the other end. "You there?"

Eugenia's face brought back the memories of what his ex-wife once said she needed from him most.

Sheldon spoke into the phone. "Chrissy has my support. While she navigates her own ship. She is her own woman. I don't think she would appreciate our getting involved."

"So you're saying you don't care?" Maddy insisted.

A windblown Eugenia marched to stand within inches of him, her razor-sharp eyes ready to slice and dice Sheldon. "What are you doing here?"

He responded to Maddy. "I'm saying it's not my place. Nor yours. Chrissy made clear to me that she doesn't want me stepping in. I've given her a confidential way to reach me if she needs. I need to go now. See you in a couple days."

He ended his call and faced the intense eyes of the girl he'd fallen for so many winters ago, when she was completing a fellowship in New York.

"Hello, sweetheart."

Eugenia's long, shoulder-length locks fell around her face, and she needled him with a fierce side-eye. "Answer."

"My son. You have my offspring sitting right there. I figured that was an open-ended invitation."

Inside the blaze of Genie's stare lay her attraction to him. He could see she was still fighting the same instincts that he wrestled when he saw her.

"What happened to notice? And who is Chrissy?" she said, waving at the other parents and marching toward the car.

"Who is Shawn?" He had time today. "And since when does our son get a sprained ankle and I don't hear about it? Chrissy is a friend."

Just like old times.

"You and your long line of friends."

"If I still had a wife, I wouldn't need so many."

She stopped and turned to him, hair swinging in the wind. "If you'd been a husband, you'd have a wife."

"Can we please not do this? I'm only here for the next couple of days. I came to spend time with Hadar since you kept him over the holidays. I figured this was a better compromise than hauling you before a judge. I just want to take him to school, do some homework, be his father. If that's okay. I'll be at the Ritz-Carlton and would like him to be with me."

She rolled her eyes. "Why didn't you wait until the weekend? It's Martin Luther King Day on Monday. A three-day weekend. Why disrupt the middle of his week?"

"In Sag Harbor, we're pitching a project, and I must be there for that. We'll be busy for the next few weeks, so I came to Chicago for a visit before things get crazy in New York. I haven't seen him in months, G."

Genie's eyes hardened. "Everything is about you and making bank, as always." She sucked in the frigid air. "You're also checking up on me. You come in here unannounced. Charm the pants off everybody, asking lots of questions. Big money Sheldon Rouse drops a few wads on the table and flies right back out."

Sheldon squared his jaw, preparing for another terse exchange of barbs that got them nowhere. He made sure Hadar was still horse-playing with friends and couldn't overhear the conversation.

"What do you want me to be, Genie? Broke?"

His ex-wife snickered her teeth, and her eyes dug deeper into him. "Maybe that would have been better. You would have tried saving our marriage with your heart, instead of your wallet."

The words stung. A revelation he'd never heard. Her explanation for disappearing had always been that she missed her family, and he'd left her lonely and abandoned in New York. That Sheldon was selfish and self-righteous. Or at least that's all he managed to glean from the last three years of bickering.

Right then, he stared into the face of an older, more mature Genie.

"You look tired," he noted.

"I am. I'm going for a promotion in the department, so I've picked up more hours lately. But Hadar's been fine," she replied with a steeliness he had seen in another woman recently.

"I don't doubt that," Sheldon said, "I'm not here to check up on you. And I don't intend to drop money everywhere and abandon ship."

Genie's gaze deepened. "Then why are you here, Shel?

Because you don't normally do this. The boring, day-to-day stuff was always my job."

Sheldon's eyes fell. "Genie, at no point did I mean to hurt you. I wanted to give you everything."

She nodded. "I know. But your ambition consumed you. It still does," she replied, her voice softening. Her eyelashes fluttered in a moment of reflection, possibly even with regret of her own. "And that was probably too much for me to handle."

She was right. Typical life had never satisfied him.

He'd wanted it all—a family *and* a high-impact tech company. Without feeling guilty about it. As well as a woman at his side who wasn't needy or scared of his drive.

Sheldon couldn't make that mistake again.

"It's cold, and we should get Hadar out of this weather," he suggested.

Genie examined him, and he felt the weight of her silent interrogation bearing on him. "No need for you to sleep in a hotel. You can stay with us, and that way, Hadar still sleeps in his own bed and keeps his regular routine." She thought further. "It'll give me a chance to do catch-up work. While you do all the boring parent stuff. For a change."

The offer lifted a cloud that had always hung over them. Perhaps they'd even find a bit of closure, finally.

"I would like that."

INSANE ASYLUM

CHRISSY

*L*anding back in New York City that Martin Luther King Day weekend, Chrissy stepped off the plane and onto shaky ground.

With Little Blake and Kara in tow, they all made a beeline through La Guardia Airport and toward the exit where Maddy waited.

Blake had surprised her with silence. Her attorney had not filed the divorce papers. And there'd been none of the blowups she'd expected.

She assumed Kevin was waiting to tell Blake about Sheldon. The entire plane ride, she fumed. Kevin was playing games, clearly trying to intimidate her by holding confidential information over her head until the best time to humiliate her.

Though scared, Chrissy still felt slightly freer. She had told Kevin no and avoided another man's control. But at what risk?

Outside the airport, Maddy had just flown in from D.C.,

and waited to drive them all to the Hamptons. They exchanged quick hugs and threw the suitcases in the trunk.

"How are things in D.C.?" Chrissy asked. She immediately noticed a change in her old friend. Maddy's joy from Christmas had stiffened. "You and your mom aren't at it, are you?"

Maddy shook her head. "No. I have a far bigger headache now." Her hands gripped the steering wheel and stared straight ahead.

"Do you want me to drive?" Chrissy asked.

Again, Maddy shook her head. "I need the distraction." She eyed the children in the backseat. "Kara and Little B, what have you two been up to? How's California?"

"We were having fun. It was warm there, and now it's cold here. I hate the cold! I don't know why we're coming back here," Little Blake complained.

Feeling her son's eyes burn through the center of her, Chrissy handed him a game.

Back in Sag Harbor, hours later, Chrissy put her children to bed. She and Maddy finally spread out at the Townsend family dining room table, where they got to work making last-minute calls and shooting text messages to neighbors about The Ivory.

"So what's really going on?" Maddy asked while pouring over her call lists.

"I'm going to file."

Chrissy kept her words cryptic, because Little Blake's ninja skills were unmatched.

Across the table, her friend's eyes lit up. "Oh, that's wonderful, Chris."

After sending a text, she shrugged. "I'm not so sure. This won't be pretty."

"Where will you all be," Maddy checked the surroundings for kids, "transitioning to?" She smiled.

Chrissy chuckled. "I like that big word you just covered with. Good job."

"Thanks. I need the practice for when my own little bugger gets nosey," Maddy replied with a slick grin that spoke volumes.

Chrissy's jaw fell slack. Questions vaulted through her brain and they stared at one another. Chrissy's gaze swept Maddy's abdomen.

Maddy wasn't drinking from a liquor glass but a mug of hot cider.

"Is there any alcohol in that cup?"

Maddy shook her head, her eyes nervous.

"Oh, my God." Chrissy beamed for her friend. "I'm going to be a godmother. Jerrell's?"

Still silent, as if continuing to process it herself, Maddy nodded, tearing up.

Pangs of sympathy shot through Chrissy at seeing her friend's mixed emotions over pregnancy. "Let's take a break and go sit outside by the fire. Does Jerrell know?"

"Not yet."

"How do you feel?"

"Terrified. Stupid." Maddy's answer was flat. "I'm pregnant and I've only known him a month."

Lighting up the fire pit, Chrissy recalled the ocean that flowed inside her, on New Year's Eve, the night of new beginnings. How Sheldon, a stranger, had rocked her. In just two nights. She connected with her friend's situation perfectly.

"Must be something about those Rouse boys, apparently," she said with a wink, trying to make her friend feel better.

They grabbed hands, giggling the way they had as teenagers. "Didn't it feel like there was nowhere else you belonged?"

Non-alcoholic cider in hand, Maddy curled into a blanket. "Woman," she whispered and peered at Chrissy. "So you and the other Rouse…"

"Girl, *did* we," Chrissy chuckled. Those two nights had played in her mind every night for the past three weeks. Sheldon's thighs still pumped, and her legs still squeezed. "I have never been so…"

"… Satisfied," Maddy finished. "Like all the others before were only practice runs. Leading up to the main hitter."

"That part." Chrissy took a sip, and let her mind wander. "How funny would it be if you and I actually became sisters?"

Maddy sputtered her cider and guffawed. "Those Rouse boys don't want that. I swear."

"What do you think Jerrell will say? When do you plan to tell him?" Chrissy asked.

"Probably never. Jerrell still thinks I'm in love with Kevin, and he wants nothing to do with me. He would likely demand a DNA. Why would I put myself through somebody questioning me like that?" Maddy stared into the warm mug as if it were a crystal ball that could foretell her future.

"Damn Kevin Middleton," Chrissy murmured. "I wish there was a way we could get rid of him."

"Now why would you want to do that?" a third voice interrupted from the side of the house. It belonged to a male.

Both women turned to find an unwanted man walking toward them. "Because we all know Sag Harbor's simply not much fun without me."

Dammit, she'd forgotten to lock the gate!

Kevin took a chair. Right next to Chrissy.

"Chrissy. Chrissy, Chrissy. You disappoint me. I thought we were better than this."

"You get the hell out of my yard!" Sitting bone-straight, she clutched her glass, getting ready to fling it.

"Aht aht! These shoes and this coat cost more than this here fire pit, girl, don't play," he snapped, and returned her ire.

Chrissy stood over him. "And my wine is still worth more than your cheap ass. But you will catch it today. You've got ears. Get. Out."

He reclined and threw his leg over his knee, nestling against the cushion seats.

"Doesn't this remind you guys of the old days? When we were kids playing on the beach, and you used to threaten to fight me until you realized what was good for you? And Maddy would sit around like a sick puppy waiting for me to kiss her? Kind of how she's looking right now." He turned to Maddy. "And, sweetheart, did I just hear you correctly that you are pregnant by a man you've only known a month? Little Miss Perfect Maddy?"

With that, Maddy leaped up and did what Chrissy had not. Apple cider flew past Chrissy and the fire, onto Kevin's beautiful Italian, camel-hair trench. He jumped up.

"But we're not kids anymore, you bastard!" Maddy screamed. "Everybody grew up, except you." She marched around the pit to confront him directly. "Get out! Now, Kevin! And I will see you at the meeting on Tuesday where I will *bury* you."

"And if I leave, what happens to Chrissy?" He turned to Chrissy, his eyebrow arching like a bow ready to shoot arrows. "You do realize I'm being pretty forgiving right now, don't you? But I might not be for long. Submit my proposal, the way you originally offered, and I accepted. And I won't make you eat that sand out there."

Chrissy thought fast. She now had leverage over Blake, so there was no need to fear Kevin telling him about Sheldon.

"Go to hell."

Maddy's anger churned into curiosity. "What is he talking about?"

Kevin snickered. "Yes, *Mrs. Mason*, what am I talking about? Or are you Mrs. Rouse now? Which will certainly be news to Mr. Mason."

Chrissy's hand shot out to slap him, but Kevin ducked. "You stay out of my business!"

"Chris, how does he know?" A confused Maddy asked.

Fury shaking her body, Chrissy could only throw herself at Kevin and start pounding on his chest. He grabbed her arms and pinned them.

Kevin's eyes flared with Chrissy in his grip. "You brought me into your business when you asked to work together. *You* asked *me*. Remember? I didn't come to you. And you reneged on your word."

"You don't need me! You're Kevin Middleton—from the almighty fucking Middleton family—and you can pitch with anybody. Your parents have even more clout than mine, so why are you hustling me?" Chrissy yelled.

"That's damn right, but my family's already got businesses around here, and these folks don't like that. Yours doesn't, so you're not a threat. Think about this. I'm giving you a chance to un-fuck yourself," he said, letting go of her and shoving her away from him.

She understood now why Blake still hadn't appeared. Kevin was holding her affair with Sheldon over her head, planning a devastating moment to drop the bomb, a time that would no doubt suit himself.

"Chrissy?" yet another male voice called.

They all turned.

Chrissy's heart conducted several somersaults. "Sheldon?"

"Mr. Rouse! Welcome. Your ears must be itching. We were just discussing you," Kevin crowed.

"Middleton," a hesitant Sheldon greeted him, still scoping the scene. "Discussing what?"

Behind Sheldon, a fifth figure stepped into view.

Maddy sucked her teeth. "Lana."

An amused smile spread across Lana's face. "Well, well. What have we here? Why weren't we all invited to the barbecue?"

"Because you do not belong here," Maddy muttered.

"From what I see, I should fit in just fine." Lana scoped out Chrissy's family's expansive gardens and rock pool.

Chrissy couldn't decide which sight infuriated her more—Kevin still standing in her backyard, or Lana strolling up in tight, ripped jeans with the man for which Chrissy had a serious jones.

As if he'd read Chrissy's thoughts, Sheldon started. "We were meeting with some neighbors a couple houses away and came to see about the yelling down here." He stared between her and Kevin, and his arm muscles tightened under his sweater. "You straight?"

Kevin pointed between them. "How do you two know each other again? I forgot. Was it the bank?"

"You were just leaving," Chrissy threatened, and hoisted a steel fire poker now in his direction.

Her longtime archenemy held up his gloved hands with

mock innocence. "Remember what I said. Whatever happens next, it'll be on you. Not me."

Sick of the entire ordeal, Chrissy huffed. "Do what you need to do."

Maddy flicked her head toward the street. "Lana will be right behind him."

She and her buddy exchanged tight hugs, before everyone cleared Chrissy's yard. Except one.

The chaos settled into popping flames and crashing ocean waves, a quiet storm in which hot and cold collided.

Sheldon's eyes glistened as if he'd found the rainbow.

"Hi," he whispered.

"Hi yourself." Chrissy wanted to go to him, but she feared someone seeing.

"Is it crazy to miss someone you barely know?" he asked.

She sighed. Her mind did not imagine him. He was really standing there. "I hope not. Or somebody might have to commit me to an insane asylum."

After she'd traveled thousands of miles, he closed the distance between them. Sensing her hesitation, Sheldon took her hand and tugged her backward, out of the firelight.

They slipped into her family's kitchen, where their foreheads touched.

His powerful scent entered Chrissy's nostrils and wrapped around her mind. Lips hovering torturously close, barely caressing, his mere presence dulled her senses. Curious, wandering hands frolicked over the other's torso. The tips of her sweater brushed Sheldon's chest.

His eyes dropped to the loose cardigan exposing her cleavage. Sheldon's hand roved across her breast like she was wild fruit. Insistent fingers pulled down her top and bra, freeing her ripe nipple. Intense waves tossed behind them.

She trembled, throbbing and ready, as she awaited his moist tongue on her flesh.

"Ah," a moan escaped her throat when Sheldon's lips took hold of her. Earth might have shaken under her feet, or maybe that turbulence was Sheldon's fingers sliding between her thighs.

A creak jolted Chrissy from ecstasy. On the wooden stairs. Her eyes flung open.

Little Blake.

Sheldon still sucked and squeezed.

Chrissy flinched, yanking her breast from his mouth. Cold air of reality hit her nipple again.

Her fumbling hands shoved the sweater back over her aching body. She murmured, "The children."

Sheldon shot up. "Oh, I didn't know they were…"

Winter frost of the real world rolled through the door, snapping both of them back to their senses.

Chrissy's hand smacked her forehead as her life resumed its tailspin. "Kevin."

A discombobulated Sheldon rubbed his head as if trying to clear it. "Uh… y-yeah… he said you and him had been discuss…" He took several deep breaths.

"He knows."

"Knows what?" He seemed to still be working out sexual frustration.

"Us. He learned I flew to Alpine for New Year's. And he's threatened to go to Blake."

His facial expression froze. "How did—?"

"I'm not sure how. The helicopter, the airport, my cell phone signal…"

Sheldon's eyes flitted around them while he put the pieces together. He whirled out his cell, holding it up and walking to the yard.

Chrissy saw the curtains move upstairs, and her pulse sprinted in her ears. What had Little Blake witnessed?

"Here." Sheldon went to her wooden chair, where Kevin had sat. He picked off a listening device from underneath it. "Your husband didn't plant the bugs on you. It was Middleton. When would you have seen him before you came to my home?"

The Ivory. She and Kevin spoke at the open house, and he'd even hugged her before they'd separated, shocking Chrissy. They had *never* hugged.

Now she understood why.

Sheldon's shoulders sank, and his forehead melted onto the tips of his fingers. "*What* is Middleton going to do with this information?"

His upset melted over Chrissy's joy to see him.

"I have no idea." An avalanche of worry tumbled into her heavy stomach. She wished they could talk it out or find a solution, but Chrissy wasn't in the house alone. "I have to go check on the kids."

"How long has Kevin known… about us?" Puffs of condensation blew from his mouth. He stared at her.

Chrissy's eyes snapped shut, and the tears squeezed from them. Kevin had known from the beginning.

"Weeks."

She watched the bullet of realization strike Sheldon.

"Chriselle, how long have *you been* aware Kevin knew?"

"Sheldon," she whispered. She recalled that evening when Kevin crashed her dinner with Neera and Cher, the same day she and Sheldon had made love at the Water Lily. Chrissy had been so livid over Sheldon's deal with Lana when she'd confronted him. Then Chrissy had tried to handle Kevin on her own. The way she'd learned to handle Blake on her own, without anyone knowing how he tried to control her.

Pain in Sheldon's face formed an icicle, piercing her.

"And you never said anything to me? I could have done something. Countered him. Protected us. Protected *you* from him. Now he has sensitive details that could hurt us both?"

She hadn't thought of her and Sheldon as an *us* needing protection. A couple. Or an entity that could attack Kevin together. For years, she had been accustomed to protecting herself, inside a dynamic of only her and Blake. This new *us* was foreign territory.

"I viewed him as my problem."

"Chris, you were so angry at me for not telling you about Lana, when there was no way I could have. But you *could* tell me about Kevin's harassment, and you didn't?"

Logic forced her to confront herself. Sheldon had a reputation to cover also. As well as history with Kevin, in which Sheldon was now at a disadvantage.

"It didn't cross my mind. I'm sorry." Sheldon's hurt formed a lake of ice cracking through Chrissy. And upstairs, she sensed the heart of her little boy freezing against her. For being with another man besides his father. "I have to go see about Blake. I know he's awake."

Sheldon started out of the yard, appearing deflated. "And I have to… go."

She desperately wanted to stop him. But she couldn't. Not until she'd dealt with her husband.

The miles separating them had disappeared. And yet, mere steps apart now, Sheldon was still so far away.

WAR

SHELDON

Sheldon hadn't slept a wink in three days. Groggy and exhausted, he threw on his gloves and scarf, charging out of Jerrell's Sag Harbor apartment.

"J! Come on, man. Time to go," he barked.

"Alright, I hear you." Jerrell followed Sheldon and locking up.

Briefcases in one hand, coffee in the other, they rolled out.

"Are we picking this chick up, or what?" Jerrell asked about Erlita as they got into his Range Rover.

"Nah, she's meeting us there." Sheldon looked over notes filled with numbers and estimates.

As they rounded the corner, Sheldon saw Maddy's car take off from her house and ride down Eastville Avenue, to Chrissy's family home. He averted his eyes, not wanting a reminder of the humiliation from three nights before.

Still sick to his stomach, Shel seethed about being vulnerable to Kevin Middleton. Sheldon had taken every precaution with Chrissy and their rendezvous. But Kevin had blindsided him.

He didn't know which of them he should've directed his upset—her for not telling him, or Middleton for his twisted actions.

Until Friday night, Sheldon thought the listening devices belonged to her husband. And if so, that would have been between Chrissy and Blake, a husband and wife. It wasn't Sheldon's place to interfere. But *Middleton*? Why in the hell was *he* tracking her? And what had he learned about Sheldon in the process?

And who planted bugs on people? To Sheldon, it was controlling and borderline psychotic. He would have attributed a lot of things to Kevin, from what he'd heard over the years—jealous, fiercely competitive, ruthless in business—but psychopath was not one of them. The more Sheldon thought of it, the more he burned to sink Kevin in the ocean until he breathed his last.

In the driver's seat, Jerrell clenched the steering wheel, and his jaw tightened.

"Man, what's up?" Sheldon needed a distraction from his own issues. "If you've got something on your mind, say it."

Jerrell sniffed. "Nothing."

Sheldon laid down the papers. "I know you better than that."

They couldn't afford to go into this meeting preoccupied or out of sync with each other.

"Maddy is pregnant."

Bleak clouds in the sky may as well have filled the truck.

"With Kevin's baby?" Sheldon cracked.

"No."

"You sure?"

A big huff escaped his little brother's terse lips. "Yes."

Sheldon cut his eyes. As if this situation couldn't get more complicated. "So let me guess. Now you're having second thoughts about competing against the mother of your child. Which, technically, you still don't know is yours."

"It's mine," Jerrell muttered.

"Wow. Really?" Sheldon scoffed. "The last time we discussed her, she was a treacherous female who worshipped at Kevin's altar, and all of a sudden, you've seen the light. You are confident that she didn't step out on you."

"Yes, she refused him. Kevin came by my store in the city. He said Maddy turned him down. Gave him his necklace back. I had it wrong. They've never been together."

"I could have told your jumpy ass that. Did I not say you were likely being a jerk?" Sheldon replied. "But, it's good. I'm happy for you. You'll be a father, it'll be my niece or nephew, and I will love them immensely. But for now, the plan doesn't change."

Sheldon might have been talking to himself more than his brother at this point. He now had to go face Chriselle.

He continued, "We go in here and give one hundred percent to getting this deal. We have the best business proposal, and if we win, you won't be a cookie salesman anymore. You'll be a cookie distributor. So if this kid does turn out to be yours, he'll eat cookies anywhere in the world he wants. Instead of in the poorhouse."

Jerrell shifted in his seat. "My relationship with Maddy and yours with Chrissy be damned, huh?"

Sheldon adjusted his tie in the mirror, irritated at the youngest Rouse who was often the most insolent. "Man, why do you always do this? Flake out on people after they set you up."

"This is all about Lana, not us, Shel. And I've got a bad

feeling about that chick and her moms. She's scandalous as hell." Jerrell squirmed.

"No, J. This is about you not going back to Wall Street and pushing paper. And me running my own tech conglomerate one day. This is about moves that are bigger than women. Get your head out of Maddy's ass so you can see that. You said you were ready for war. They are showing up for war. Especially Middleton. Chrissy and Maddy are grown. They can handle a little pressure," Sheldon replied and got out.

Every muscle in his body was tense as the knots tying up yachts in the harbor.

He marched toward the building, pulling up the collar of his coat to shield him against the cold. Inside awaited Brent and the other investors. Lana strutted in with her mother, Erlita.

"So, who is this special guest you mentioned?" Brent asked Sheldon as they all hovered.

"She's coming. Don't worry. She carries a lot of weight in this community, and she agrees with us that Sag Harbor needs to innovate and grow."

Eager for a new adventure, Brent slapped Sheldon's chest. "Dude, we'd better win this. We passed up that nightclub."

"We will. Have I ever been wrong?" Sheldon asked, getting a high off of Brent's energy, just like in the old days when they'd rowed together in college.

"No, you have not, my friend," Brent said, his eyes as bright as a Christmas tree.

Chrissy, Maddy, and another woman entered the lobby, alongside several of the neighbors whose doors Sheldon had knocked on over the previous few nights.

When Sheldon passed Chrissy, he averted his gaze. He could not afford to be foolish any longer.

Since he'd already been silly enough, he now had to upgrade the security system in his house. There was no telling what private information Kevin had hacked and shared, and with whom.

Chrissy was a wonderful woman, but between her husband and Middleton, he couldn't get caught up.

To Shel's surprise, when Kevin arrived, he did not huddle with Chrissy and Maddy. They had split into separate teams, proposing a different business from Kevin's. That would have explained all the chaos and fighting the other night. The two camps had apparently fallen out. Sheldon hoped their old divisions would benefit his team.

The leader of Village Council called them all inside. Six final businesses made their pitches and endured grilling from the individual council members.

"Ms. Lana Gilley, you are from Texas, you currently live in Washington, D.C., and you're proposing *Escapade by Erlita*? But why can't the escapade occur down South? What brings you all the way here, to the Hamptons?" one member asked.

"Well, ma'am, I admit I only visited for the first time this Christmas. And I am in awe of this cute little town and the kind residents. I love Texas, but Sag Harbor is different. Affluent but still humble. A good place for growth and diversity. I loved hearing the stories about the historic black communities here, and it broke my heart to learn they are struggling now. I believe my mother's business would help with that. We can bring in young professionals from diverse backgrounds who want healthier, fuller lives. We would commit to keeping your neighborhoods quiet but thriving."

It relieved Sheldon that Lana spoke well. Her Capitol Hill chops had come through. He and Jerrell exchanged satisfied expressions.

Kevin also presented, flaunting his family's ties and other properties and interests in the Sag Harbor area. But the council members' faces did not light up the same way for a kids' babysitter club. To Sheldon, that's how it sounded.

Finally, Chrissy rose to present *Racquel's Rack*, an online clothing company with a warehouse in Sag Harbor that would be open to the public. Women would rent eccentric, high fashion and worldly attire, and then ship it back. After so many wears, other customers could buy it.

Not bad. Sheldon understood why Chrissy jettisoned Kevin for this. It had been a smart play. The council members' faces were hard to read on this one.

"Ms. Gilley," another member began. The councilwoman's name was Celeste Newman. With a sharp, interrogating demeanor, Councilwoman Newman leveled Shel with a piercing glare. "We have several people here who have deep ties to Sag Harbor. This is their home. Why should we take a chance on outsiders possibly disrupting the peace and relationships here?"

With that, Chrissy, Maddy, and Maddy's mother nodded alongside other members of Sag Harbor's black establishment.

Sheldon inhaled.

Lana started. "Well, Councilwoman, all you have to do is look around. The generations of yesterday are not active in Sag Harbor anymore. Most of the children who grew up here own vacation spots in other cities. Take for instance, Chriselle Mason over there. She's been living in Los Angeles for the past ten years. And didn't visit Sag Harbor for about five of them."

The room grew quieter while the drumbeat between Lana and Chriselle became loud.

Still eying Chrissy, Lana continued, "A lot changes in five years. Technology evolves. Opportunities and social priorities shift. A prime example is the new wellness revolution that's happening. Organic food, chia seeds, and overnight oats weren't hot five years ago. But they're all the rage now. Natural hair wasn't hot five years ago, but everyone is trying to live kinky and free today. So what makes Chriselle more knowledgeable about the needs of *today's* Sag Harbor than me?"

Chrissy's glare could have drilled a tunnel in the ground.

Councilwoman Newman leaned in. "But, Ms. Gilley, her family has roots here. Her parents come here. Her grandparents and great-grandparents were here. They literally helped build this town. We don't know you. So even if your high-tech business is promising, how can we trust you to respect our integrity? That's the heart and soul of *this* part of the Hamptons—integrity."

Maddy, Chrissy, and their contingent of neighbors clapped.

Sheldon stood. "But, Councilwoman, we do have a witness from this community who will tell you about the necessity of *Escapade*. Without us, your neighborhoods may get an influx of strangers whom you truly don't know. And that unknown is a bigger threat to your peace than us."

Councilwoman Newman approved Sheldon's speaker.

Chrissy and Maddy turned in their seats, concern plaguing their faces.

Sheldon stepped toward the door and motioned to the older woman who waited on the far side of the lobby. He stepped back for the matriarch to enter.

From concerned to appalled in milliseconds, Chrissy shot up.

"What are you doing here?" Her face aghast, she turned to Sheldon. "Bastard!"

"Mrs. Mason, control yourself. Anymore outbursts and I will have you removed," Councilwoman Newman chastised.

He hadn't wanted to do it, but it was necessary.

Sheldon squared his shoulders and moved to the microphone to stand alongside Lana and his guest: Mrs. Townsend, Chrissy's mother.

MOTHERF—

CHRISSY

In disbelief, Chrissy stumbled to the front of the room. "Mom, what are you doing testifying for them? You should be over here where you belong."

Sheldon moved between them, blocking Chrissy. "Chris, calm down and let her say her piece. Just as you did."

Fury brought her voice to a low snarl. "You are so low. Snake!"

"Mrs. Mason! To your seat!" Councilwoman Newman bellowed to the security officer, "One more outburst, grab her."

Her muscles taut, Chrissy mad-dogged Sheldon as Maddy pulled her away. She turned to her mother. "Mom."

Chrissy's fingers immediately started texting her father, her uncle, her grandmother, anybody who would talk sense into Mrs. Townsend. Appalled, she stood helplessly as her mother adjusted the microphone. She hadn't even known her mom was here from the city.

"Yes, members of the Village Council, it is good to see you all again. It surprised me when Mr. Rouse here reached out to me. But I was willing to hear what he had to say, as should you, because he is correct. Sag Harbor Hills, Ninevah, Azurest, all neighborhoods I love, are not what they once were."

Her mother swallowed, eying Chrissy before laying out the case for Erlita's beauty spa and hair salon.

Councilwoman Newman raised an eyebrow of her own. "And you would oppose your own daughter, and Maddy, another legacy of this neighborhood, why?"

"Understandably, Councilwoman, our children who grew up vacationing here, see competition. That's the reason for their fresh energy. But they have built nothing these past few decades. Only now do they come. I am happy my daughter attempts to defend Sag Harbor. But she's lived on a different coast the last ten years. And I don't believe she can maintain that commitment."

The words were a Mack truck driving over Chrissy's insides that lay on the expressway of her mother's callousness.

Maddy's hand remained on Chrissy's leg.

"Madam Councilwoman, in that case," Maddy started, eying Sheldon and Jerrell, "we have a witness to call also."

"Relevance?" Councilwoman Newman asked.

"A vacationer in Sag Harbor frequently and who knows the Rouse brothers very well," Maddy explained. "He can give insight on their commitment to the peace, or lack thereof."

After the councilwoman approved a brief time allotment, Maddy stepped outside.

Even Chrissy was in the dark about this person's identity. But she did enjoy the sight of Sheldon and Jerrell stiffening with tension, after the stunt they'd just pulled.

An aging, handsome man entered the room, and now it

was Sheldon's face that fell slack. This gentleman looked like an older version of them both.

"Yes, I am Charles Rouse, the father of Sheldon and Jerrell Rouse." He proceeded to make his case for the peace and tranquility of Sag Harbor as it is.

"Sir, why do you oppose your sons?" Councilwoman Newman pressed.

"Because my sons are talented, and they devote themselves to money. It's how I taught them. My boys will not concern themselves with your peace. They will, no doubt, do what it takes to pursue wealth. Regardless of the harm that brings to your community. You should not allow them to destroy the peace that previous generations have built here."

Minutes later, walking out of the meeting, Chrissy reeled.

A decision would not come for weeks. Her raw nerves had lost all feeling in every part of her.

Maddy had proven she could play on a treacherous level with Wall Street bankers, and of course, that came as no surprise with her Capitol Hill background.

But Sheldon's tactics had knocked Chrissy on her ass.

The men hung back as the women exited. Passing by Sheldon, she fought the urge to punch him.

His steely eyes answered Chrissy. At his side stood one bubbly Lana Gilley.

"Mom!" Chrissy hissed the moment they entered the lobby, grabbing her mother's arm and pulling her away from Sheldon and Jerrell. "What are you doing here?"

Chrissy's father burst into the corridor. "Georgette, what is this? What are you doing?"

Mrs. Townsend turned to them both. "Getting our child and her family back to L.A.! Where they belong. This whole stunt of trying to start a business in a community you don't even live in is dumb. You have a husband. Stop shirking your responsibilities."

"That's Chrissy's business, not yours," her father replied.

"It *is* our business." She faced Chrissy. "How will you take care of yourself? You live under our roofs, in comfort we provide. And that Blake provides."

"How can I make any money for myself with you always suffocating me?" Chrissy snapped, louder than she'd intended.

Every head in the room swung toward them.

Her chest rising and falling, airways clogged with a years-long storm spinning inside her, she muttered, "You have always acted like my life was over because I had kids young. And I'm tired of it. If you can't support my new life, then stay away from me."

Mrs. Townsend didn't blink. "You live in my house, young woman, so that will be hard to do. And watch your tone."

Chrissy bit her tongue to prevent anymore fury from spilling. She could not say too much more about her plans, fearing if she did, her mother would take steps to block her.

An arm slid around her waist.

Maddy. "Come on. Let's bounce."

"Bye, Chrissy," Kevin called out with a smirk, then turned to Sheldon. "And bye, Sheldon. It was good seeing you guys this weekend. Maybe we can all go out to eat at the Firewood Village Inn sometime."

Before anyone could stop him, Sheldon left Jerrell and their father, and practically flew at Kevin. "Motherf—"

"Sheldon, no, man!" Jerrell bellowed. He shoved his brother off the rat.

"If I find out you hacked me *once*, just once, you fucking psychopath, I will—" Sheldon yelled.

"You will what?" Kevin asked, chin thrusting up. "Go on."

The room waited for the answer.

"Shel, not here. He's not worth it," Jerrell muttered, and jerked on Shel. "We're supposed to be cool, remember?"

With Kevin's coat still in Sheldon's grip, they were all unsure if he'd heard.

He threw Kevin off of him like trash. Sheldon then stormed toward the door, boiling on his way out. But not before blowing past Chrissy.

"I was stupid for fucking with you."

THAT DAY HAD BEEN the children's first missing school. Every buzz of the phone or notification on her computer, Chrissy jumped. Her frayed nerves shook in her arms and fingers as she served the kids their dinner.

Though she'd planned and planned, her preparations didn't stop her from glancing at the front door every few minutes. Headlights illuminated the street, stopping her breath each time they passed.

When would Blake arrive? How?

She attempted to relax and work, lining up talent showcase appointments for the next few weeks. But Sheldon's words ricocheted through her mind. *I was stupid for fucking with you.* How had this been the same man who had loved on her so passionately? Who had introduced her to love?

Sipping a glass of wine, sending out more emails, she tried to push his furious face from her mind. Maybe he was right. They both had been fools.

Upstairs, Little Blake refused to go to bed or do his evening reading, and she knew why.

Though her son didn't tell her when she asked him, his

attitude was more distant since Friday night. He'd asked for his daddy, ran to the windows to look for strangers, and bugged her about who was calling.

Again, her phone buzzed, breaking up her thoughts. *Caller Unknown.*

Shit. It was too late in the evening for this to be some government call. Blake had likely blocked the number. She got up and turned off the lights, peeking through the curtains, up and down the street, where several dark cars sat. Where *Blake* might be sitting in a car.

"Mama, aren't you going to answer it?" Little Blake peered down at her from upstairs.

"Blake, to your room. Now, please." She halfway expected to see her husband jump from the bushes or burst through the window. If she answered the call, and he was standing somewhere nearby, he might hear her voice.

Lifting the phone to her ear, she kept her voice low. "This is Chriselle."

"Yes, Mrs. Mason, I am Jonathan Torres, a social worker with Los Angeles County Department of Children and Family Services."

She almost dropped the phone. Blake had called the county on her!

"Sir, u-um, I can explain why the kids weren't in school today. I can assure you there is a perfectly good explanation."

"Actually, ma'am, I'm calling to check that you have properly protected them."

She fell into a chair. "Protected them?"

"Yes. From their father. After his arrest last night for the assault of Giselle Brown. We have removed Ms. Brown's daughter from her care for her failure to protect the child from escalating violence in the home these past few months.

It was brought to our attention that Mr. Mason has small children whom he cares for, so I am contacting you with a few questions."

That's why Chrissy hadn't seen Blake. Upstairs, light escaped from the crack in Little Blake's doorway. Answering one question after another, Chrissy was careful with her words. Anything that happened to his father, Little Blake would certainly blame her.

"When do you plan to return to Los Angeles? So we can interview the children in person?" the social worker asked.

She sucked her bottom lip. "I don't plan to. I've already made arrangements… for our welfare. Because of the reasons you just stated."

She ended the phone call, shaking with a sense of emancipation. Her instincts had been spot on. The social worker would not open a case on her kids, because she had already taken steps on her own to protect them from Blake. The social worker warned her she could actually get in trouble if Blake contacted them without a monitor before he took anger management and mental health classes.

A prayer floated from Chrissy's grateful lips. Her biggest fear had been the hatred Little Blake would have for her, and how Blake would poison him against her. But she could now put all of this squarely on Blake.

Her next call was to her attorney. "File it."

"What happened?" Attorney Nelson asked.

"Can't talk," Chrissy murmured. "Run a criminal background and you'll see."

Attorney Nelson chuckled. "Shall I make this public? Anonymously, of course."

"Please," Chrissy answered, breathing a sigh she thought she would never release.

"Mama, who was that?" Little Blake called.

"Nosey, it was somebody who is checking to make sure we're safe."

"I don't need anybody to worry about me. Daddy takes care of us. When are we going back home?" he asked.

"We'll talk about it later, but for now, young man, take your bath and stop worrying about grown people's business."

"I want to talk to Daddy."

Chrissy rubbed her head. "You know he's been busy lately."

"You're lying! He said nothing is more important to him than me."

She shot up from the chair, marching up the stairs, and snatched her son. "Blake Mason—"

"You're lying! Daddy's not busy! You just don't want me talking to him, and you want that man who was kissing you to be my daddy!"

"Blake, quiet!" Kara came into the hallway now.

"You shut up talking to me, bitch!" Little Blake yelled.

A nuclear warhead exploded in Chrissy's chest, and she grabbed his arms. "No, Blake! That is unacceptable. Do you hear me? You will not talk to anybody like that."

Furious, he wriggled inside her grip. "You can't tell me what to do."

"Where did you learn that language? Who told you that?"

As he grimaced, his eyes could have fired lasers at Chrissy. But he remained silent. He would protect his father and not speak. Chrissy didn't need him to.

"I am your mother. An adult. You will show respect. And you are to respect your sister. What you just did is wrong, Blake."

"I want my daddy."

She calmed herself to avoid using the same anger for

which she'd chastised him. "This is not how you behave to get what you want. I'm sure your father will call you soon. I would never keep him from you. But if disrespect is what you learn when you are around him, I will do something about it." She looked into her son's eyes.

Within an hour, she'd set up counseling for the children, with extra sessions for Little Blake. That's where she would drop the news that they weren't returning to L.A.

With their father now having an open court case, he probably could not leave Southern California. That allowed her a little room to make plans and relax. She still didn't know what she would do for her own money while building a client base on the East Coast. And there was also tuition payment for the children's new school, because Blake would certainly freeze the account again as soon as he left jail. If he hadn't instructed someone to do it already. She had some savings in the bank but would still need to call her dad.

Despite the hurdles ahead, Chrissy finally envisioned a new life for herself.

When she'd moved out of hers and Blake's home months before, it had mostly been a warning shot. Chrissy had expected to be back in his bed within a week, certainly in a month. But she had surprised herself. Blake's begging hadn't worked. After years of living in his shadow, she relished freedom too much to relinquish it.

This sudden turn of events in her favor might be the escape route she'd always longed for.

In her thoughts of the future, hovered Sheldon's face. His body, arms, broad back towering over her. She tried to shove him out of her mind. With that stunt he and her mother pulled, and the lowdown way he'd talked to her at Village Hall, any further feelings for him should have died. His teaming up with Lana, and weaponizing her own mother against her, proved he was a heartless Wall Street shark who just might have used Chrissy to get ahead.

For that reason alone, they were over. No matter how badly she wanted him. After years of her getting railroaded by Blake, no man would ever use her again.

DON'T INTERFERE

SHELDON

From one bank to the next, Sheldon was in a mood. Maybe even nervous.

Every few minutes he looked over his shoulder, or at the front door of the branch, searching for angry faces. More specifically, for jealous, enraged husbands coming to confront him. At his house, while eating his dinner, he peered into the security monitors of his property. But all week long, no husband appeared.

Instead of a raging man, he fought only with memories. Of Chrissy's voluptuous nipple, hard and thick in his mouth, and her heart pulsating under her flesh.

But those fiery moments had come at a dangerous cost. Her son may have seen, and if Kevin didn't tell Blake Mason, that boy surely would.

This was the very drama he had always avoided. No married women, and only mothers whose children were older. Yet here he now struggled. And she had a violent husband.

He'd put his life and career on the line, all for a couple of nights. Sheldon rarely ignored his instincts, and his schoolboy attraction to Chrissy led him to throw each of them out the window.

Styled regally, passionate with a cool reserve, she'd seemed so perfect. Yet, since landing in his life, she'd only brought chaos. Sleepless nights had tormented Sheldon the entire week as he reminisced about every part of her underneath him—her skin, her wetness, how she laughed, or shrieked with surprise when he showed her something new. In an odd and unsettling way, Sheldon felt comfortable with Chrissy. For some years, he hadn't let his guard down with anybody. Now he couldn't get her off of his mind, and it distracted him.

Chrissy's fury at him had excited Sheldon. He didn't know what words the mother and daughter exchanged personally, but he felt no guilt for going after what he wanted. Of the many doubts occupying his head, his decision to take off the gloves was not among them. That was business, and Chrissy had decided to play. If she couldn't handle a few light scuffles in the ring, she wasn't the powerhouse Sheldon had hoped.

The number one reason he'd reached out to Mrs. Townsend was because he was so impressed with Chrissy. A woman who'd caught the attention of the *Wall Street Chronicle*, for making moves in Hollywood after ten years of being a housewife, clearly had a few tricks up her sleeve. She had picked off her husband's clients right under his nose, so she knew how to play her hand close to the vest. Chrissy was clever and strategic. The woman had to have learned it somewhere. So Sheldon had called her mother to feel her out. He discovered the woman was the unofficial social director of the Hamptons. It had been perfect. Chrissy would have to forgive him.

Now, at the end of the week, he considered his next moves

during his entire drive from the city across Long Island, toward Sag Harbor. The Southampton Frost Festival was this weekend, and Sheldon and his team needed to be front and center, pressing flesh with the village council members. Lana was back in town from D.C., her mother, Erlita, now house-shopped for a permanent place to show her commitment to Sag Harbor, and Brent was returning with his crew.

Chrissy should have returned to L.A. already, and Sheldon would take advantage of her absence to gain an edge with council officials. His team of outsiders needed to improve their chances over the locals.

He stepped out of his car and into a winter wonderland. Festive streets welcomed him, all lined with smells of choco-late and sugar, roasting pork, and boiling seafood. After settling in and changing clothes at Jerrell's place, he headed down the street for hobnobbing and food.

"Mr. Rouse," Lana said, greeting him with Erlita alongside him.

"Ms. Gilley." He shook her hand. "Have you heard any news about our position?"

They walked through the crowds of families. "Some members are having a private gathering among themselves at Councilwoman Newman's house. They're forming a voting block. So they can narrow the options down to just a couple of businesses they'd prefer to see here. And then they'll join at the meeting next month to defeat all other companies."

"Good detective skills, Ms. Gilley. I'll have to keep you in mind if I ever need a private eye."

"You must have forgotten where I work," she said with a wink. "And it just so happens I'm having tea this weekend with Councilwoman Newman."

"Get out!" Sheldon gasped.

"More like come on. She's no fool. She knows a damn good idea when she sees it. But more important than that, she hates perfect little Madison Page. Councilwoman Newman is just fine with these longtime black neighborhoods being broken apart. She does not want to see them become active again, so she likes that young outsiders will come in who can shake up some shit, and toss out the old ways."

At that part, Sheldon reeled. "Are you serious?"

Lana grinned. "As a heart attack. Ms. Newman only fronts like she wants peace. And for the black neighbors to be strong. But the tea is that she craves that new money too. And she doesn't give a damn about the black folk."

Sheldon scanned around him to see if anybody had overheard her saying that. "Be careful who you tell that to. Our entire selling point is a stronger black social class."

"Of course," Lana muttered.

At that moment, as the two of them pow-wowed together, their heads leaning in close, Sheldon caught a sight.

Whoa. She's here. He peeped up again, trying to stay discreet. Chrissy was staring right at him.

"What's she doing here?" The words escaped faster than his brain intended.

"Who? Chriselle? Same as you." Lana eyed their mutual opponent. "I was hoping her kids would be ugly, but I guess they're not half bad."

"What kind of person would say that?" he asked.

"Somebody like me, who is extremely petty." She sucked her lips and walked onward. "Drink?"

"Definitely," he responded.

As they sipped some good cognac while eating smoked, well-seasoned turkey legs, a bulky man who could have been a football player approached Lana. He kissed her mouth, rubbing his hands around her possessively.

"Hi, baby." Lana turned to an increasingly nervous Sheldon. "Mr. Rouse, this here is Desmond. He's a friend of mine whose family is in construction. If we get the deal, I wanted him to talk with you about doing the work on The Ivory and making it into what I want."

Sheldon stuck out his hand with caution. Something about this situation didn't sit right. When he'd conducted extensive research on Lana—to see if she was married, if her mother was married, if they had any crazy people in their family, or other barriers that would prevent his working with them—he had not seen a boyfriend.

"Desmond, pleasure to meet you. I'm happy to review your work. Of course, Erlita and Lana are not the only deciders here. They've reached out to others for help financing this deal, so there's an entire team that must weigh in," Sheldon explained. He hedged so this guy wouldn't get any idea that he was a shoo-in.

"But our decisions carry the most weight." Erlita strutted up. "Remember, it is Escapade by *Erlita*."

Sheldon chuckled. "Oh, I don't forget. As long as you recognize this isn't Texas, and Erlita will need a lot more capital if she's going to have an escapade anywhere near Sag Harbor."

"I'm doing ya'll a favor. You know that," Erlita replied.

"The better way to put that is we're all doing each other a favor," Sheldon countered.

Suddenly, whooping and cheering emanated from one area of the festival. They all turned to see the focus of attention.

Boinnngggg! A loud gong sounded throughout the street,

followed by hooting and clapping. Another ball flew into a pin, knocking it down and sounding the heavy bell once again. More cheering broke out.

Two people seemed to take turns at throwing hard balls to knock down a single pin. One thrower was a council member. The other was Chrissy.

"What's this?" Erlita asked. "Isn't there something unfair about that?"

"Woman, please," Sheldon muttered.

She hit the pin head on and knocked it down.

Next, the councilperson did the same.

"Which councilperson is that?" Sheldon asked.

"Roger Carr," Lana responded.

Chrissy's children leaped, their eyes stretching, and filled with pride for their mother. Those kids must have eaten jumping beans for dinner, because they had more energy than circus performers with those leaps. Meanwhile, their mom was a vision, cloaked in a cranberry-colored outfit, like she could have been fruit hanging from a tree.

"You and her have a thing, huh?" Lana asked.

Clearing his throat, coming back to himself, Sheldon tried to change his face. "What?"

"You heard me. That's really why you went down to her house the other night, when you told us you were making sure it wasn't your brother, Jerrell. And Kevin must be onto the two of you. You seem to be a man who moves undercover, so of course, you and him must have beef." She sipped her cognac.

"And you concern yourself with my affairs, why?" Sheldon asked. He shifting away from her and assessed this how her nosiness might impact business. Jerrell had warned him before the council meeting that she was scandalous. And Chrissy had warned him before that.

"I'm not. So long as your little escapade with her won't interfere with our priorities."

He suddenly remembered what else Jerrell had told him about Lana. "You should tell yourself that. You are messing around with somebody's future husband, are you not? That could get sloppy. I would hate for Desmond's fiancée to show up and see that her man is diving for dollars in all the wrong places."

"Marriage, schmarriage. When they're married, it makes things more fun," Lana replied, her eyes studying Sheldon over the rim of her glass. "Doesn't it?"

"I wouldn't know." With that, he walked off to shake some hands and meet more residents. He'd have to deal with his and Chrissy's fling becoming common knowledge later. For now, Sheldon couldn't get distracted and allow Chrissy to gain leverage against them.

He spent the next hour working the event, moving through the booths, stopping to play games, tasting apple pies, peach and blueberry cobblers, sampling chowder and dipping shrimp in numerous sauces. He even learned a couple of line dances and joined a fun song that involved spinning, jumping, and switching partners. Friendly residents clapped and cheered, and the live band stomped on the street.

"Now grab the dancer to your right and spend them round and round!" the guitar player yelled.

Sheldon reached to his right side and found himself grabbing his wide-eyed, beautiful new enemy. They were linking hands before either fully realized who they'd grabbed. Too late to let go without it causing a ruckus, they both started off to the left.

"And round and round! Don't drop 'em now!" the guitar player crowed.

Sheldon could look nowhere else but into Chrissy's grimacing eyes, or both of them would have fallen to embarrassment.

"Now swing 'em to the right!"

They reversed, holding hands and clasping one another. Chrissy seemed to strain as she bit her lip.

"What's the matter? You're out of shape? Can't keep up?" Sheldon asked.

An evil gleam flickered on her face and, suddenly, her hands were not inside his anymore. She'd let go.

Sheldon's legs tumbled backward, too fast for him to stop them, and the momentum sent his ass onto the smooth asphalt.

"Oh!" the crowd cried, including Chrissy. All of the dancing stopped.

In the greatest act of fake sympathy he'd ever seen, Chrissy clasped her mouth, and her fish-eyed shock could have rivaled Lucille Ball. In her alligator skin leather boots, she rushed toward him.

"I don't know what happened! My hand slipped. Are you okay?" she rattled off, dropping to one knee before Sheldon, with a vindictive glint in her eye. "I didn't hurt you, did I?"

She immediately jumped up again. In front of everyone, she offered Sheldon a hand, pushing it right in his face. So close she stopped short of slapping him.

The entire village of Sag Harbor looked on, waiting for whether Sheldon would take her extended hand.

From the ground, he mad-dogged her.

But Sheldon took her hand, or he would have appeared to be an ass. With a strength he hadn't been expecting, she hoisted him up. Then, from nowhere, a firm slap against his back pushed him forward. Chrissy clawed her nails into his shoulder.

"And that one was for the shenanigans with my mama," she muttered low so only he heard. Faster than Shel could say "ow," she pivoted toward the crowd. "I think he's going to be okay, everyone. Nothing a little hot cider won't fix. My treat. Spiked, of course."

The other dancers clapped, before the officials moved in to thank sponsors and announce raffles and prizes.

Chrissy hadn't allowed him to get the best of her and apparently could give as good as she got. How was Sheldon both irritated and somewhat impressed?

Tossing him a ferocious side-eye that ignited his own fury, Chrissy pivoted and strutted from the dancing square.

Sheldon pursued.

He marched in front of her once they stood behind a cotton candy stand that concealed them.

"What the hell was that? You could have hurt somebody. It was irresponsible," was all he could think of.

"Now you know what'll happen the next time you cross me," she muttered, jamming her finger into his chest.

"You played a grown man's game, and you got stung," Sheldon insisted.

"But my *mama*? And you didn't tell me?" she shrieked a little too loud.

They both scanned around them to ensure no one had heard. People were still listening to the prizewinners being called.

"Tah! I know you're not talking. You brought my dad."

Her finger swished in front of Sheldon, and he wanted to bite it.

"That was Maddy. Not me. If she'd told me, I would have shut it down."

Despite hot coals heating Sheldon's face, he still turned down. "It doesn't matter, and I'm not offended, because this is *business*. I thought you understood that. You make the decisions you need to make for your project, and so will I," Sheldon replied. "If you're going to compete, at least don't be soft. Be a *woman* about your shit."

Chrissy got in his face, her eyes so vicious he expected her to stab him. "And if you're going to compete, *play fair*. The whole time, you were using me. You only brought me into your house, into your bed, to distract me while you got the knife ready. You caught me slipping. Once. It *will not* happen again."

Her chest heaved as it did when she got emotional. Burgundy lips curled to make a point, the sweet smell of dessert circling her, Sheldon studied her.

Sheldon, bounce. It was the smartest thing to do. The only thing.

"That's not true. Not at all. I wanted to be with you. End of story. There was no other motive than that. I expected you to handle this bid situation like a woman and not a child," he huffed.

Her hand flew up to hit his face. But Sheldon caught Chrissy's wrist, pulling her to him. The scent of sweet berries wafted into his nose from her coat, and the smell weakened his discipline. She squirmed, and he held on, even though her wild eyes sought to crush him.

Still holding her, Sheldon whispered against her forehead, "You kept me in the dark about Kevin. You know he and I have a beef. And you left me exposed. I've hired a security company, in case Kevin passed my information to your husband. But to hell with that, because I will also deal with *both* them myself."

"No."

"All I've done since we met is protected you, Chris. Why wouldn't you do the same for me?" By the end, his vocal cords were shaking out his words. "I don't want to believe that you would see me hurt."

Chrissy's eyes told him what her mouth wouldn't.

"Are you scared of Kevin?" he pressed. "Did he threaten you?"

Her gaze fled from his, darting everywhere at the carnival except to Sheldon's face, inches from hers.

"Chriselle."

He understood so much more now. How could he be mad at her when she was terrified? Two men were yo-yoing her between them.

"Don't interfere, Sheldon."

"Chris, I've got your back and I said I would handle it. All you have to do is say the word."

"*I* have to handle it myself." Those big doe eyes flared at him. "You just told me to be a woman about my shit. So *let* me. I've known Kevin my entire life, and Blake is my husband of ten years. I'll deal with them. Stay *out* of it, or you and I are done." She pulled away, and in silence, she stumbled from him.

Sheldon rubbed his chest where she'd poked him relentlessly. But his body hurt in more ways than one. Every time they left each other now, she took a bigger piece of him with her.

I JUST WANT PEACE

CHRISSY

The first glass of wine disappeared within three minutes. That took off some of the edge.

"It was so hard not to just tell him," Chrissy muttered, leaning her head against the cool mantel that was not yet heated over the fireplace. "He seemed like he truly was hurt about Kevin. But he brought in my mother. My *mother!*"

Maddy took Chrissy's glass and poured in more wine. "That's business, Chris. It was a boss play. If you plan to work in the agent industry especially, you can't take this stuff so personally."

The concern on Sheldon's face earlier that evening left her feeling caught in a spider's web of betrayal. Which Sheldon would she get next time? The one who stabbed her in the back, or the one who wanted to protect her from Kevin? He'd looked so sincere. She didn't know what to believe.

Maddy looked up the stairs where Chrissy's children were doing their evening reading. "How's the, uh, transition going?"

Chrissy rubbed her eyes and spoke in partial code, keeping her voice hushed. "They still don't know. We have a counseling session tomorrow afternoon, and that's where I'll do it. The boy already had a session this week, to get him ready. Little Mama is easy. She will always follow me, but the boy favors his dad."

"You still haven't heard from Big Man?" Maddy coded her conversation about Blake also.

"There's a good reason. You'll never believe it." Chrissy eyed the upstairs. "Later."

"Good or bad?"

"A miracle. My lawyer is making moves as we speak."

Maddy's eyes widened.

"My prayers are finally being answered. I was starting to think the angels hated me in the Upper Rooms," Chrissy joked.

"Have you thought about how you will get on your feet and live?"

"Start looking for work at the talent agencies and studios here, work my way up, and build a client list of my own. Stay in-house for a while, until I build up my industry contacts, and then open an agency."

"And that won't take long for you at all. You were in the *Wall Street Chronicle*. Agencies will fall all over themselves to have you." Maddy held up her hot cocoa.

"Send me all the good vibes for that, sis," Chrissy replied and toasted. Her gaze dropped to Maddy's abdomen. "And what about your little bun? How's it cooking? Does the juvenile brother know yet?"

A smile spread over her friend's face that only a woman expecting could have, and her fingers hugged her belly. "Yes, ma'am, he does. And it's been hard to shake him from my side ever since I told him."

Chrissy burst out laughing. "Really? So he's no longer tripping on you still, about Kevin?"

Maddy shook her head. "No, apparently, he and Kevin must have had words after I went back to D.C. Kevin told him nothing ever went down between us. So then, of course, like the genius he is, Jerrell came back with his tail between his legs."

Chrissy needed this comedy for the night, to laugh at something and distract her from her own shit storm. After doubling over with laughter, Chrissy inspected her friend from childhood.

"Yeh, girl, I can see it all over you too. You're falling in love with your baby's daddy. You've got that *we're having a family* dreamy face."

Maddy's smile deepened, and she shrugged. "Mmm… maybe."

Chrissy smirked. "Maybe my ass. But don't worry. You won't be looking like that after the kid gets here, and you want to kill Jerrell those first few months." More chuckles.

In her head, she recalled the tense meeting at Village Hall earlier that week, how Sheldon had behaved, and how stunned she was.

But Maddy had taken it all in stride, as if it were another day at the office. That boss play of bringing in the Rouse father—how Maddy had matched Sheldon, move for move —priceless.

"It doesn't bother you that Jerrell is playing on the same team as Lana? That he's working with her against *us*?"

Maddy thought for a moment. "I don't see it that way. He can't stand Lana. But he's got a brand-new business, and Erlita's idea is a lucrative shot for him. I can't begrudge him that. He's not working against us, so much as in his own interest. Chrissy, you are my friend, and I will say it to you again, girl: if you're going to play with high rollers, leave your feelings at the door."

Chrissy sipped her wine as she recalled Sheldon saying the same thing. *It doesn't matter, and I'm not offended, because this is business. I thought you understood that. You make the decisions you need to make, and so will I. If you're going to compete, at least don't be soft. Be a woman about that shit.*

So maybe it was possible that Sheldon could protect her personally and still be her business rival. And she needed to put on her big girl panties.

Suddenly, loud bangs at the front door startled them out of their seats. Gripping the chairs, Maddy and Chrissy exchanged glances.

"You expecting company?" Maddy asked.

Chrissy wished she could have said no. But she knew the time had finally come. Blake had gotten the divorce filing. Or either Kevin had finally informed him about Sheldon.

Her body leaped into action, leaving behind her every vital organ suspended in space until she was moving without thinking. Chrissy's legs were swift as they took her to the bookcase, where she snatched off a large fake book.

Once she placed her hand on the digital finger touchpad, the book popped open, and inside lay a gun.

More insistent bangs against the door, and she almost jumped from her skin.

"Chrissy Mason! Get out here now! Or did you forget you were married while you've been here all week with my kids? Open this goddamn door or I will knock it down!" Blake's furious voice declared.

"Daddy! It's my daddy! Let him in," Little Blake cried, zipping down the stairs.

"Blake, no!" Chrissy huffed. "You can't see him right now."

Suddenly, Maddy was on her phone.

"Who are you calling?" Chrissy asked.

"Chriselle! Don't make me knock again," he screamed. "I'm trying to respect your family's house. Just give me my kids. I don't give a damn what else you do."

"I'm calling police," Maddy whispered.

"Don't arrest my daddy. Daddy!" Blake screamed happily.

Chrissy's thoughts whirred through her head at a hundred miles a minute. "Maddy, no! Don't call police."

"What? Are you crazy? He is talking like he has lost his mind," Maddy replied.

Pressing her eyes shut and opening them again, Chrissy called out to her husband, "Blake. Wait a minute. I will open the door, but you have to calm down. Do not let these kids see you act a fool. We will keep this cordial."

"You've got ten seconds to bring my kids to me," he said from the other side of the door.

Chrissy's arms wrestled Little Blake from the door. She whispered to Maddy, "Take the kids and leave."

She wouldn't allow Little Blake to see his father humiliated and led away in handcuffs. Or at least, Little Blake couldn't be present when the call was made. And she especially couldn't violate her agreement with children services, that she wouldn't allow them around him.

"I want my daddy!" Little Blake cried.

"Go out the backdoor, use the back path," Chrissy instructed Maddy. "Head to Emma Vincent's house and get her husband. He hasn't moved out yet."

"I don't want to go!" her son bellowed.

Her daughter, Kara, shook in confusion.

"We shouldn't leave you," Maddy insisted.

"Mommy, are you coming, too?" Kara asked.

"Baby, I'll meet you in a minute, but follow Aunt Maddy now," Chrissy muttered. She lay the fake book containing her gun on the hallway coffee table, so she could have it close. Then she dialed 911 and slid her phone behind a lamp where it wasn't visible, just as her lawyer had instructed.

A strong Maddy dragged Little Blake's squirming body out the backdoor and into the backyard, his screams loud enough to horrify the entire block. A trembling Kara trailed him. Chrissy welcomed the disruption.

This time, Chrissy had locked the gates on either side of the house, so no one could get through. After Kevin had slipped into the yard, she'd prepared better for Blake.

Glass shattered across the living room window, the shrill noise destroying her eardrums. Covering her head, she moved toward the table where her concealed gun sat.

Terror racked her at the sight of Blake crawling through the ground window.

She and Blake stood face to face.

"What did you do with my kids?" he asked.

Her arms quaked as she tried to control them, "They're safe."

Her husband stepped forward, and Chrissy held out her hand to stop him. "Don't come near me. I just want peace, and custody of the kids."

"It'll never happen. You can't even afford to take care of them without me. You're not shit outside this marriage, Chrissy. What… you thought because I had a little dust-up, that you were rid of me? That you would erase me just like that?"

He started toward her again.

Chrissy braced herself. "You can't haul me back to California, Blake. No matter what you do. All the screaming and violence on Earth won't make me afraid of you."

He grabbed her hair and yanked her toward him. The snarl from his mouth ricocheted through her ears. "Well, maybe I should do something else so you learn some respect. All I've done for you these years, and this is how you act. Go upstairs. Pack your bags and get ready to go."

Closing her eyes, silencing her doubts, she remembered every humiliation and insult over the last ten years, from discovering him with an actress laid out on his office desk to the pairs of panties she'd found in his Escalade.

Opening her eyes again, she stared him straight in the eye. "I got a call from a social worker, Blake. You want to know what he told me? I'm not allowed to let the children see you. If I give you any visits, the State of California will charge me for failing to protect my children from you."

The flow of Chrissy's blood returned to her, and Blake's blood seemed to drain from his face.

"They will remove our rights and place our kids in foster care. With strangers. You won't have any say over them, and Blake will go to bed in somebody else's house. Every time you call to talk to him, you'll have to ask the foster parent's permission. When you visit him, someone will monitor you. A stranger will listen to every word you say. How do you think your son will look at you then, Blake? How do you think that will affect both him and Kara?"

Chrissy spoke mostly in terms of their son, because she knew that's who Blake lavished attention on, their child who worshipped at Blake's feet and desperately sought his approval.

What Blake hated most was feeling he had no control over his possessions.

"You're lying! And if you're not, you called the social worker on me." He pulled her hair tighter, sending pain shooting through Chrissy's scalp.

Wincing through the torment, Chrissy replied, "No. Giselle doesn't have her daughter anymore. The county took her kid, and the social worker called me for a welfare check on mine."

Apparently stunned to hear this, Blake held his grip. He looked as if he hadn't known, so he had likely gotten on a plane as soon as the jail released him.

"Why should I believe you, Chris?"

His wife swallowed. "Because the kids love you, especially Blake. Very much, and I'm willing to work with you for *him*. So our son will be okay, and won't turn into…."

His eyes flared. "Finish what you want to say. So he won't turn into me."

Chrissy shuddered but felt no fear. "You and I were young. I know you resented me for what our parents pushed us into. And you did what was necessary so you could come up."

Blake's mouth curled. "*We*. So *we* could come up."

She shook her head. "So *you* could come up, Blake. You've always controlled the money and what we did with it. The limelight has always been yours."

"You're my woman, and it was yours too. You selfish b—"

"But I didn't go to Spelman to live your life for you," she muttered, hot tears rolling down her cheeks. "Or to spend my every day sacrificing to prop you up." Her soul might have poured out also. "You never wanted me. I never wanted you. Let's end it."

He stared as if, for the first time, her words were finally processing for him. "Fine. I'm happy for you and this new life you want. But my kids are *my* life. So what if I don't agree to let them move way the hell out here? Cali is their home. Not this cold-ass place with all this snow and shit weather, and these uppity people."

Chrissy stiffened her shoulders. She just needed to keep him calm and talking, long enough for cops to arrive or a neighbor to come.

"We can work out a schedule to share the kids."

"Or I can keep them where they belong—with me, cut you off from the account so your mommy and daddy have to keep feeding you."

"The accounts are ours, Blake. You'll have to split everything and pay me alimony. All of it, I earned."

"The hell you did."

"It's true. And you know what else? My attorney has information about the extra money you made under the table these last few years. Where a lot of those cash deposits came from. The girls you arranged in Atlanta. And what you do to wash the cash at your office."

His face sank. "You don't know shit."

As she'd anticipated, he slapped her. And when he did, his grip loosened. Chrissy bolted for the fake book and pulled out the gun. Switching off the safety, she cocked the hammer and aimed.

He laughed. "You don't even know how to use that thing! What do you know about guns, Chris?"

Blake lunged, and she fired.

She struck the thick outer sole of his boot, almost sending Blake's bones leaping out of his skin.

"I can use it. That was your only warning."

Chriselle had spent her time in California practicing—after her lawyer had given her the number to a gun instructor.

"Walk away, Blake. Give me the children without a fight.

Take some classes and counseling, and I won't bring up your illegal business contacts in court."

"You are my wife, the mother of my kids. What the hell kind of lowdown-ass woman does some shit like this to her husband?"

Watching his every move, her finger hugging the trigger, Chrissy spoke one of her greatest truths. "The kind of woman who never loved you in the first place."

GRATEFUL

SHELDON

"Sheldon! Sheldon! Open up, please."

He threw his laptop on the couch and ran to Jerrell's door. Who in Sag Harbor knew him and where to find him? Especially at 9:30 at night. Suspicious, he looked out the peephole to see a disheveled Maddy staring back. She banged once again. Her knock was certainly strong for a person so slender.

He opened to a woman breathing as if she'd run all the way to him. "Maddy, what's up? Where's J? And don't you have a key to get in here now?" he asked, peeking around her.

Her trembling hands reached to him as she released puffs of condensation. "Shel... come on... Chrissy needs... help. I had to leave and... forgot my keys." She started pulling on him.

Sheldon tensed up. "Help with what? Chrissy doesn't want me involved in her marriage." She had made that much painfully clear, and he didn't want to risk losing her.

Maddy grew emotional. "It's Blake."

Sheldon saw red. *"What?"* He was already moving for his keys.

How many times had Chrissy told him in no uncertain terms that she would fend for herself? But he had given her plenty of time to resolve her issues the way she wanted. He'd hoped she would use the phone he gave her, but she was too stubborn. Now he was stepping in. Chris would just have to be mad.

He admired the way Chris wanted to assert her own power. Hell, it was attractive. But she needed him, and he sure as hell needed her.

His doubts and equivocations out the door, he followed Maddy, no coat, in only his flip-flops. "I'll drive. Get in."

"Oh, God," she muttered as they faced blue and red spinning lights a few blocks down. Next to it was an ambulance. Maddy jumped from the car before Sheldon stopped it. Neighbors had gathered around the house.

Fear ensnared him as he pushed the brakes. Every outcome rushed through him. Where was she? *God, please, don't do this.* He shoved past the emergency responders, searching for her. He recalled Chrissy's determination the first time he'd met her at the bank. At the front of his mind was her steely will to survive. Her intention to live on *her* terms. Sheldon had to feel her once more, even if it was to slap some sense into him.

But she didn't appear. Not in the yard. Did she lay on a gurney? Had his pigheadedness cost him? *Again?*

An unshaven, dismayed person walked out in handcuffs. As officers led him from the house, Sheldon briefly passed the man who must be Chrissy's husband. For a fraction of a moment, they exchanged eye contact.

Chrissy's past departed as her future arrived.

"Hey!" Mr. Mason called at Sheldon, twisting as police pulled him away. "Who are you? Who are you? I don't know him. Who is that dude going to my wife?"

Sheldon kept walking toward his destination.

Several breaths cascaded from his lungs. His heart might have stopped as Sheldon approached a ravaged house. Shards of glass lay throughout the yard, and the spectacle shattered Sheldon's insides. Some neighbors taped garbage bags over the large broken window.

Sheldon followed Maddy inside.

"Yes, I'd like to press charges," a familiar voice spoke.

There she sat in an armchair, perfectly cool. Her cheek was slightly red.

Sheldon's lungs squeezed out his oxygen at seeing her bruised.

But her shoulders squared, her tough chin thrusting up.

"Please send me those photos you've taken as soon as you can. And also the transcript of the 911 phone call."

The officer studied her. "Certainly. I'll upload and log them at the precinct, and we'll email you and your attorney digital copies in twenty-four hours. The 911 transcript will take longer, a few days, probably sometime next week."

Chrissy nodded before they left.

Maddy looked at Chrissy. "I thought you said you weren't calling the police."

"I didn't want Little Blake to see me do it. My phone was on, with the volume down, the entire time. Now I have a long 911 audio recording of Blake. And if my lawyer's information is correct, he could go to prison for a lot more than assault. The actresses he represented and manipulated can see him put away. With no damage or embarrassment to them."

Sheldon marveled. So he was right. The little firecracker was conniving.

"You planned all this? By putting your *life* on the line," Maddy pressed, unhappy about it. "This could have been so much worse, Chris."

"She's right," Sheldon added, his eyes unwavering when she glared at him. Although it was impressive, it was still deadly.

Chrissy held an icepack to her cheekbone. "Worth it. Now I have a basis for a five-year restraining order. He can't come within a hundred yards of me. Monitored contact only with the kids. That gives me time to work on Little Blake, without Blake around to screw with his mind. Both my children will learn what strength is, and what it is not. Besides," Chrissy said with an exhausted smile, "this is Sag Harbor. We look out for each other. I knew our friends would get involved as soon as they heard what was happening."

Sheldon watched them hug, not knowing what to do with himself.

"Girl, you are still badass Chrissy Townsend and have not changed one bit," Maddy whispered.

"I'm glad you're alright," Sheldon finally spoke. More like overjoyed she was standing in front of him, as stalwart as ever.

Her eyes told him she was happy to see him, but even so, she scoffed. "I'm glad that you're glad. You're still a snake."

Maddy smirked, staring between the two of them. "Uh-oh, lover's quarrel alert. That's my cue. I'll head to the Vincents, where I left the kids. We'll hang out until your parents come."

"I should go," Chrissy said. "Explain to them what's up."

Maddy scanned Chrissy's open living room that now had

no window. "You should stay here and watch this big security issue, so no passersby get any ideas."

Once she'd left, Sheldon turned to Chrissy, who muttered, "You can leave with her. We don't keep reptiles in our house."

He grinned, and so did the muscles in his chest cavity.

"You're right. I am a snake. But I'm asking you to consider having a pet."

He placed his hand over hers and gently took over the job of holding the icepack to her cheek. "This needs some mustard, so it'll control the bruising and swelling."

Chrissy's guffawing shook her shoulders, an easiness sliding over her bruised face. "Are you seriously suggesting I spread food on myself? Like a backwoods Louisiana home remedy?"

Sheldon welcomed her laughter again, how she seemed to melt as he was melting. "You're laughing, but it works. Gram used to put mustard on us all the time when we fell and busted our knees back home."

While they cracked up, her eyes illuminated the corners of Sheldon again. He left for the fridge to get the mustard, and they moved to the kitchen. He leaned over her as he applied it.

She started. "So while you had me at the Water Lily for a high-energy afternoon, you had no clue your boys were making a deal at the same time? You hadn't met with Lana's mother that morning? Something you might have mentioned."

Sheldon paused, thinking of the words he would say, and how. "Chris, that Saturday, I had a full day scheduled. You knew it wasn't likely I would work with Kevin. I told you as much. So of course I was meeting with Erlita. But when your cousin called me, I dropped everything. There was nothing else. I put everything on the line and walked out. Erlita was already irritated with me. She could have said she'd take her concept somewhere else. And I wouldn't have cared because all I needed was just five more minutes with you."

He stared into Chrissy's eyes, watching their steeliness melt.

"It wasn't smart of me to walk away. Erlita called Brent after I left. And Brent closed the deal. He and I go way back, so it's cool between us, but even he wondered if I was in my right mind. So don't think for a moment that that deal was more important to me than you."

"But that stunt with my mother. Why would you—?"

"Because I knew you could handle it. You're not weak, Chris. Don't pretend you are. A woman who steals her husband's clients, no. Your fierceness is a drug to me. I knew it from the moment I found you raising hell at the bank, without lifting your voice even once. You had my officers' asses in a snare, and I loved every minute. I never told you this, but," he smiled and placed the lid back on the mustard jar. "I stood and watched for a full five minutes before I went and offered to help."

She snorted while chuckling, her fluttering eyelids signaled he'd caught her off guard. "What? You let me suffer, for your entertainment?"

"For my admiration." He blew the mustard on her skin so it could dry faster.

Her cheeks lifted in a grin.

"But what about the Village Council meeting? What you said? About being stupid for—"

"I spoke out of anger, and I apologize for my tone. It was mean. I'm sorry for hurting you. Not that it's any justification, but Kevin had pissed me off, and his actions worried me for both of us. But I wasn't wrong. We were foolish, Chris. We should have waited. *I* should have respected your marriage.

But damn, I wanted you. Like Maddy said, it might have ended with your life. And that, I could not bear."

She studied him. "But those nights with you, after my children, were the greatest gift I have ever received. Like the universe was telling me things would be just fine without Blake. If not for you and me being together, that clarity may have missed me. Our New Year's together put a nail in the coffin of my old life."

"It gave me new life," Sheldon replied. After bandaging her, his hand remained on her face, running his thumb over her mouth.

"Us," she corrected. "Gave us new life. I'm sorry for not telling you about Kevin. I was so worried about Blake, and I should have remembered your end of the danger."

"I knew." His finger traced her nose and along her eyebrows, and he relished finally holding her. The past few weeks, he'd laid awake and imagined her. "I wish you would have let me help you."

She stared at him, their eyes inches apart. "It had to be me. Nobody else."

"I get it. And I will deal with Kevin. As for you taking all that risk yourself..." Sheldon winced at the horrors that crossed his mind. "Please don't ever do that again. Promise me."

A tear skipped onto her cheek. "I promise."

He held Chrissy's face with both hands, his fingers sliding along her temples and then her scalp. Their breathing intermingled once he drew her closer. His tongue grazed her lips, promising her more gifts ahead.

In the back of his mind was Genie's voice.

"Chris, you should know..." He inhaled. "Sometimes, money and opportunity drive me really hard."

The crystals of her eyes shined at him, maybe even through him, her lips twitching in a tiny smile. As if she already knew. "Sometimes? Or *all* the time?"

He shrugged, grinning. "More often than not. Still, I could have warned about what I was doing with your mother."

She laughed. "You definitely keep things interesting." Chrissy's face turned serious, and she eyed him. "Are you telling me this because you think it'll scare me?"

Sheldon's breathing slowed. Inside him, he heard the drum of loneliness his heart had banged for years. "It ruined my marriage."

Soft fingertips brushed his jawline, while Chrissy's eyes stroked his pain. "I don't think that's what ruined your marriage."

He kissed her fingers. "So does it? Scare you?"

He needed the answer. The loaded moment formed an expressway from one pair of eyes to another.

Her head shook slowly. "No. It turns me on." She sucked his lips. "And I want you to teach me."

A wave of relief rolled over Sheldon, and he brought her head to his. "Are you even real?"

Gazing at her, into her, he kissed Chriselle with his eyes open. So she could see all of him. As their tongues slowly danced, she didn't flinch.

GROWN

CHRISSY

Sheldon's kisses were the sweetest reward after such a hellish night.

From her forehead down to her pulsating skin just at her collarbone, he left soft kisses, his hands escaping under her sweater and kneading her flesh. How would she control this throbbing between her thighs while she managed the kids these next few weeks and months?

And, sweet heavens, when Sheldon kissed her with his eyes open, he could have been arresting her soul. She could look nowhere else, too mesmerized. No one had ever done that. His stare penetrated her, so unnerving that she thought he was casting a hoax. It just might have been working.

He moved a deft hand underneath her wool skirt, inside her panties, where his fingers thrust upward, and Chrissy gasped. He still kissed her with his eyes open.

"Ah," she moaned against his mouth.

"What's the matter?" He smiled and talked shit. They both laughed at how weak she was for him.

Chuckling and moaning simultaneously, she whined, "Ahhh.... Asshole."

"Mmm. You're ready. We'll have to do something about that."

A car entered the driveway. Headlights flashed against the trash bags.

Sheldon yanked out his hand and moved toward the bathroom to wash.

"Chrissy!" Her mother cried from outside and a door slammed. "Oh, my God, Chris! Baby, are you in there?"

She went to let her parents in, and they threw their arms around her.

"We came as soon as Maddy called us." Her father eyed the bandage on her cheek. "What happened?"

Chrissy shook her head. "Nothing. It turned out fine."

"Where is Blake?" Mrs. Townsend did a quick scan for him.

Irritated that her mother had barely noticed her bruised face, Chrissy eyed the woman with a hard stare. "In jail, where he should be, Mom. Out of mine and the kids' lives."

"Well, you need to get him out," Mrs. Townsend retorted.

Chrissy huffed. "No, I don't have to do anything."

Mrs. Townsend raised her hands. "All he needs is a good talking to. For his family to sit down—the Masons and us—and we all talk him back to himself. And you all will be just fine. Every marriage has its complications."

"Mom, it's *over*," Chrissy snapped, with all the finality she could muster. "I've already filed for divorce. This is Blake's second assault in a month." She watched her mother's mouth gape open. "That's right. I got a call from a social worker in L.A. He hit his mistress last weekend. And she lost her daughter to child services. Blake is getting worse. I will not live this way. And more important, my son can't grow up thinking this is acceptable."

"For better or worse, Chris, those are the vows you took," Mrs. Townsend muttered.

Her father cringed. "Georgette, I'm not sure I agree with—"

"Not for the price of my *life!*" Chrissy shook now.

Mr. Townsend blinked several times. "Hold up. You mean this isn't the first time? Blake's been… hitting you? When? For how long? Why didn't you tell me?"

"Because Mom said I had to woman up and handle it for myself. That he would grow out of it. And I was ashamed." Chrissy's voice quivered as she spoke.

Mr. Townsend turned to her mother. "Georgette, *no.* This is our child. How could you?"

Chrissy continued, "You have always treated me like some kind of nitwit for messing up young. Because I wanted my baby."

"You made your choice when you decided to keep it," Mrs. Townsend shot back.

"No, *you* chose for me," Chrissy replied, shoving an accusing finger between them. "I didn't know any better, so I listened. But I followed your rules, and I took your path, playing little Suzy Homemaker. And look where it got me. Not anymore. I head to L.A. in a few days to wind things up, and I'm getting a restraining order for five years. If you bring up Blake's name again, I'll find my own place and you will not see the kids or me."

"That won't be necessary," her father interjected.

Her mother's eyes flared. "You will struggle, Chris, and you've never had to struggle, little girl."

Chrissy's pulse ping-ponged between her ears, and blood

gushed in her arms. "Maybe struggling will turn this little girl into a grown woman. And maybe you'll finally show her some *respect*."

In the tense face-off against her mother, Chrissy's lungs clawed for air.

She continued, "Now. The children need to start school here in New York. I could use some help keeping them stable while I'm out of town. But I *am* doing this. With you, or without you. The choice is yours, Mom."

Her mother's frazzled face searched between Chrissy and her father.

Her parents jumped at the sound of shuffling behind them, and they turned around with surprise. There stood an uncomfortable Sheldon.

He raised his hand in an awkward greeting. "Good evening, sir. Mrs. Townsend."

"Mr. Rouse," her mother stared, confused. "What on earth are you doing in our house? And why are you coming from our bathroom?"

His mouth dropped, and he seemed scattered for a moment. "I was rubbing… mustard on Chrissy's bruise there. Got a little messy." He looked to Chrissy, clearly uncertain about what to say, and how much.

"You put food on my daughter?" Mrs. Townsend asked.

Chrissy shoved down a laugh. Among other things he'd put on her…

"He was down the street when Blake came, and Maddy ran to get him." Chrissy pointed to the bandage on her face. "He patched me up."

Mrs. Townsend examined them both with a long side-eye. "Of all the neighbors Maddy could have gotten, why him?"

Chrissy and Sheldon exchanged awkward glances, before their gazes played hopscotch on the floor.

"Wait a minute." Her mother put two and two together. "Is *this* who you were with over New Year's? Who had you missing in action for two days, while you were lying to us about being with your friends? *That's* why you were so pissed at him, at the Village Hall meeting. I was wondering. You two have become an item!"

Chrissy's teeth bit down on her grin, like she was sixteen.

Sheldon offered his hand to her father.

"Sir, I'm Sheldon Rouse. I meant no disrespect toward your daughter."

"Apparently, you've been disrespecting something," Mrs. Townsend snapped, with a cocked neck. "And check how she's all hot and bothered. You were disrespecting it a lot."

Sheldon's head dipped in embarrassment, while Chrissy's amusement sputtered out.

Chrissy's father observed his child's face and his own lips spread. "Look at her. My baby's beaming. I've never seen her like that. He must be disrespecting it better than her husband ever did."

Chrissy let out a big huff. "Okay, you two, I'm standing here. Knock it off, please?"

Her father leaned over and kissed Chrissy's forehead. "You have our word. Your mother will stay out of your business from now on." Mr. Townsend's good nature evaporated as he turned to Sheldon. "But not so much that we won't protect our daughter. If necessary."

Sheldon nodded. "Of course, sir. I wouldn't expect anything else."

Her father cast a warning glare at her mother. "Georgette?"

Mrs. Townsend sucked her teeth. "Fine. You won't hear a peep from me... not even to say I told you so once you start feeling the heat."

Chrissy didn't believe that statement for a moment. She and Sheldon exchanged embarrassed expressions before he shifted to assess the house situation.

"Until you guys replace the window, you're in for some chilly nights."

"We can't go to a hotel and leave it open this way," Mr. Townsend chimed in. "I'll call a company in the morning, but for now, we're stuck here."

"And it's probably best to sleep down here, so you're ready if somebody tries to slip in." Sheldon paused, staring at Chrissy and sweeping his hand over her shoulder. "If it's alright, I'd like to stay with you all for the night, help guard the place and make sure there are no more surprises."

Chrissy's father eyed him. "She's still married. So you can sleep next to me."

FREEDOM

SHELDON

"Come and live with me." Sheldon wrapped his legs around Chrissy, who lay against his chest in his jacuzzi. Picking up some water, he poured it over her breasts, and his hands poured over her glistening skin.

"Mmm, that sounds amazing," she murmured while he nibbled her ear.

"It will be. You'll not want for anything. I'll see to it. I'm probably being a fool by asking you. Again." He watched her moist flesh ease between his fingers. "There's certainly no pressure. I know you're not divorced yet, and there are the kids to think about." He sighed, and kneaded her breasts that he loved. "But the connection we have is real. It's getting harder to be here without you."

She brought his hand to hers and kissed it, staying silent, as if considering the possibility.

"I would love to be with you in your castle." She clasped her hands around his. "But I *do* want to want for something."

A pang of disappointment shot through him. "How did I suspect you would turn me down?"

"I'm not turning you down." She kissed his hand again, massaging each of his fingers. "Only saying I need time. I've lived under other people's roofs my whole life. I want to know how it feels to come home to mine. All me. Something I pay for. With money I earned."

Her reason reminded him why he was so crazy about her. She couldn't care less about Sheldon's wealth or trappings. "And then, of course, you need time to finish your divorce. How do you feel so far?" He had to check in and make sure she wasn't having second thoughts about ending her marriage. A decade was far longer than a drop in the bucket.

"I don't believe my predicament the last ten years has been a marriage. More of a terrible mistake that would not end. I've never been in love before. Never."

"You didn't have a high school boyfriend?" he asked in disbelief.

"I dated a couple of guys, but nothing serious. Mom stayed on me like white on rice," she said laughingly. "So naturally, I was naïve when I got to college. Blake was a crush. One of those dudes who looks good and then, when you get to know him, you want to vomit. But by the time I vomited, it was too late."

A small, sad chuckle shook her chest.

"So I've been like a zombie for a third of my life, living on autopilot, doing what I need to survive. When my classmates were graduating and picking apartments and jobs ten years ago, I was already married, with a baby on my hip, and jumping into our first house. It feels like I'm starting so much later than everybody else. To the rest of you, it might be a small thing because it's already behind you. To me, this is finally my turn to feel... alive. Freedom."

Sheldon's heart was heavy, but he understood. He wanted

her in his bed all the time, to wake up next to her, feel and hold her, smell her, wrap her in his arms and make sure no one ever tried to hurt her again. More and more, he was becoming certain that she belonged to him. And he wanted to show her.

But for now, he would have to accept these dalliances they snuck into their schedules. His lips pressed against her hair. "You enjoy your freedom. You've more than earned it. I look forward to watching what you do with it."

Sheldon stopped himself from saying something else and pouring out his heart. There would be time.

"Once I've breathed and lived for me a little while, yes. I'd love to make a life with you."

Too many nights had passed when Sheldon questioned if he would get this chance at happiness again. It had only been a couple of months, and he wouldn't blow it. She would have her space.

"I'll wait as long as you need me to. You're worth waiting for." With that, he stood and dried both of them off before carrying her to his bed.

Where Chrissy surprised him, pulling him down onto the mattress. And she straddled him. Her supple ass opened so her moist valley rubbed against his dick that quickly saluted. Sheldon stared up at her full, perfect breasts poking over him, smooth curves boasting their sexiness and flat, fleshy stomach that he rubbed. His girl stared down at him.

"I swear I want you as much as you want me. And when my divorce is behind me, and my children have adjusted, I hope the fantasy in my head will become real, Shel."

Her fingers caressing his chest burned little trails of heat across him. And through his heart.

"Fantasy?" he murmured.

"Mhmm." She rolled her damp hips over him. Chrissy's tongue crested her bottom lip while her stare grazed his body. Damn, she drove him nuts when she looked like that.

Sheldon explored her womanhood, where his thumb rediscovered her clit. They both gasped—her at his touch, he at her wetness. Gazing at her, he licked his lips.

Rising, Chrissy positioned his shaft at her slick opening. She'd never ridden him before. Slowly, she sat on his shaft. Both of them drew quick breaths at the feel of him entering her. Since they trusted one another and she was wearing an IUD, they were skin to skin. Although frankly, Sheldon would have gladly gotten her pregnant, he knew she was a long way from that. Instead, he stared at Chriselle, savoring her mind-blowing heat, its moist tightness as he sank into her. She gyrated her hips and was a little uncertain, but he would talk her through it. Sheldon loved that she even wanted to please him. Every time they connected, she left another piece of her inside him.

"Tell me about this fantasy. What kind of fantasy, baby?" He palmed her hips and guided her so his length didn't hurt her. But her sweet strokes were already milking him.

Her head fell back as she found her stride. "The kind where you teach me to disrespect you. A lot."

CHILDREN DIVED into the party jumper, one of the few warm spots at the President's Day fair.

"Dad!" Hadar ran to Sheldon with excitement all over his face.

"Yes, sir," Sheldon took a break from helping Jerrell and Gram with pastry sales.

"Can I go out on the dock with Blake?" Hadar huffed and puffed from all the activity, his eyes shining.

Sheldon eyed both boys. "I don't have time to watch you right now."

"I'll do it. If I stand here and eat one more Pecan Roll, you will roll me out of here tonight," Maddy replied and took off her apron.

"Where's Kara?" Sheldon scanned around for Chrissy's daughter. She still jumped in the party jumper. "Blake should take his little sister with him. And all three of you stay together."

"Aw, man, why does she have to come?" Blake whined. "I always get stuck with her."

Sheldon cracked up with laughter. "That's the same way I feel about this dude." He motioned next to him at Jerrell. He slid his arm around young Blake, seeing this as a moment to show Chrissy's son the positive example he didn't receive from his father. "Sorry, my man, but let me explain to you the rules of being a big brother. See, your duty is never over. You must loan them money. Help with homework. Get them out of trouble when they do dumb stuff." Hadar laughed as Sheldon continued. "Because you're older, that kind of makes you a superhero, and you have to be available at all hours. Anytime, day and night. Sucks, I know, but somebody has to be the strong one." Sheldon reached over and pinched Jerrell's cheek. "Isn't that right, baby brother?"

Jerrell jerked away. "Ha ha, very funny. You do not save me." He and Maddy kissed.

"You wish I didn't. You're only alive because I always save your butt from Dad and Roland." Sheldon continued laughing.

"I'll grab Kara," Maddy said.

Sheldon kissed Hadar's head. "But avoid the water, and

please do what Miss Maddy asks you. Don't let me hear you're giving her a hard time."

"Don't worry. Hadar and I are going to hit these arcades, and then we'll see who gives who a rough time," she replied. "How about we start with *Star Blaster*?"

Hadar's and Blake's faces lit up in shock.

"You play *Star Blaster*, Aunt Maddy?" Blake asked.

"Brother, I grew up on that dock. I used to eat guys like you for breakfast," Maddy bragged.

"You can't beat me," Hadar replied with a big grin. "I'm the master."

"I'll bet you a pizza that the master is me," Maddy challenged.

"Yes!" the boys crowed. "Let's do it!"

As they took off toward the festivities, Chrissy marched up to Sheldon, wearing a troubled expression.

"Babe, straighten your face. Before you scare off the customers," he cracked.

She held up her phone. "I just got a text message from the secretary for Village Council. They want to see all the bidders. Now."

With that, they left the pastry sales to Gram and Jerrell's new assistant manager before rushing off. Chrissy called for Maddy to come back with the kids, and all of them hurried into Jerrell's Range Rover.

"So is this good or bad?" Jerrell asked.

"I have no idea," Chrissy muttered. "But my hunch is there's an issue. They already scheduled a meeting where they're announcing approvals in two weeks. Why is this coming out of nowhere? Something new must have happened."

Parking the car, they all rushed up the steps and into the building.

Sheldon's instincts also told him the situation was off when he entered to find Lana and Erlita already inside.

"Well, well," Lana cackled. "Look at all of you. One big happy family."

"All of you, please, sit," Councilwoman Newman began. "Thank you for coming on such brief notice." She turned her attention to the children. "This conversation will be... heavy. We have a conference room, right behind us where they can wait awhile."

Sheldon and the others sat on edge, as a secretary escorted the kids out. Maddy, Chrissy, Jerrell, and Sheldon all exchanged nervous looks.

"I have Mr. Middleton here on speakerphone, so he listens in," Councilwoman Newman said. "Now, it's come to my attention that two of you have been engaging in an intimate relationship throughout this entire process." Her eagle eyes sharpened on Chrissy and Sheldon. "Is this true?"

He and Chrissy froze, stiffening next to each other.

Goddammit.

Middleton.

"Um," Chrissy stammered. "Yes. It is. But, I don't understand."

"Let me clear you up then," Ms. Newman started. "That's a serious potential conflict of interest that you should have disclosed."

Sheldon shot forward in his seat. "We didn't mean any... never intended to deceive anybody. It's just... well... Chrissy... Ms. Townsend is married. Separated, but still married, and—"

"Sheldon, I can explain my own life, thank you," Chrissy

interrupted, and blinked away her annoyance. "Council-woman, there is no ill intent here. No deception, or secret scheme, or anything. We only met in December. While we both investigated this process. It hasn't even been two months, and… we… our relationship is in its infancy."

"But not so infant that you all are not watching each other's kids now, meeting at each other's houses, holding family gatherings," Lana noted from the other side of the aisle, with Erlita nodding in agreement.

"Lana," Sheldon started, with all the damn restraint he could muster, "do you really think I would work so hard to raise money, and invest my own, simply so I'll screw… *myself?*"

"I wonder what you two might be planning. Maybe to join up and outvote us at some point, so you can combine the companies, or undermine ours," Erlita retorted.

"That's crazy," Sheldon objected, unable to believe this was happening.

"Not really. You and I both know hostile takeovers occur all the time," Councilwoman Newman replied. "So you see why some parties here express concern for your intentions."

"Ms. Newman, you've known me my entire life. I would not screw over the city or my neighbors," Chrissy said, her voice trembling.

The Councilwoman nodded. "Yes, that's true. But some other bidders here do not. It's why we gave you the benefit of this informal meeting in advance, to tell you personally, rather than denying your proposal without an explana-tion." She looked at her fellow council members. "We realize this could be error or oversight, that your intimacy may be still quite new, and this issue possibly did not cross your minds. So we will not reject the projects altogether.

But the two of you must remove yourselves from this process."

"But wait," Maddy interrupted. "Jerrell and I are seeing one another. We didn't disclose. Why are we not being penalized?"

"The filing documents do not list Jerrell Rouse as a principal of Escapade by Erlita. He is merely a vendor, and not a decision-maker. Not the same level of oversight or responsibility. So it's unnecessary," Ms. Newman explained.

The sky might have been falling on Sheldon's head. He turned to Lana again. "If I walk, I take my connections with me. How will you fund this?"

Lana snickered. "I've spoken to Brent. He's still on board. I'll manage."

Councilwoman Newman stared down at the phone. "And is it my understanding that Mr. Middleton has a request?"

Sheldon's fists tightened in his lap.

"Yes, Madam Councilwoman, I intend to withdraw my project proposal. And as full disclosure to the Village Council, I am considering making Erlita and Lana an offer."

And there it was. Sheldon fumed.

"They worked together," Chrissy muttered the moment they stepped outside the doors. "*That* was the collusion!"

"Of course, they did," Maddy said.

"It's why Middleton was gathering intel on us. All this time, we thought he was waiting to go to Blake and cause drama. But he was going after this. Kevin knew his idea wasn't good enough, so he came for ours," Sheldon thought aloud, inwardly chastising himself for not seeing it.

"And Kevin's money and influence are long. Something Lana cannot turn away," Maddy added.

Lana and her mother strutted down the steps, gloating as their Texas-sized purses dangled from their arms. They pulled their coats tighter and put on their shades. "Hope there's no hard feelings, folks. You all can still come to the grand opening and welcome your new neighbors to Sag Harbor like the classy people you are."

Sheldon held a furious Chrissy. So neither of them would start anything that might cause their arrest.

But her phone buzzed, and she checked a fresh text that arrived. Sheldon couldn't help seeing it.

I told you I would destroy you. Enjoy being Mrs. Rouse.

"Destroy you?" Sheldon asked, turning Chrissy to face him. His blood heated. "It's time for you to tell me everything that went down between you and him."

She hesitated, and he sensed her shame in Kevin intimidating her. Maddy and Jerrell listened.

But Sheldon insisted, keeping his voice soft. "Chris, don't keep things from me. He planted bugs on you. We need to know what we're dealing with here."

Maddy gasped. *"Bugs?"*

Chrissy rubbed her head. "At the Ivory Open House, right after Christmas, I asked Kevin to work with us. But when he saw Sheldon and me talking, he was suspicious. So he told me he would destroy me if I screwed him. Later, Maddy found someone we were more comfortable working with. But Kevin wouldn't let it go. He demanded that Maddy and I stay on his project, so the clout of all our family names would strengthen his position." She turned to Sheldon. "It's why you heard the fighting in my yard."

Maddy touched her arm. "Why didn't you tell me? You know I would have dealt with him."

"I thought he meant to sabotage *me* with Blake, and me alone. And that's my marriage, my problem. So I went to L.A. to take care of Blake myself. Then you and I would be free to work with who we wanted. And I didn't want you fighting Kevin, because he does have his uses. We may need him for something else down the line."

"No, you won't." Sheldon's fury jackhammered his head. "We were both so focused on the Blake situation that we didn't think of how Kevin could manipulate this. The bids. Taking me off the project, so he could slide in."

How could he have let Kevin pull the rug from under him not once, but twice?

Maddy sucked her teeth. "This isn't over."

"Far from it," Sheldon said. "This just might be perfect. I've run some deeper background on Lana. And I learned how she has the money to come here."

Maddy's eyes widened. "Really now? You don't say."

"I do say," Sheldon replied and squeezed Chrissy's shoulder. "Taking them down isn't a question of if, but when."

THANKFUL

CHRISSY

*C*hrissy wrapped up work, putting away the actors' files and grabbing her coat. "I'm heading out, Mr. Goldberg."

"Alright then, thank you so much for all your help today. You are absolutely amazing. Please come back tomorrow," he said in a singsong voice.

Laughingly, Chrissy replied, "It's my pleasure and I can't wait."

The administrative assistant had already headed out for the day, so Chrissy took out her key to the office and locked up.

She glanced at her watch. 7:15 p.m. now. Her mom should have been giving the children baths before they started reading.

In her purse, she felt her phone buzz on the way down to the street. It was Karema Jackson. Elated and exiting the elevator with a hop, Chrissy answered.

"Well, well, stranger, you've moved on to bigger representation, and I thought you'd forgotten about little old me," Chrissy joked.

"Ha! Girl, stop playing. How could anybody forget you? Ever!" Karema bubbled through the phone. "Oh, my goodness. This is so awesome! We could never forget!"

Chrissy laughed while bouncing through the shiny glass doors of the office building on Fifth Avenue. "Do you like it? How did I do?"

"How did you do? This is phenomenal. It's everything. You are a badass. I worship at your feet," Karema replied. "I will never forget this. None of us will."

Chrissy's boots trotted toward Sheldon's Mercedes that awaited. She was too giddy to walk. He threw open the door as she got in, and they exchanged a kiss.

She pulled out her copy of the *Hollywood Tattler*, and there, in a corner of the front page, was Blake's mugshot from his arrest. Holding it up like a trophy, she displayed it to Sheldon as they drove off for a celebration dinner. On the inside spread were photos of Chrissy's reddened face, and the shattered windows of her family's home with the surroundings blurred out.

"I know," Chrissy spoke into the phone. "And I'll never forget you. Just remember me when you ladies get big, okay?"

"You took one for the team. For real. And put yourself out there for us." Karema choked up. Suddenly, the other actresses Chrissy and Blake had represented chimed in. "Thank you, Chrissy!" they took turns saying through the phone.

She placed the call on speaker so Sheldon could hear their clapping and joy.

"You're more than welcome." Chrissy beamed. "I miss you guys. Each one of you will be fabulous. And hit me up if there's anything. I mean it. *Anything.*" Her voice also shook with emotion now.

Minutes later, she and Sheldon were dining at *The Waterfront Cafe,* facing the water across a glowing New York City.

Chrissy didn't stop raving about how great her lawyer was, how much she loved her new boss, how she couldn't believe the people she was meeting, the atrocious nerve of this one actor, and everything under the sun when Sheldon chuckled over the table.

"Oh," she said with a deep giggle. "Sorry, I've really been running my mouth, huh?" She popped a shrimp in.

Sheldon's face glowed over the candlelight. "And with good reason. I haven't seen you this ecstatic. Especially not since that day at Village Hall."

"Oh, please don't."

"Okay, okay." He held up his hands to surrender, his gaze dashing behind her. "They're bringing our drinks. Excellent."

The server set down her Moscato and his cognac. And a grateful Chrissy immediately began to take hers to the head. She had been waiting for this drink ever since this morning, when she reached her desk, and found that the administrative assistant had left the paper in her chair.

But Sheldon cleared his throat before she turned up, stopping her, and offering a toast. "To the brilliant and badass Chrissy Townsend."

Rolling her eyes, she chuckled, clinking her glass against his. Finally, that precious first sip. Turning it up, she relished the sweet liquor flowing down her throat. Shamelessly, she took a long, celebratory swig, sending him into a laughing fit. After a disgustingly big dinner with too much eating and laughing, he smiled at her as if she were a rare gem. Every time he looked at her like that, Chrissy feared her heart would give out. She wasn't sure she would ever get used to him drinking her up like that.

"This feels good," she murmured.

"Yes, it does," he replied.

After dinner, he helped her up from the table. Putting on their coats, they headed out for a stroll on the boardwalk, their leather-gloved hands intertwining. Brisk air hitting their faces, they stopped to take in the city skyline. Lights shined as stars, stringing all around them, as if they stood among the galaxies. Sheldon wrapped her in his arms.

Chrissy couldn't have been more jubilant to be back in her native New York, and to be spending weekends in quaint Sag Harbor.

"A lot of people never feel this." She breathed into the cold air. "I count my blessings every day, to be starting over again."

"That you're starting at all is why I love you so much," he murmured into her hair.

She shuddered against him. Maybe she'd misunderstood. She hadn't just heard what she thought. "What did you say?"

He turned her around. "I said," he swallowed, his leather gloves caressing her face and warming it in the cold, "it's why I love you. So much. Already."

Chrissy gasped. Though the words echoed in her ears, she needed to process them. "Sheldon."

"It's okay if you need more time. But if I don't say it, I would be lying to you, lying to myself. And I'm too old for that," he said, his illuminated eyes reflecting the city behind her.

She shook her head, grabbing his face. Her gloved hands stroked the strong jaw she liked to kiss, and her eyes found the question in his.

"I love you every bit as much, if not more. You are one of

the best things to ever happen to me," Chrissy said, starting to choke.

Sheldon trembled, bringing her face to his.

She continued, "I only needed a minute to thank the heavens that you're real. Sometimes I can't believe this is finally happening for me. And I really have to accept it and be thankful."

"It's really happening, baby. And then some." His arms tightened around her. "The closer we become, the harder it is to be without you. But I'll wait."

As always, his experienced tongue did not disappoint, sucking her into him. His eyes open, they opened her. With the passing of every wintry day and night.

She doubted if she could really hold out on his offer of living together. But there were still the children. Little Blake was finally coming around to accept that New York would be home permanently. He was even enjoying Sheldon, Jerrell, and their boys' activities without Mom. Right now, it might have been damaging to rock the boat.

In the meantime, she could look forward to plenty more hugs by the fireplace, outings on the yachts, and the quaint and humble peace of Sag Harbor. But there were a few clouds hanging over this new happiness.

Lana. When he left jail, Blake. And that damn Kevin Middleton.

"A penny for your thoughts," he said, his breath stroking her skin.

She shook the worry from her mind, determined not to let it ruin what had been an awesome day. An awesome revival of her life.

"Thinking about the future. Us. The children," she replied while snuggling against him.

Sheldon kissed her forehead, his warm lips lingering. "So am I, baby. In more ways than you know."

In his pocket, his cell phone buzzed, and as he pulled it out, they both stared at the name. Shel's expression took a dive, though he instantly tried to hide it.

"Baby, everything good?" she asked.

Shel shoved the phone back in his pocket. "More than good. Perfect. You're shaking. Let's get you back inside." He escorted her toward the restaurant.

But now he seemed uneasy and Chrissy detected a change.

His phone screen had read, *Eugenia*.

Now Chrissy could only wonder, what did his ex-wife want?

THE END?

BOOK 3 EXCERPT

FLINGING ALL SPRING

ADELLA

Dr. Adella English pulled off her bloody operating gloves and squeezed the arm of her eight-year-old patient, before she left the operating room. "I want to see him again in twelve hours. A little concerned about his stability, given his diabetes."

She released an exhausted sigh, unfurling her hair from the ponytail she'd worn the last two days. Her next to last shift before the Thanksgiving holiday brought a smile to her lips. One more round of twelve hours, and she was free for four days.

In the doctors' locker room, she showered and threw on her street clothes. Then, a pair of familiar arms circled around her waist. Her bottom lip slid under her teeth, and she leaned her head back, feeling his warm breath on her neck. And then his lips.

"Good morning," her boyfriend Wes murmured, since it was 9:33 a.m.

"Good morning yourself," she twittered like the birds on the windowsill outside the locker room.

"How was surgery?" he asked.

"Successful for now. But I'm coming back early to watch the little guy, make sure he remains stable. When do you think you'll be out?"

"Probably midnight," he replied, turning her to face him. "And then I'd like to take care of somebody else for Thanksgiving. My most special patient." He kissed Del, and the rapid beat of her heart might have flown her from the floor. After devouring her lips, he gave her a final peck, sweeping his finger over her brow. "And I'm hoping this holiday, we can finally…"

His eyes slid over her figure, a subtle reference to all he hadn't seen yet.

A giddy heart surgeon gazed back at him, rubbing his shoulders, and trying to forget the slight tension she now felt in hers.

She doubted how much longer she could hold him off. How many thirty-five-year-old men waited for a virgin?

"Have I not shown you how I feel about you?" Wes asked, referencing the ring he'd bought her, that she couldn't wear at work. His eyes examined hers.

"Of course, you have," she said, stroking his cheek. "But how many times have we talked about my family?"

His head fell. "Adella, it's the twenty-first century. We're no longer delivering our mail by horse and buggy."

"Can we please not talk about this here at work?" she asked, lifting his head and bringing his gaze back to hers.

"Sure, I'm sorry, I was just hoping…"

"I know, and so do I. And we *will*. I can't tell you how much it means that you're so patient."

Wes's eyes flared. "I seriously can't wait to meet this family of yours that has such an iron grip on you. My family adores you, Del. They can't wait for us to wed, and you to become their daughter. So when will you tell your folks?"

Her breaths became shallow.

"The next time we're all together. Everybody's headed to Cape Cod for Christmas. Come with me then, and that's when we'll tell everybody."

Wes kissed her hand, a smile returning and his eyes shining again. "Really?"

Del swallowed the anxiety clogging her throat about her family's reaction when they learned that Wes was white. But she wondered if that was her only fear.

Still, Del nodded. "Yes. Really."

At that moment, her phone buzzed in her purse. Her eyes fell to the screen.

Solomon. Del's oldest brother. He rarely called her.

"I have to grab this."

A happy Wes put a final peck on her lips. "See you tonight then."

"Yes, tonight," she replied, picking up the phone.

"Solomon, hey! Happy Thanksgiving! It's been too long, big brother!"

His heavy voice greeted her. "I know, Adella, and I'm sorry to deliver bad news, but you will need to come to the Cape. Papa is sick. In the hospital, and they're not sure he'll make it. Woke up for a bit. And he wishes to see… you."

She plummeted to the changing bench, dropping her purse. "What happened to Papa?"

"He had a heart attack two nights ago. They fear his condition may worsen. So the elders have summoned us for a family gathering."

"Two nights! Why am I just now getting a call?"

"The elders only called the grandchildren today." By the elders, he meant Papa French's eight children, including Del's mother.

Del blinked as if her eyelids were windshield wipers that could clear her confusion.

She'd just spoken to eighty-six-year-old Papa a few days before, and he'd sounded fine.

Del and Wes had planned to stay in town for Thanksgiving, dine with friends and take in a couple of shows. Now, she strategized making the drive that would likely take three hours.

She tore out of the doctors' locker room, with her purse and keys, hoping she could reach Papa's hospital by early afternoon. She made a pit stop by the cafeteria, to inform Wes of the emergency.

A big smile crossed his lips. "One more goodbye kiss before you go? How did I get so lucky?"

"I'm so sorry."

"What do you mean? Sorry about what? You look like your dog just died, and you don't have a dog, my love."

Del reeled as she forced herself to say the words. "I just got a call from home, and it's my Papa. He had a heart attack over night. His condition is not stable."

"Whoa, oh wow, babe. You shouldn't go through that alone. I'll go with you and support you," Wes offered. "I can tell the chief to pull somebody else in here to cover me. I know how much your grandfather means to you. I'd like to meet him if I could."

Del looked into the eyes of the man she'd been dating the past year. Her insides screamed that that was not a good idea. She cleared her throat.

"You know what? For right now, let me feel out what's happening with my family."

Wes rolled his eyes, his shoulders slumping. "So now's not a good time either? We were going to go at Christmas anyway."

Her worry for Papa was mounting inside her, as she fretted over whether each moment of her delay might be the last that Papa breathed.

In the haze of her anxiety, she saw Wes's disappointment.

"Meet me there in a couple of days. I'll go first, be with my mother, and help her. And on Saturday, come and join me. How's that?"

A tender, grateful kiss was Del's sendoff. Wes's fingers stroked her neck as his eyes poured into hers. "I love you. My prayers are with you and your family. Call me and tell me when you've made it safely."

She nodded and sucked his lips one last time, breathing in the familiar mixed scent of closeted doctor scrubs, latex and medical-grade sanitizer. To the rest of the world, the scent might have been a horrendous reminder of a Halloween house of horrors. But to Wes and Del, it was the smell over which they'd bonded the past year.

"I love you too. I'll call you." Their fingers clasping a final time, she didn't want to let go of his eyes still holding her. Del forced herself to turn away, and she made a hasty dash for the doctors and nurses exit.

The drive to the Cape gave her ample time to stress over how she would prepare her traditional family for a white country guy in the form of Wes.

It was the last thing her Papa needed after a heart attack. Her grandfather had always made clear to his family that roots and heritage were everything. In fact, the *only* thing worth preserving.

While the Manuel family's wealth may have placed them among mostly whites in their professions, neighborhoods, and country clubs, they were to always remain committed to their Black American ancestry. So for her to bring a white man to her Papa's *dying* bedside... she cringed at the tornado of angst forming ahead.

Arriving in the Cape, she didn't stop by her grandparents' home but headed straight to Cape Cod General Hospital. After her cousin texted her the room number, seconds later, she was entering a parade. Cousins, aunts, uncles and extended relatives filled the corridor outside her grandfather's room. Many who had flown into town overnight, had not visited Cape Cod in years. Their faces visibly waited for his last breaths so they could get to the distributions of the estate.

Adella greeted her cousin Afi. "Afi, how is he? Any changes?"

Afi shook her head. "He's awake, but weak. Hooked up to a ventilator."

Del took off her mental heart surgeon hat, and settled into obscurity as the anxious granddaughter. Even if she possessed insight into her grandfather's condition, her mother, aunts and uncles likely would dismiss it.

A long line of relatives waited to see him. Adella prepared to wait her turn, greeting relatives she had not seen in a while. Second and third cousins had flown in from colleges, graduate schools, and jobs across the country. Even a long lost brother appeared. And more relatives trickled in every few minutes.

"Del! I've been waiting forever. Get in here." Her mother's frustrated voice called to her from Papa's room.

"But Mom, I'm skipping the line. What is it? You have a medical question? His heart?"

"No. We are waiting for *you*. He has asked where you are," her mother replied, hands gripping Del and pulling her inside.

Confused, she followed as her mother maneuvered Adella past her grandfather's seven other children.

"Pa," her mother whispered into Mr. Manuel's ear. "She is here, Pa."

Del went to his bedside to find a frail man who seemed to have been stricken by a comet and eaten by its radiation, since she'd last seen him three weeks before. "Papa."

His eyes formed slits, as their pupils rolled around in a dazed state. They found her. "Del... ba... by," his hoarse voice creaked.

She leaned closer, and his fingers shook to find hers. Cracking a joke, she asked, "What are you doing in here? I thought we were going golfing this weekend?"

Hard as Del tried not to cry, tears slid down her cheeks at this tall, strong man now rendered so feeble.

A thin smile cracked around the corners of his lips. "The..." he slurred, and Del's surgical mind presumed his tongue was likely dry and its muscles impacted by heavy sedatives. "The lllaww..."

"The law, Papa?" Del tried to clarify.

"Law... yer. Talk to... lawyer. K?" He managed to nod his head an inch. "I tr... tru... st... yyy..."

Del's eyes blinked numerous times. "Stop trying to talk.

Preserve your energy for healing. You will get up in a couple of days and walk right out of here, and we will go hunting. Nothing else."

He smiled, a tear running down his face. "Proud." Another slight nod of his head. "Pr…" His chest heaved up and down.

She started to check his vitals and heart monitor.

"Papa!" Del cried.

"Pa!" Her mother pushed Del out of the way. As did each of his scurrying children, until Frenchie Manuel's grand-daughter found herself the furthest from the man who might have been closer to her than her own father.

The guttural wails and cries that rang out around the room confirmed her fear.

As she made her way back outside, her cousins crowded around her.

"Well? Did he speak? What did he want?" Afi asked.

"Why you?" another relative asked.

A sea of faces surrounded Del, but she was still trying to decipher his strained last words. Talk to a lawyer about what? She wasn't one of his children, so why did she need to concern herself with his legal affairs? Her mother and Aunt Lizelle, and Uncle Bryce could handle all that. She simply wanted to mourn that her Papa's strong voice and stronger spirit were only a memory now.

"He's hooked up to monitors and could hardly breathe. I only made out that he said he was proud," she lied.

"Proud of what? Proud of who? Did he say anyone's name?" a flurry of voices asked, one after another, until they fused together.

"Excuse me. Doctor?" a single voice rose above them all.

Del ignored it, assuming someone called for a doctor and

nursing staff to come and perform standard resuscitation protocols, before pronouncement of the death.

Swirling in a windstorm of grief, she grabbed her forehead. Maybe Wes should have come with her, because her grandfather's loss was hitting her like a wrecking ball she hadn't expected when she drove in.

"Dr. English? Adella English?"

When she lifted her heavy head, a lone arm extended toward her. It offered her a sealed envelope.

"Yes?" she asked.

"For you, madam," a mail courier responded. "Would you sign here please, confirming your receipt?"

All eyes fell on her.

Did she open this document in front of everyone?

Adella stood up to trudge away, having no clue if this was private or something intended to be read in front of the family. She decided she would inspect it first.

"Where are you going?" Afi asked.

"This envelope is addressed to me alone."

After reaching a small chapel, she sat on a pew before her shaking fingers opened it.

"Adella English, you have been named the sole heir to the estate of Charles Francis Manuel. With conditions. Please present yourself on tomorrow, the day after your grandfather's death, November 24, 2021, at 9 a.m., at the office of Attorney Scott Walden, 90329 Bishop Street, Cape Cod, Massachusetts."

She sat back. On Thanksgiving Day? The man wasn't even cold yet.

No.

DESMOND

Seated in the plush leather seats of his mother's boardroom, an exhausted and hungover Desmond fought sleep.

"Did you hear a word I just said to you?" Mrs. McLain asked.

He opened his eyes. "You were speaking?"

"Take this seriously. This is real life. Our business needs you, and now is not the time to slack off and screw everything in here that has a hole! Grow up!" she hissed. "I brought you in, and gave you a job. One job. You had one. Vice President of Public Relations. Get off your ass and do it."

"Did it ever occur to you that I have interests of my own? And construction isn't it?" he asked.

"Whoring and foam parties are not a legitimate business profession."

He longed for his football days, the only escape he ever had that allowed him to forget his family name, family business, and family commitments. Of him and his two siblings, he was stuck in the middle, and as such, it had allowed him to fly under the radar for most of his life.

"Now," his mother began, setting her hands on the conference table. "You have an opportunity to redeem yourself if you don't want me to cut off your balls financially."

Here it came. The point of this meeting.

"Finally," he huffed, closing his eyes again. Whatever she wanted, he would go out and do his normal routine where he half-assed it, before returning to say at least it got done. Then she could shut up, and he would go on with his life.

"We need to elevate our presence in certain parts of the

country, specifically the Hamptons. It's been one of our hardest markets to break into. Very exclusive communities that operate behind the scenes and based on name recognition. Longtime friendships and reputations. Without increasing the size of our clients' money, we will struggle by end of next year. We need richer clients. We have found one inroad."

"Okay?"

He didn't bother opening his eyes until his phone buzzed. He swiped the screen to smile at a nude photo of the girl he would, for sure, be pounding on that night.

"Manuel Realty & Company Owner is Frenchie Manuel, a longtime Hamptons operator since the seventies, whose commercial properties have been on the ropes for a few years now. Vast real estate holdings throughout the eastern and southern parts of the United States. Maryland, Massachusetts, Virginia, Alabama, the Carolinas, Georgia. But he never quite made a full recovery after the 2008 housing crash. Since then, his holdings have teetered, particularly as shopping malls and big name physical stores go under."

"And?"

"We need his name brand and prestige, and he needs our money. There is one best way to achieve this." She moved to take the seat directly in front of him.

"What? Public relations tour? Photo ops? Shake some hands at a party? Ribbon cutting? Some new shared property somewhere? Just tell me the date and time, and I'll put on the clown suit and show up."

He nestled his back inside the seat, waiting for her to bore him with her next pointless assignment.

"Marriage."

Desmond's eyes popped open, his head reeling as if one of

her bulldozers had hit him. Rarely had anything she'd said ever shocked him. In fact, never had his mother shocked him.

"Mm... *what?*"

"You will marry Mr. Manuel's granddaughter. Or I cut your lazy ass out of my will. You meet her in two days. Sober up and get shaved."

THANKS FROM LULA

Thank you for reading *Sag Harbor Black Romances*! If you enjoyed this story, please leave a review at your favorite retailer.

If you were feeling the Rouse family and the characters in Sag Harbor, here's how you can stay connected.

Web site: www.lulawhitebooks.com

Email: lula@lulawhitebooks.com

Join Lula's Luxe Suite Reading Group:

www.facebook.com/lulawhitelounge

Read the stories before they go on sale:

www.patreon.com/lulawhite

Lula's stories are available weeks to months in advance as she writes them on her Patreon.

Books In The *Sag Harbor Black Romances*

Brown Sugar This Christmas - Maddy & Jerrell

Hot Chocolate This Winter - Chrissy & Sheldon Part 1

Flinging All Spring - Adella & Desmond

Overheated for Summer - Chrissy & Sheldon Part 2

Rouse Family Christmas - All Couples

Books in the Sag Harbor spin-off series *Explore Men of the Hamptons*

Explore You - Kevin & Cher

One Tasty Night - Solomon & Chaitra

Taste You - Solomon & Chaitra

Drink You - Lion & Kamila

See Through You - Keenan & Eugenia

Find You - Roland & Neeraja

Book related to Sag Harbor and *Explore Men of the Hamptons*

A New Life for Christmas - Odell & Tazima

The Young & Luxurious Series

Love & Fire — Kori & Easton